Critical Acclaim for *Traded Secrets*

"New author Victoria Presley is a storyteller in every sense of the word! *Traded Secrets* is a one-sit must-read!"

—Debra Dixon, Bestselling Author of
Hot As Sin

"*Traded Secrets* is a fresh, unique, and marvelous read! Ms. Presley draws you into the story with a swift, ingenious hook and keeps you there. This is a touching, tender love story destined to captivate readers. I loved it!"

—Virginia Brown, Bestselling Author of
Jade Moon

"A delicious blend of past and present! Captivating and clever. A fine read!"

—Patricia Potter, Bestselling Author of
Diablo

PASSION DENIED

Jacob pushed Savannah onto her back and deepened their kiss. His hand reached up to tickle against her neck causing shivers to flame over her. He released her lips only to drop tiny kisses on her eyelids with a feather touch more erotic than raw passion. Her resolve to maintain a safe distance from this man faded into a hazy fog.

"Jacob," she breathed.

He lifted his head to look at her, his eyes passionate with need. She returned his steady gaze as each silently asked the other the unspoken question.

"It's not right, Savannah," he said, kissing her once again then slowly backing away from her body. "Too many things stand in our way right now." He disentangled himself from their embrace. "If we consummate this marriage, I want it to be because of love, not because you want to comfort me."

"Jacob," she interrupted.

"Go to sleep, Savannah," his voice took on a ragged edge.

Savannah closed her eyes and listened for the sound of Jacob's breathing. He was silent, although the unsteady rhythm of his lungs proved he was not resting. She buried her head in her pillow. It was going to be a long night.

*For my mother, Jerry Turnipseed,
and for my friend, Cindy Sargent—
two great encouragers.*

LOVE SPELL®

May 1996

Published by

Dorchester Publishing Co., Inc.
276 Fifth Avenue
New York, NY 10001

The name "Love Spell" and its logo are trademarks of Dorchester
Publishing Co., Inc.

Printed in the United States of America.

TRADED SECRETS

VICTORIA PRESLEY

LOVE SPELL NEW YORK CITY

Chapter One

Savannah's knuckles turned white as she clenched her fists. The overbearing figure standing before her said nothing, but skeptically met her gaze over ancient spectacles.

"Where did you come by this collection, miss?" the old woman asked coolly, looking back to the case of watches on the counter. She lifted a magnifying glass to inspect a pearl-faced wristwatch.

"They were my father's."

"I see." Her tone indicated she did not see at all. Savannah cast a worried frown around the musty antique shop, stifling a catch in her throat. She hated to sell her father's collection, but she had no choice. No choice at all.

"Your shop came highly recommended," Savannah said in a voice that boasted more confidence than she felt. "I'm certain you know collectors who would pay dearly for a group this valuable. My father was passionate about antique watches. He found them all over the United States." She watched the woman's pudgy hand close around an exquisite gold pocket watch. It had been her father's prized piece.

"Vintage 1860," the woman speculated, sounding impressed by her own knowledge.

"Actually," Savannah said, "the date is engraved on the works inside. It's an 1854 Dennsion, Howard, and Davis. One of the first they produced, mint condition, too. This particular watch has been in my father's family since shortly after the Civil War. It's what inspired him to collect antique watches."

Behind the counter, the woman glanced up sharply, clearly displeased at having been corrected. "Why do you want to sell them if they're so valuable to you?" she asked, her eyes narrowed in suspicion.

"I . . . I need the money."

"Humpf!" The woman shut the first of six leather cases. "You don't sell collections like this just for the money!" She glared at Savannah, obviously waiting for a better explanation.

"It's the truth," Savannah said in a small voice. "I'm hoping to enroll in medical school this fall. With my inheritance and the money from Dad's collection, I should be able to make it through my first year. After that, I'm hoping for a scholarship to finish." She forced her hands to relax on the counter. Selling the collection was harder than she'd imagined. Savannah pushed a strand of her hair away from her face. Reaching for the cases, she sighed. "Before he died, my father told me to come to you if I ever needed to sell. He said you were a conservator—"

The woman looked up sharply. "He did?" she asked incredulously. "I'm known as a conservator in other places, of course, but I had no idea my reputation was renown. I'm delighted." She softened a bit, then looked closely at Savannah's face, as if finally seeing her for the first time.

"He said you were always interested in things from the past. I assumed he meant antiques."

"Of course he did," she agreed quickly, then stared silently at Savannah, her eyes narrowing again. "Your father must have been a special man if he knew I am a conservator. For that reason, I'm going to give you a little free advice. It's obvious you're desperate to sell. Written all over your face. That's a big mistake in my business. Be nervous on the inside, but calm on the outside." She came from behind the counter, her rotund body barely squeezing through the slim opening.

"I'm going to do you a favor," she went on in a grandmotherly voice. "And don't ask me why or I may change my mind. Your collection is worth far more than I can afford to pay, but I do know a gentleman who might be interested." She gestured around the store in a sweeping motion. "Take a look around while I call to see if he's interested." She rushed off to the back room, the pocket watch still in hand.

Savannah's gaze followed the shopkeeper until

she disappeared behind a ragged curtain covering the doorway. She hoped she was making the right decision. Becoming a doctor had been her dream throughout high school and college. She had been well on her way, too, until a handsome first-year medical student turned her head, and she fell hopelessly in love. Despite her father's warnings, Alan had convinced her to become a nurse before going to medical school. It made more sense, he had told her confidently. She would gain vital work experience while he got his degree. After he graduated, they would be married; then it would be her turn.

Only her turn had never come. Her smooth-talking fiance completed his residency and walked out of her life, leaving her with nothing but a cheap diamond ring and his spiteful cat.

Savannah let out a long breath. At least her father hadn't lived long enough to see the mess she had made of things, she thought sadly. It would have broken his heart. He had always said she was meant to be a doctor, and it was time to correct the past.

Turning, she considered the antiques surrounding her. The dim overhead lights cast a yellowish glow around the room, lending a mysterious air to the store. The hot, musty smell gave no hint of the pleasant spring day beyond the dirty plate glass windows. And yet, despite the poor lighting and humid air, the store was oddly charming. Although covered by a layer of thick dust, most of the antiques appeared to be quite valuable and in impeccable condition. Some even looked unused.

Savannah's eyes settled on the dozens of antique hats filling the window display. Tattered old hats were everywhere. An old racing derby sat atop a wooden shelf beside an elegant silk top hat. Several sequined ladies' hats adorned the heads of old mannequins and dress forms, and an antique fireman's helmet hung suspended from the ceiling with string.

A small cedar wardrobe was also in the window. Its doors were open, revealing shelves filled with crocheted baby bonnets, gingham sun hats, and even an old leather football helmet. A tiny brass sign on the door read CONSERVATOR in small elegant script.

At the very top of the wardrobe, carefully placed across the corner of the door, was an antique nurse's hat. It was hard to see in such an inconspicuous spot, but it caught Savannah's eye. She leaned closer for a better look.

Hanging just within reach, the hat was shaped like a pillbox with white lace sewn around the edges. A pale blue ribbon was woven through the lace and tied into a little bow at the back. Impractical for an emergency room nurse like me, Savannah thought curiously. It was so familiar though, almost as if she had seen it somewhere before. She traced her fingers around the fragile lace, trying to imagine who it once belonged to.

"Careful with those," a warning voice called from the back room. "That's a very special collection. Quite valuable, in fact."

"What makes them so valuable?" Savannah asked, more to make conversation than from actual interest. She continued to finger the yellowed lace. "Are they for sale?"

"No, these are priceless." The rotund woman walked toward Savannah, shaking her head. Taking the fragile cap, she replaced it lovingly on the vanity, brushing a speck of dust from a gray fedora before glancing at Savannah. "Your luck is charmed today, miss. Not only is Mr. Evans interested in your collection, he's rushing right over to meet you.

"That hat belongs to someone," the woman continued without pausing. She pointed to the nurse's cap now hanging back on the corner of the wardrobe door. "I'm only the conservator." The late-afternoon sun peeked through the lace with an enticing dance of light, almost as if calling to Savannah.

"Belongs to? You mean they really *aren't* for sale?

"Oh, no. Each hat belongs to someone different. When a person realizes it's missing, they come in and find their hat. My family has been the conservator of this particular grouping for years." Her double chin tilted with pride.

"You mean you just keep the hat until they remember it's here?"

"Well, yes and no. The owners don't necessarily know they have a hat. They walk in one day and see it, and they know it belongs to them. Simple as that." She picked up a dirty pink feather duster and swiped a nearby marble-topped vanity, darting a glance at Savannah. A bell tinkled in the background announcing the arrival of a new customer. "Since your father knew about me," the woman added, "I assume he also knew about the hats. It wouldn't surprise me if one of those were yours." Without waiting for a reply, she headed toward the customer coming through the door.

Savannah grinned at the old woman's poorly veiled attempt to sell her a hat. It was unlikely one belonged to her. She didn't look good with anything on her head, not her own nurse's cap or a pretty Easter bonnet. Without thinking, she reached again for the lace-bound hat. How could someone just see something in a window and know it belonged to them? While it was a great sales pitch, it didn't seem as simple as the lady made out.

Savannah walked to the heirloom vanity near the window and sat down on a tapestry-covered stool. The cool marble top felt cool on her arms as she studied the yellowed lace on the hat. The odd shopkeeper was happily occupied with the new customer, her father's gold pocket watch still in the woman's chubby hand. Savannah tossed her hair over her shoulders and placed the hat gingerly on her head. Looking into the mirror partly clouded with age, she giggled at the sight of the pillbox perched precariously over her bangs.

"There, that's better." She tilted it to a jaunty angle and grinned at herself in the mirror, sadly realizing how little she smiled lately. She had been a fool to trust a man like Alan. She had sacrificed everything for him, for their future. And now both were gone. Never again would she allow herself to be used like that. The decision to give up nursing and complete medical school had been a difficult one. But now she was committed. Savannah Stuart was taking control of her life, of her future.

She could feel the worry dissipating with her resolve. She hated to sell her father's collection, but he would want for her to do it. Medical school had been just as important to him. His watches would go a long way in paying for her first year. After that, who knew? It was a gamble she had to take.

Reaching up to remove the hat, Savannah looked at her image once more. A wave of peace settled over her, bringing relief that she hadn't felt in weeks. She dropped her hands back to the marble top and leaned her chin down on them, enjoying the relaxed feeling for a moment longer. It had been a long while since she felt such peace. A long, long while.

The dim overhead lights buzzed a comforting tune as Savannah's eyes closed in contentment. Just a moment longer, she thought. . . .

"No, Doc! No!" A vicious scream shattered Savannah's musing. She bolted at the sound, her nursing instincts taking over. A man was hurt and needed help. She jumped to her feet, knocking over the vanity stool.

Hearing the scream again, Savannah turned to race to the scene. What she saw stopped her instantly. Her heart beat wildly in confusion. She was not in the antique store anymore. She was standing in what seemed to be a hospital. Although bed after bed filled the room, it was not the clean, white hospital she was accustomed to. Instead, this looked like someone's home, with a grand staircase and beautiful heavy draperies lining the windows of a massive oak-paneled room. She stood in what appeared to be a foyer, looking around in confusion. Her breath caught in her lungs as she saw the vanity from the antique shop standing against the wall. This time there was no dust. Fresh bandages sat folded in neat piles across the marble top.

Savannah shook her head to clear it. This had to be a dream. Was this really a hospital? The scream pierced the air again, this time fading to a guttural moan as the intermittent grating of a saw's teeth ceased. She clutched her throat as a uniform-clad attendant approached her, carrying a bloody blanket under one arm. His eyes were downcast as if he couldn't force himself to meet her gaze. As he passed her, the blanket shifted to reveal the bottom half of a badly injured leg still bleeding from its amputation. Nurse or not, Savannah knew she was going to be sick.

She turned and rushed out the front door, collapsing on the ground as she reached the bottom step. A horse standing nearby shied away in fright. Savannah gasped at the scene, not comprehending what she saw. Horses, wagons, dirt roads, barefoot children, long-skirted women, and men in uniforms filled her vision.

Where am I? she thought. What have I done? Where's the antique store? The pull of hair across her face reminded her the nurse's hat was still atop her head. She snatched it off before it could fall, and her eyes widened in disbelief. The cap was no longer yellowed with age. The dainty blue ribbon was not tattered and frayed. It was crisp, nicely starched, brand new.

Savannah stared at it in horror. One minute she was wearing an old hat and gazing into a mirror. The very next, she was retching outside a make-shift hospital, facing a street that looked as if it were a movie set. That flicker of explanation died as quickly as it arose. This was too real, far too real, to be a Hollywood production.

Sitting on the steps in front of the house-turned-hospital, Savannah looked in confusion at the scene before her. Gone were the the normal street lights and speeding cars. People on this dirt-packed street bustled about their business, casting worried glances at her. Dusty air filled her lungs as heavy horses plodded along pulling cumbersome wagons. The burly men holding the reins nodded as they passed by. It was obvious they had no concerns about the street or where they were. If anything, they appeared to be concerned for her.

No, something had happened at that antique store, and Savannah was caught in the middle. Where she was, she didn't know, and the only thing she carried with her was a silly little nurse's cap.

Suddenly she remembered.

The hat. Savannah held it up in front of her with shaking hands. The old woman had asked if it belonged to her. At the time, the question amused her. Now the power of it left her breathless. Could it be possible the peaceful feeling she sensed with the hat held a power that—she struggled for the thought—a power that sent her here? Wherever she was. Was it her hat after all?

"Pardon me, ma'am," a deep masculine voice drawled sarcastically near her ear. "If you have a minute, I require assistance with the soldiers inside." Strong hands lifted her to stand. As they released their hold, Savannah's still-shaking legs folded quickly to the ground. The hands reached for her again, this time firmly pulling her up until her eyes faced the expanse of the man's broad chest.

Savannah forced her legs to hold steady as she drew a deep breath to regain her composure. Holding onto the man's hands for support, she looked up into the clearest blue eyes she had ever seen. Instantly, she jerked her hands away.

"Where am I? Who are you?" Savannah nervously brushed a strand of her hair away from her face.

"Where are you?" he asked incredulously, his cool eyes staring in disbelief. "Where do you think you are? You're at the army hospital in St. George. You *are* the new nurse, are you not?"

"No . . . yes . . . I don't know," she stammered, her lip quivering, her pulse beating wildly. A million questions raced through her head, but she was too frightened to speak. She looked about again, still uncertain of what she was seeing. "What . . . what year?"

A flicker of compassion crossed his rugged face. He reached into his vest pocket and pulled out a handkerchief. "You must have fainted and hit your head," he said, his Southern voice softening as he handed it to her. "Of course things seem confusing. It's the first of March, 1862. My name is Jacob. Dr. Jacob Cross. I sincerely regret you had to see that . . . situation, earlier. Couldn't be helped." He looked down at her, obviously expecting her own introduction.

"Savannah Stuart," she managed to sputter.

He smiled slightly, nodding back toward the hospital. "It's hard on all of us, but especially on newcomers. I should have been more considerate." He looked truly apologetic as he ran his hand across his bristly square jaw.

"Newcomers?" Savannah whispered softly, her senses in turmoil. She looked at the street, then back at the tall man. Whether it was because of her surroundings, or because he stood so close, everything was overpowering, even his presence. His mahogany hair struck a blazing contrast to his vivid blue eyes, and he wasn't even dressed properly to be a doctor, although several damp red splotches on his shirt indicated he had just come from some type of surgery. Savannah shook her head in frustration. Of course, she didn't know him.

"You will stay?" The tone of his voice changed slightly. There was almost a plea in it, very faint but still there. "I need a nurse desperately. The fighting hasn't let up for weeks, and our beds are full."

"Fighting."

"Yes." He looked at her quizzically. "The Union has taken parts of Tennessee, true, but there has been no surrender here or down south in Mississippi." He shook his head bitterly. "Even though I have very little to treat them with, more and more wounded arrive each day. Frankly, Miss Stuart, I must have help."

Mutely, Savannah continued to stare as realization began to dawn. She was standing in a town called St. George, probably in Tennessee, in front of a makeshift hospital, talking to a doctor about the . . . *Civil* . . . War.

"You will stay." This time his words were more of a statement than a question.

"I—I . . . don't . . . know." Savannah hesitated, her mind refusing to recognize the significance of his words. "You see—"

The doctor's impatience instantly flared. "I've got wounded men inside!" he snapped, pointing to the house behind them. "They are waiting for me. For you, too. Either come inside and help me, or go home. The last thing I need is an indecisive female getting in the way!" He brushed past Savannah and stormed up the steps.

"No! Wait! Dr. Cross!" Savannah cried, racing up the steps on his heels. "Please don't leave me out here."

He stopped just before the door.

"It's just . . . I have no idea what to do. I've

never been here before." The words rushed from her mouth.

Jacob shrugged. His expression didn't soften. "Then come inside and help me. I'll show you what I need." As he held the door open, she could see the rows of beds and hear the sounds of wounded men calling for help.

Savannah stood for a moment to consider her situation. She obviously had more pressing matters to worry about than assisting this irritating stranger with patients she wasn't even sure existed. However, he was her only connection with this strange place, and that left her with very few choices. She looked back at the street, considering her options. A night on the street in her time could be deadly. Was it any different here? She was out of her world, away from all she knew. At least the hospital would be safe until she figured out what to do.

Forcing her confused emotions into order, Savannah turned to face the doctor waiting by the opened door. With a deep breath, she gathered every shred of courage in her soul and squared her shoulders. Holding her head high, she walked past the doctor into the waiting hospital.

He had been relieved to see a new nurse standing by the doorway. As one of the only doctors within fifty miles, Jacob desperately needed help. His relief had quickly fizzled and turned to irritation when he saw her cover her mouth and rush to the door. He had requested a trained nurse, not a squeamish female who would faint at the sight of blood.

Glancing over his shoulder, he saw the young woman making her way behind him. She was definitely not a Southerner. No genteel Southern lady would dress that way, war or not. Her blouse revealed most of her creamy shoulders, although it was not daringly low cut. Her skirt didn't reach the ground; the boldly flowered pattern was harsh on the eyes. And riding boots! Jacob was torn between shock and intrigue. From the stares that followed her, so were the patients she'd be tending.

Despite what she was wearing, he had to admit that she was a vision. Her face was framed by long thick hair, loose tendrils brushing her forehead. Was it red or blonde? he wondered. It had been a long time since he had seen a woman with such gentle beauty. War had taken its toll on most of the women around these parts. Their once-soft Southern faces had become hard and caustic as they watched husbands, brothers, sons, and lovers give their lives for the Confederacy.

With an irritated shrug, Jacob forced his thoughts back into control, pulling his practiced reserve to the surface. What was he thinking? He needed a nurse, nothing more. It didn't matter what she looked like.

"We'll begin over here." His tone conveyed nothing of his musings as he led the new nurse to a group of wounded men waiting in the next room.

* * *

Savannah watched as he quickly went to each patient, checking injuries. According to the doctor, most of these soldiers had been there since early morning, the more seriously injured tended to earlier, leaving others to wait in pain. It was obvious this man did need help. As upset as she was, Savannah's professional nature understood why he had no time for her questions. The room was filled with row after row of restless men smarting in fever, their discolored flesh evidence that bullets were still inside them and serious infection threatening. Briefly, she wondered if they even used bullets during the Civil War. Whatever it was, she knew they needed treatment. Instinctively, her nursing skills took over, allowing a brief respite from her own terrifying situation.

Question after question raced through her mind, not only of where she was, but why these men were not receiving better medical care. She remained silent, though, unwilling to ask the sullen doctor. Quietly, she worked alongside him, cleaning injuries and bandaging wounds with what limited supplies there were. An inner fear continued to tug at her, but she found strength in performing her professional duties.

For the most part, Dr. Cross ignored her, speaking to her only as a physician would to a nurse. His abrupt attitude irked Savannah, but she accepted it. He obviously carried a heavy burden, trying to care for these patients single-handedly.

It touched her that he acted genuinely concerned about each soldier he treated. She watched as he leaned close to hear the whispers of a badly injured man who wanted to tell someone his fears for his brother still on the battlefield. For a moment, Jacob stopped his work and held the man's hand, offering what little comfort he could. Most likely, the man would not recover to see his brother again. Her heart skipped a beat as she watched the handsome doctor with the patient. His low baritone voice and deep Southern drawl sent a prickly sensation down her spine, even though his words weren't meant for her.

Leaning over to hear the man's whispers, Jacob's dark hair fell into his eyes. "He needs a haircut," Savannah mumbled.

Jacob glanced up, his blue eyes locking with hers. "I guess I do," he replied with a smirk, clearly amused by her embarrassment from being overheard. His attention returned to the patient before she could respond.

As impressed as she was by Jacob's bedside manner, Savannah was astounded to watch him move from bed to bed without so much as washing his hands or cleaning his instruments. It was clear that the people here knew nothing of germs, not to mention infection control and other modern medical developments. The doctor's own lack of medical discipline was terrifying. Twice she had asked to scrub up; twice he had glowered at her for not attending to the matter at hand.

"No surgical gloves, either, I presume," she had snapped right back, not allowing him to intimidate her. That was her own personal rule of nursing, something she had learned to do to protect herself from Alan's sharp tongue. She may have to respect a doctor's knowledge, but she would never allow him to bully her.

Considering the man before her, Savannah recalled from her college history classes that medical treatment during the Civil War was appalling, especially compared to the advances in her own time. Kindness and a few ineffective and often addictive painkillers were about all this dignified doctor could offer, since the practice of medicine was not to see dramatic improvements for several generations. Maybe she could offer some modern medical skills while she figured out how to get back to her own time.

Leaving Jacob to finish wrapping a wound, she moved to the next patient.

"How do, ma'am," an adolescent voice squeaked as Savannah reached to undo a hastily bandaged shoulder. "A Yank's bayonet got me before I could fire. I got him, though. Shot him right through the eyes." Pride swelled his chest.

"You were in the battle? Why, you're just a boy!"

The lad recoiled as if he had been stabbed again. "I'm fourteen," he said defensively. "Man enough to kill Yankees."

"You're right, young fella," Jacob agreed, coming to stand next to Savannah. "But it looks like I'll need to clean your wound and stitch you up if you're going to use that shoulder again."

Savannah gasped as Jacob bent to prepare the needle with fine silk thread. "Surely you're not going to stitch without giving him an anesthetic!"

"A what?" Jacob looked up from his work.

"You know, a painkiller."

"I know what an anesthetic is, Nurse Stuart!" he snapped sharply. "What little laudanum and chloroform I have are needed for amputations." A muscle twitched in his cheek, indicating his irritation. "Whiskey, like everything else, is also in short supply around here." He turned to the boy, kneeling close to the injured shoulder. When he spoke, his tone was more encouraging. "This rifleman has been through more aggravation than stitching. You'll be fine. Right, soldier?"

"Yes, sir." The look in the boy's eyes did not match his words as he watched Jacob thread the needle. The young man clenched his jaw as Jacob pierced his skin with the needle and came up the other side. His face became ashen as unshed tears gathered at the corners of his eyes. He grabbed Savannah's hand, gripping tightly again and again as the needle repeatedly pierced his flesh.

"I'm sorry," Jacob whispered softly. Concern filtered across his face and was gone before Savannah was sure of what she saw. Jacob met her glance, his blue eyes obviously sharing the boy's anguish. Her heart went out to both of them.

She had to admire Jacob Cross. Apparently, he was the only doctor in this hospital, he had practically no drugs or painkillers, and he had no help. No wonder he needed a nurse. Savannah didn't know what had happened to her, or why she was here, but she was a nurse—and a good one. She could easily bring at least some progressive medicine to these folks while she figured out how to get back to her own time.

Thinking it best to remain silent until she knew more about Jacob Cross and his hospital, Savannah decided to hold her questions, even the ones relating to medicine, for the time being. She cringed each time he used the same needle to stitch up a wound, but took heart in knowing she could bring about a few changes for the good. She touched the little white cap on her head. Perhaps there was a purpose for her being here after all.

Stepping back to grab a bandage the doctor had asked for, Savannah walked right into a gray-haired woman wearing spectacles and an annoyed expression on her face and carrying an armful of towels. Jacob was still focused on stitching the boy's shoulder, paying no mind to the woman.

"Just who might you be, missy?" The woman placed her free hand on her hip, her toe impatiently tapping the floor.

Savannah saw Jacob looked up at the sound of the high-pitched voice, then glance at her. His brows rose in interest, although he remained silent. It was obvious he was going to be no help. She lifted her chin and assumed a professional air.

"My name is Savannah Stuart. I'm a registered nurse."

"Humpf! Registered, are you? And with whom, pray tell, are you registered? The Yankees?" Her eyes narrowed.

Savannah's mind raced as she struggled to formulate a suitable response. She couldn't possibly tell the truth, that she was from the future. They would promptly escort her to the nearest institution for the mentally deranged. As she rummaged through her memory for a bit of Civil War history that might help her charade, a flash of inspiration struck her. It was so brilliant, she had to contain a giggle. *Gone with the Wind!* Surely everything one needed to know about the Civil War was contained within the reels of the classic film.

"Of course not," Savannah replied, mustering up as much indignation as she could. "My family is from Georgia. We have a plantation north of Atlanta," she added with smug satisfaction. It felt awkward lying to the old lady, but if she intended to create a new identity, she'd have to make up a few things at least.

"Georgia!" The woman's expression softened instantly as she smoothed her long white apron and put her load down. "Well, then, I do apologize for being so abrupt. It's just you were a bit clumsy there, and we can never be too sure about who they send us, and for what reason. We haven't had much luck getting nurses, or keeping them for that matter." Her eyes narrowed again. "You wouldn't be just stopping off her on your way back to Georgia?"

"No, ma'am." Savannah smiled. She was definitely not headed for Georgia.

"Jacob, where are your manners?" She thumped Jacob on the head with her long skinny finger. "I'd like a proper introduction to our new nurse! Doctor or not, you should at least be polite."

"Miss Emma," he said, grinning as he tied off the last stitch, "I'd like you meet Miss Savannah Stuart. Miss Stuart, this is Miss Emma Long, owner of this fine establishment. She has graciously allowed us to use her home as a hospital during this relentless war. Without her, this hospital would not be," he said with obvious affection. He stood and walked toward them. "She does everything for me from making sure all the men have enough to eat to making wraps and bandages." Jacob leaned toward Savannah with a conspiratorial whisper. "She may not be able to cut off a leg, but she can sure bite off a head!"

"Jacob Cross! I do declare you are just like your father!" Although she pretended irritation, it was easy to see the older woman was very fond of him. Miss Emma wagged her finger under his nose. "You're incorrigible! Don't come looking for me the next time you need clean bandages, young man."

She reached to clasp Savannah's hands in her own. "It's nice to meet you, my dear. Just let me know if Jacob gets out of hand. I've known this boy since he was knee-high to a grasshopper. He's still not too old to take behind the woodshed." With that, she headed back the way she had come, stopping frequently to adjust a pillow or offer a kind word to a wounded soldier.

"Wow," Savannah said, watching her go. "What a lady."

"Wow?" Jacob repeated with a puzzled look.

She stared at him until she realized the source

of his confusion. "Yeah, wow. It's a new term, I guess. It means . . ." She struggled to find the right word. "Amazing." They both watched Miss Emma holding the one good hand of a man missing the other.

"You're right." He smiled down at Savannah, obviously pleased. "Wow."

Although she tried not to show it, Savannah was frightened. Scared to death, in fact. She had been in this strange place since early afternoon. Whatever force had brought her there was not in any hurry to send her home. She leaned back in the white rocking chair to collect her wits and to figure out what to do.

She sat secluded at the far end of Miss Emma's porch. The sun had just set with a brilliant burst of copper energy, one of the most beautiful sunsets Savannah had ever witnessed. The colors appeared to be so much more vivid than in her own time. The house was situated at the far end of town, surrounded by other homes of distinction. The street in front of the porch was deserted except for an occasional soldier who tipped his hat as he walked by.

The words of the antique dealer echoed in her mind. "Would one of those hats happen to belong to you?" She fingered the lace of the white hat in her lap. Was it possible this hat did belong to her? Was it possible the hat had brought her there? The idea overwhelmed her.

"Evening, ma'am."

Savannah gave a soft smile to a gray-clad soldier passing on the street. The people were much friendlier than those at home. That was, except for the moody doctor. He had spoken very few words to her during the afternoon. When necessity demanded conversation, he was curt and to the point. Still, he was downright nice when Miss Emma demanded an introduction, proving he could be pleasant if he chose. In spite of his manners, he did need a nurse, and she was, for whatever reason, the only one around.

Savannah had been at a loss for what to do when he stood by the door and demanded she come inside the hospital. After staring at the sights around her, she had followed him simply because it was less frightening than the streets. There, horses raced by with riders clinging tightly to the saddles, and soldiers strolled, carrying side arms and rifles. She closed her eyes and sighed in bewilderment. At least she knew what to do and how to behave in a hospital, even if it wasn't a modern one. There looked to be safety in that at least.

It had taken every ounce of courage she possessed to walk through the carved mahogany door. The scene on the street had scared her, but so did the irony of the situation. Less than a day after promising herself to become more self-sufficient, circumstances were forcing her to rely on someone else. Another doctor for that matter. Once again, fate had dealt her a losing hand. This time, though, it was becoming more and more obvious that there was nothing she could do but put on her best poker face and play the game.

Rocking back and forth, Savannah reached a decision. She would not sit by and allow circumstances to control her. For the first time in many years, Savannah Stuart was taking charge of her life. Jacob Cross wanted a nurse, and that she could be. Tomorrow she would not remain quiet. She intended to use her full modern medical knowledge to treat these patients. She might not be a doctor, but it was obvious her world of medicine had taught her more than they were practicing now. While she desperately wanted to go home, to go back to what she knew, Savannah also knew she could help immensely, and she would no matter what Jacob Cross might have to say.

As dusk faded into the darkness of night, Savannah yawned, stretching her arms. She needed somewhere to stay for the night. Miss Emma had retired to her room long before they had finished treating the wounded, and most of the others she had met during the day had left the hospital, including the handsome doctor who had barely acknowledged her as he put on his coat and reached for his hat. A small group of men, obviously hospital stewards, had remained to care for the soldiers. No one had given any thought to the new nurse, assuming she had somewhere to go just as they did.

She rose from the rocker, the nurse's cap in hand, and headed back into the hospital. Surely she could find a place to rest there. Near the vanity she stopped; the resolutions made only a moment ago wavered. What if her traveling through time was related to the vanity, instead of the hat? She ran her hand across the marble surface. She was certain it was from the antique shop. It was newer, more lovingly polished, and the mirror was no longer cloudy, but it was definitely the same. Could the vanity have something to do with her being there? She had been sitting on the same cloth-covered stool when she had closed her eyes for only an instant, and wound up in the "Twilight Zone." Maybe, just maybe, it could take her back. Hearing no sound from the adjacent room full of sleeping soldiers, she placed the lace-edged cap back on her head and sat down. Looking into the mirror, Savannah positioned her hand on her chin just as she had only hours ago. She waited for that peaceful pleasant feeling to steal over her consciousness and take her back home. Closing her eyes tight, she tried to imagine the inside of the musty old store.

Nothing.

She tried again, but no relaxed feeling drifted over her as it had earlier. Savannah sighed and opened her eyes as a sense of hopelessness hovered over her. Whatever had caused her journey was clearly not about to send her home. Until she could figure out how to get back on her own, there was little she could do but make the best of things.

Lifting a small oil lamp from the marble surface, she tiptoed through the hallway. Patients filled every available inch of the room to the right. Climbing the creaking stairs to the second floor, she held up the brass fixture, illuminating the hallway. It looked more promising. The light bounced off a long rug that graced the floor. Several dark wooden doors lined each side, and small wooden tables stood between the openings, a few fresh flowers on each one. Quietly, she stopped at the first door to the right, listening for any noises before she turned the knob. Pushing softly to prevent a squeak, Savannah peered inside. A patchwork quilt was thrown across a wooden bed in the corner. A small dresser sat to one side, a large wardrobe on the far wall, and a rocking chair between them. Savannah breathed a sigh of relief as she entered the room. Since there were no knickknacks or personal items, she doubted it was occupied. She'd be safe up here, at least for the night. Tomorrow, she would find her own place to stay.

She opened the two windows, allowing a cool breeze to filter in. Savannah hesitated briefly about undressing for bed. This wasn't officially her room, but common sense overcame her wariness. It wasn't as if she had packed or anything. These were the only clothes she had in this strange time. They'd be messy soon enough if she continued to work in the hospital. Sleeping in them would only hasten the time they wore out completely. She unbuttoned the waistband of her skirt, caught it before it fell to the floor, then gently folded it over the footboard of the bed. Her blouse followed next. She started to remove her silky bra and panties, but thought better of it. Just in case this was someone's room, she didn't want to be caught completely naked.

The breeze from the partially opened window caused light prickles on her skin as she climbed into bed, pulling a blanket over her and clutching the little white hat in her hands. She laid her head on a soft feather pillow, and although it was wonderfully comfortable, she could not rest. Gunshots fired in the distance, the faint sounds of a barroom brawl filtered up through the window, and the moans of the wounded and dying below called out. Her imagination began to torment her each time the old house creaked and the wind howled. Very slowly, the tears began. Something strange had happened in that antique shop, and why it had happened to her, Savannah had no idea.

One thing was certain. She could not tell a soul who she was until she figured things out for herself.

Chapter Two

Jacob lifted the forkful of fried catfish to his mouth. He usually disliked the strong, distinct flavor, but it was about all that was left in any quantity around these parts, and that was only because the Tennessee River flowed about twenty miles to the east of the city. Once war had been declared, the Confederate army had needed virtually everything for the war effort, including food for the soldiers. If they could figure out how to get it to the front line, the catfish would probably be sent, too, Jacob realized. He took another bite. He didn't begrudge the situation; compared to the meals most of the soldiers were eating, he was partaking of a feast.

At his table in the far corner, Jacob surveyed the restaurant as he'd done every night for the past year. Rose's Boarding House and Restaurant was one of the few establishments in town still open for business since the fighting began. It was to have been a brief war, the Southerners thought, a war easily fought and won. The fact that it was quickly becoming a lost cause was illustrated each night when the restaurant filled with frustrated Confederates.

Not too long ago, the North had converged on a small town located right on the river quite a bit north of St. George. Since St. George served as the army's rear echelon staging and supply center, control of the city was vital. Each day more and more soldiers arrived as the companies of Confederate forces began to congregate in St. George before heading on to battle. The situation was coming to a head in the surrounding areas. There would be bloodshed, that was certain. When and where, Jacob didn't know.

It was late. The usual crowd of boisterous soldiers had already dined and now probably relaxed with a game of cards in the saloon. The restaurant was quiet and the crowd minimal.

It amazed Jacob that the restaurant survived so skillfully since the beginning of the war, especially seeing how the rest of the city suffered. Rose Taylor's husband had enlisted early and had been killed shortly afterward, leaving her with two small children to raise. Rumor was that she consorted with a married officer to keep her business running. Jacob scratched the bristly hairs along his jaw in irritation. Most of the town considered Rose a fallen woman and deliberately snubbed her at every opportunity. The shortsightedness of the townsfolk did not set well with him. He knew firsthand that they all had to do what it took to survive, Rose included.

As one of the area's few remaining doctors, Jacob was welcome at most any home for dinner, but he preferred the solitude of Rose's where he paid for his meal with coins. If he dined in the homes of others, he paid with pretended polite interest as anxious mothers displayed their marriageable daughters. Most importantly, at Rose's he usually didn't have to answer the painful questions that eventually arose about his family and his plantation.

"Evening, son. Mind if I sit a spell?"

Jacob had been so immersed in his thoughts he didn't realize anyone had approached. "Of course not." He motioned to the chair beside him as Arthur Kent tiredly sat down.

Arthur was his father-in-law, as well as his own father's neighbor and closest friend. Riverlawn's southernmost fences bordered the Kent Plantation before the war. Now, it remained to be seen what would become of their lands. Jacob considered the gray-haired man before him. He looked much older than his fifty-four years; his once-proud bearing sagged a little as if the weight of the war were on his shoulders alone.

"Good to see you, Arthur. How's Mrs. Kent?"

"As best as can be expected, I suppose. Robert's death came as a blow to all of us, but she's taking it especially hard. He was our last to die in this godforsaken war." The older man shook his head in resignation. "We've lost everything now. Anna, all four of our boys, and probably our home, too." His voice cracked as if he were fighting for control.

Jacob understood Arthur's grief only too well. Anna had been his wife.

"Who would have thought it would come about like this?" As he offered a small cigar to Jacob, once-steady hands now trembled slightly at the effort. "What about you, son? Have you heard any word about the men who murdered Anna and Nathaniel?"

"No. I doubt we ever will," Jacob replied, bitterly steeling himself with reserve. "All I know is that everything's gone. My wife, my father, and my home. Just like you and Mrs. Kent. Everything." He lit the cigar and watched the blue puff of smoke dissipate.

"My biggest fear now is running the hospital," Jacob continued, steering the conversation away from such painful things. "They can't keep bringing me wounded from the front if I have nothing to treat them with. The Yankees have made it virtually impossible to get supplies now that they've reorganized Nashville and control virtually all of the Tennessee River. I'm still able to get laudanum, iodine, and a bit of morphine down river, but even that's unreliable."

"What about Sanger? Can't he get what you need?"

Jacob shrugged. "You and I both know that he could, and we both know why he doesn't."

The two men smoked their cigars in silence,

each lost in his own thoughts.

Finally, Arthur stood and stretched his tired muscles. "I used to have a lot of influence with the governor, son. I doubt that will get us very far, but I'll make some inquiries for you. Now that the army has taken over our town, your hospital, the church, and Rose's are about all we have left of our own. I'll be damned if we lose them, too."

"Be careful of Sanger, Arthur," Jacob warned. "You've lost too much already."

Arthur nodded, then slowly made his way to the door, a once-proud man reduced to desperate grief.

God, how Jacob hated this war.

His thoughts turned back to the hospital. A nagging feeling had tugged at him since the new nurse arrived. His first impression was not good. He desperately needed a trained nurse, preferably a male nurse to assist with the soldiers, and look what he'd got instead. Her reaction at the sight of the amputated leg indicated the army had sent another irrational female volunteer who had no concept of the blood and gore that filled an army hospital. The moment he saw her, he had fully expected her to flee, and she had.

When he had followed her outside, her angelic face and the subtle glow of her hair had caught him off guard. Loose and free, it was unlike the severe chignons of other female nurses he knew. This nurse was beautiful, no doubt about that.

"Beauty doesn't matter," he chided himself softly. He needed a strong male nurse, someone who could really help. When he had approached her on the steps, he had fully intended to send her packing, back to where she had come from. Instead, he had taken one look into her fearful eyes and his heart had stopped. Without warning, she had stirred in him some unexplained emotion he couldn't resist. Instead of rebuking her fear and sending her on her way, he had asked her to gather her courage and come back inside the hospital. The anger he had felt quickly dissipated when he saw the struggle on her face. It was obvious she was courageous and, in spite of his misgivings, he admired her tenacity. There was more to Savannah Stuart than met the eye, something he couldn't explain. After the long uneasy moment when he had looked into her hazel eyes, he felt a connection . . . some kind of unexplained link. When he had touched her arms to hold her steady, Jacob had the oddest sense that they had met before. He knew her somehow, he was almost sure of it. Just how he couldn't remember.

Other thoughts stirred inside him as well. Images long buried and best forgotten. He had not so much as thought of another woman since Anna, and it annoyed him to think a stranger, no matter how striking, could so quickly attract his attention. All afternoon Jacob had tried to maintain his distance with his usual gruff manner, but he had found himself slipping each time he looked her way. She was so out of place, so alone. Another person just like me, he thought wryly.

It was clear that she had been terrified, standing in the foyer. And a look of absolute horror had filled her face later on the marble steps. She was lost, and that's all there was to it. Jacob had had to quell an urge to take her in his arms and whisper words of comfort. He had not felt emotions so intense in a long, long time. That annoyed him greatly. What was it about this woman that affected him so?

He countered his feelings with impatience. The only thing he had left from this brutal war was his work at the hospital, and he needed a nurse to make sure the work was done. From the skills and knowledge she had used this afternoon, it was obvious she was extremely experienced. For that he was grateful. Her clothing was unusual and her speech was odd, but her knowledge of medicine was far above what he expected. Whoever she was, she was no stranger to a hospital. Nor was she hesitant, as most ladies would be, to work with male patients. Her confidence was almost aggressive, and that made her priceless.

Jacob shook his head to clear the image of her long flowing hair. All he needed was a nurse, not the responsibility of another woman. Lord knows, he hadn't been able to protect the one he once had.

He pulled his gold pocket watch from his vest to check the time. A quarter to ten. She was probably tucked into bed somewhere, dreaming peacefully. In spite of his supper, an empty feeling settled deep inside. He laid his watch on the table to finish the last bite of pie. The second hand of the timepiece circled slowly. His life had changed dramatically since he had given the watch to his father years ago. It was about the only thing to survive the fire, and now it was the only thing he had left of his father, of his family, of his life.

He fingered the etched gold. His conversation with Arthur Kent dredged up unhappy thoughts of Riverlawn, his family's cotton plantation. All that remained was charred embers and ruined land. The ironic part was that his home had not been destroyed by an act of Yankee aggression. A casualty of war would have been much easier to accept. No, Riverlawn had been burned to the ground, and his wife and father murdered by one of his own. A Confederate officer, a fellow Southerner, a supposed gentleman.

His father had been a tolerant, reasonable man who wanted peace between the states above all else. Nathaniel Cross had been kind, easygoing, and proud of his Southern heritage. Confident the North and South could compromise and settle their differences without war, he had spoken out against it and had been labeled a Yankee sympathizer.

Once Tennessee had joined the seceding states and war had been declared, a zealous group of Confederate soldiers had come to the plantation supposedly with orders to requisition all horses for the cause. In reality, the trip was meant to be a lesson—teaching barn burning ordered by the Confederate officer commanding St. George, and the destruction had been harsh.

Jacob had been in Nashville when it happened. The conflict had not yet begun, but skirmishes between the growing forces had been severe enough to require his skills as a doctor. His father had wanted him there in case war broke out. "If it does happen," he had said, "our boys will need a good doctor, son. You must be there for them."

Jacob blinked to calm his emotions. He had gone as his father had wished, leaving Riverlawn and his family unprotected. Later that month, Nathaniel Cross had died, shot through the back trying to protect his home from his own Confederate soldiers. The bullies had fled, leaving his wife, Anna, still inside the burning flames of the house. She never had a chance. That vision haunted him more than any of the others.

The army officers commanding St. George had insisted the men involved had not been operating under any orders. Their actions had been their own. They had been quickly tried and all but one had swung from the gallows. It hadn't been fast enough, though. Faced with meeting his Maker, one of the condemned had named the man who had issued the orders.

By then it was too late. The war had begun in earnest, and attention had turned to protecting the land. Now that this part of Tennessee was targeted by the Yankees, justice for a prewar murder was not a high priority of the Confederacy. More than likely, the man responsible would never be punished, a fact that filled Jacob with bitterness.

Even after all that had happened, Jacob knew his father would have wanted him to fight with the Confederacy and defend their Southern heritage. Nathaniel Cross had not wanted war, but neither had he been a coward. He would have protected his lands and way of life like any Southerner would. Any Southerner, that was, except his own son. Anger ate at Jacob with a sharp edge. He cared for their wounded, but he refused to fight for an army that would kill their own.

Some in town considered him a coward, especially the Confederate officers, but most of the townspeople understood. Either that, or they were too afraid of losing their only doctor. That was certainly the case with the army. They might think him a coward, but the garrison had no doctor without him.

Jacob reached into his coat pocket and pulled out a small book about California. A soldier had given it to him just before he died. After reading about the land of opportunity and adventure, Jacob had decided he would leave this place. He would go west when this war was over. Go west and forget all the pain of the past.

It was well after midnight when Jacob headed back to the hospital. Opening the front door of the house, he nodded to the stewards on duty. Tonight was oddly quiet. No deaths. Fortunate. Jacob tossed his hat onto the marble vanity by the door. He admired the vanity for a moment, noting what a beautiful piece of furniture it was. This whole `house was filled with treasures. Even though she had put up a fuss when her home was commandeered for a hospital, Miss Emma fought a dignified battle to keep it homey and comfortable for her boys. She might be a tough woman, but she was certainly a true Southern lady.

Jacob walked through the maze of hospital

beds, checking patients. Most were asleep, but some nodded to him with weary eyes. The cacophony of painful groans were common at all hours. Sleep brought relief to many, but not to all. An occasional "Evening, Doc" rose from one of the nameless faces in the beds.

He stopped by the bed of the young soldier he stitched that afternoon. His face was relaxed in sleep. So young, Jacob thought. Within a week he'll be back to the battlefront. Sadly, he realized the brave boy probably wouldn't make it next time.

With a rueful shrug, Jacob mounted the stairs and headed to his room. Like many of his patients, he welcomed sleep to escape, at least for a little while, the horrors of the day.

A terrified scream shattered the quiet night air, not a scream of pain but one of outright terror. The sound tore through the hospital like a pulsating alarm, waking everyone in the house. It sounded again just a second later.

Jacob jumped at the shriek. It came from his bed! From right beside him!

It was late, and no moonlight filtered in from the window. Damn! He couldn't see a thing. Instinctively, he groped for the oil lamp on the small table beside the bed to see what was causing the commotion. Another scream began and was quickly halted as a set of teeth sank firmly into the side of his hand and refused to let go.

"What in h—!" His other arm shot over prepared to fight. The momentum brought the entire length of his body in hot contact with the entire length of . . . He still couldn't see clearly, but his body certainly knew what it felt. Those were the curves and silky skin of a woman. He had a sinking feeling he knew which woman those curves belonged to. His new nurse.

"Would you please let go of my hand so I can reach the lamp?" The calmness in his voice surprised him. The teeth released their hold, and Jacob leaned further over the cowering woman, groping for the lamp. He tried to ignore the response in his body as skin touched skin. Lord! Wasn't she wearing anything?

His fingers had just reached the still-warm lamp when three stewards burst through the door. Their own oil lamp was held high, obviously fearful of what they would find. A half-dozen patients followed as quickly as their weakened limbs allowed.

"Excuse us, Doc, we thought the lady might be in trouble or something," the first mumbled. His glance skipped between Savannah's wide eyes, her obvious state of undress, and the naked Jacob leaning over her on the bed. Jacob didn't have to look at the surprised man to know he was clearly torn about what to do.

"This is not what you might think." Jacob reached for more of the blanket to cover his body, inadvertently pulling it off Savannah's breasts. The shiny lace of her undergarment glittered from the glow of the lamp.

Savannah snatched the blanket back to cover herself, leaving Jacob's backside fully exposed to the men. He glanced quickly at the woman beside him and saw the fear in her eyes. As angry as he was, there was no sense letting the men have an eyeful of his new nurse. He leaned toward Savannah, trying to hide her from the interested eyes of the men.

Wrong move, he thought a second too late. From the corner of his eye, he saw a small smile form on the faces of those in the doorway. He glared at them all in irritation.

"Not to worry, Doc. We understand," snickered another voice. Nervous chuckles filled the room and leering glances darted toward Savannah.

"What is the meaning of this disturbance? Can't a woman get a good night's sleep in her own home?" Miss Emma forced her way through the maze of burly men. She caught sight of Jacob's backside and Savannah's fearful face. She took the oil lamp from the amused medic and lifted it higher.

"Jacob Cross, what have you done? Your mother, God rest her soul, raised you better than this. Why—"

"No!" Jacob said sternly to Miss Emma and the grinning stewards behind her. "Miss Stuart has been compromised in a situation not of her making. I walked up the stairs without a lamp and wandered into the wrong room."

"But, Doc, this *is* your room," reasoned a voice in the back.

"Gentlemen"—Jacob's voice grew low with a threat—"I repeat. Miss Stuart has been compromised in a situation not of her making. You will forget this incident and not mention it again. Do I make myself clear?" He deliberately met the eyes of each man, his stare just as forceful as a menacing step. One by one the stewards backed out of the room.

"Sure, Doc. Whatever you say . . ." Whispered laughter filled the hall as they descended the stairs.

Jacob turned his head to face Miss Emma. Wariness filled his eyes. He could handle a group of patients, but Miss Emma had scared him ever since his twelfth birthday when he had stolen an apple pie from her window ledge. She had snatched his ear and made him confess his deed to his father. A trip to the woodshed and a sore behind had been his punishment.

"Miss Emma, you have my word as a gentleman that nothing unseemly has occurred here tonight."

The elderly lady stared intently at him, and then at Savannah on the bed behind him. Her expression was unreadable, but Jacob knew that look. She was about to take matters into her own hands.

"Jacob, may I speak with you a moment?" She turned and walked regally out the door, carrying the oil lamp with her. "And put on your pants, young man," she commanded over her shoulder.

He felt his face flush. "Yes, ma'am. Be right there." She shut the door with a quiet click. Jacob leaned back against the pillow in resignation. Why, he thought, do these things always happen to me? He threw back the blanket and stood reaching for his pants. He had never lit the lamp, so he reached for his pants in the dark without glancing at the woman in his bed.

"What was the meaning of this, might I ask?" Savannah demanded. "I don't know who you think you are but . . ."

Jacob clenched his teeth and ignored her. He would deal with her in a minute. Right now, he felt like he was making a trip to that woodshed again.

He reached for his shirt, then cleared his throat for silence as Savannah began to speak again. "If you so much as move from that spot, madam, I will be hanged for murder." He ground out each word, making sure she understood his meaning, then slammed the door behind him.

Miss Emma waited in the hall, the oil lamp illuminating her thick cotton gown like a curious apparition. "Jacob," she said softly, her expression serious, "you know that I did not want this hospital in my home, but I allowed it. I did it for our cause, true, but I agreed mainly because of my friendship with your dear mother, God rest her soul." She set the lamp down on a table and reached to hold his hands in hers. "However it may appear now, this place is still my home. No matter what happened between you and Miss Stuart, I will not have rumors spread that unbecoming conduct is allowed here. Our honor and our way of life is the main reason we are fighting this war."

Jacob nodded silently. She was right, of course.

Her home and dignity were to be protected.

"You know as well as I," she went on, "those stewards and soldiers will talk. Before noon tomorrow, the entire town will believe that you are . . . shall we say . . . taking liberties with the only nurse we have. We simply cannot have that." She shook her head to stop his argument. "No, don't interrupt. You know this is so.

"I realize Miss Stuart is new to us, but that makes it all the more urgent. She seems to be a fine young Southern lady, and her reputation has been compromised." She looked meaningfully at his face. "Far be it from me to insist," she said, squeezing his hands for emphasis, "but you must marry this young woman, and do so quickly. Her honor, yours, and mine, are all at stake." She dropped his hands, picked up the oil lamp, and made her way back to her room. Before entering the door, she turned to the stunned man leaning against the wall.

"While you are making your decision, Jacob, consider these words, also. There are Confederate officers in town who would love a reason, no matter how unjust, to teach you a lesson, too."

Speechlessly, Jacob watched the small figure as she shut the door behind her. Pounding his fist on the paneled wall, he thought about the woman in his room. It had taken only minutes for the course of his life to be altered dramatically. Through no fault of his own, he was honor bound to that woman. Miss Emma was right. Sanger made no secret of his hate for Jacob, and no secret of the fact that he needed just one good reason to close the hospital and send Jacob packing. If the small-minded folks in town believed he had taken the nurse against her wishes, Sanger could easily get what he wanted. Jacob could not let that happen. He could not let the hospital be destroyed, and he would not let Sanger destroy him. Not when he was so close to the truth.

This is too much, Savannah thought as she rose from the bed, her heart still pounding furiously. In less than twenty-four hours she had been transported in time, away from everything she knew, confronted by suspicious people, horrified by the conditions in this supposed hospital, and now this. In spite of it all, the corners of her mouth lifted slightly. If it hadn't happened to her, it would be pretty humorous. She fought to bring the thundering of her heart under control as she waited for Jacob to return from his confrontation with Miss Emma.

She reached for her clothes and pulled them on. She hadn't forgotten the feel of his skin next to hers, and if she was going to fight with the man, she'd better be prepared. Walking to the window, Savannah looked out on the quiet street considering her situation. More than likely, the doctor had walked in on her accidentally, and he was now standing in the hall, paying the price for his error with a severe tongue-lashing from Miss Emma.

She had been floating between dozing, dreaming, and fitful sleep when a sudden weight had dropped on the bed beside her, the heat of a definitely masculine body brushing against her thighs. Had she been in her time, she would have reacted the same way and screamed. Only at home she would have then reached for the mace she kept in her nightstand. Although she'd be pressed to convince him of it, Jacob Cross was a lucky man not to have eyes full of the burning chemical while he listened to Miss Emma's lecture. Savannah took a deep breath to calm her nerves and to face what was about to come.

She was surprised and unnerved when the door opened softly, having expected it to be flung open in a rage. The handsome doctor stood in the doorway, not moving. His looming figure filled the opening and blocked the dim light from downstairs, preventing Savannah from reading the expression on his face. Her heart resumed its pounding; a flicker of fear tingled up her back.

"What do you think you are doing slipping into my bed in the middle of the night?" His voice was perilously soft. Savannah sensed the danger in his words. She set her shoulders and prepared to meet the challenge in his voice.

"What do you mean 'your' bed?" she asked, tossing her head and glaring at him.

"This is my bed, madam, so the question remains. What are you doing in my room, in my bed, in the middle of the night? If you had wanted to spend such . . . time with me, surely more discreet arrangements could have been made."

Jacob shut the door behind him and walked forward until his body was only inches from hers. She could feel the heat from his skin, an unwilling reminder of the electric warmth from their encounter in bed.

Savannah tilted her jaw in a defiant stare. "How dare you! This wasn't planned!" Never in her life had she been accused like this. "No one had the decency to show me to my room, so I found one on my own. I didn't know it was yours." Her eyes dropped from his, down to the front of his shirt, awkwardly mismatched as he had hurriedly buttoned the wrong hole. Savannah forced herself to repress an angry smirk as she remembered feeling his naked lean muscles pressed tightly against her body. She had felt his response to this contact too.

"Planned or not, this is indeed my room. And you have caused quite a stir." Jacob must have sensed her thoughts as he walked stiffly to the dresser, reached into the top drawer, and drew out a box of matches. Without looking at her, he lighted the oil lamp, which filled the room with an eerie glow. He sat down in the rocking chair, leaned back, and considered her thoughtfully.

Savannah breathed a sigh of relief. He was calm, at least. Something else was going through his mind, though, and she had the distinct feeling she wasn't going to like it.

"Surely you must know every inch of this house is filled with wounded men. Did you expect us to provide you with a room, too?" His tone took on a suspicious air, irritating her to no end. "A lady does not innocently wander into the rooms of a strange home in the middle of the night. What are you really doing up here?"

"I thought this was being used as a hospital, not someone's home, and I do not appreciate the insinuation that I was up to something." This time Savannah's voice sharpened with the edge of anger. "You said you desperately needed a nurse, and you asked me to stay. The least you could have done is inquire about my well-being and made sure I had somewhere to sleep for the night." She glared at him accusingly.

Seconds ticked by as they stared at each other from across the silent room, each sizing up the situation between them. The silence intensified as Savannah met his steady gaze. She would not cower to this man, no matter who he was. In her own time, she had not allowed herself to be intimidated by every ill-natured doctor she knew. She wasn't planning to now just because she was in another century.

Finally, he coughed slightly, breaking the tension. "You're right, Miss Stuart, I should have ensured your lodgings for the evening. For my negligence, I apologize."

Stunned, Savannah stared at him. The last thing she expected was an apology.

"Be that as it may," he continued, "we have a slight problem."

She watched him apprehensively. "What do you mean, a problem?"

"Every soul in this hospital heard your scream, Miss Stuart. Several men saw us both without clothes in a very compromising position. Within a very short time, the entire town will know of your indiscretion."

"*My* indiscretion! How dare you!" She felt her anger flash through her like wildfire. He had lulled her with his false remorse, making her think that perhaps he wasn't so bad. She jumped forward and made a move to strike his face, but he was too quick. Still sitting calmly in the chair, he gracefully caught her arm mid-swing and held it with one hand.

He looked at her, clearly surprised. "Surely you understand what I am saying? Whether or not anything occurred here is beside the point. I have compromised your reputation." He continued to hold Savannah's wrist. "I am honor bound to repair the damage."

Anger still raging inside her eyes, Savannah stared at him, not understanding his words. "*You* are honor bound? What do you mean?"

"You and I must marry, and we must do so immediately."

She gave a sharp tug to her hand and he released it. Nervously, she rubbed the warm circle left by his touch. "Try another line, buster," she said indignantly. "That one's not working. Why in the world do we need to marry simply because one of us was in the wrong room? It makes no sense."

"Perhaps not," he agreed, his eyes never leaving her face. "Lord knows, it's not my idea. But, not only will it protect your honor, it will protect Miss Emma's as well."

"What in hell does Miss Emma have to do with it?" she sputtered.

Jacob opened his mouth to speak and shut it

abruptly when he heard her words. Clearly, women did not use such language in his presence. Too bad, Savannah thought as she continued undaunted.

"I said, what in hell does Miss Emma have to do with it?" she asked, deliberately repeating her words to annoy him even more.

If he was offended, he hid it well. "I refuse to believe you don't understand what I am saying. This is about propriety. You and I were found pressed together in the same bed. Even though it was you who came to my bed, from all appearances, it would appear that I was forcing myself on you.

"This is Miss Emma's home, and I value that above all else, including the fact that it is serving as a hospital right now. This is much too big of an event to assume there will be no repercussions. People like to talk, and the town likes to look down their noses at anyone who dares to cause dishonor or break tradition."

He reached forward to clasp Savannah's hand and looked deeply into her eyes as if willing her to comprehend. "I also have to consider how the army will view the matter.

"Make no mistake, Miss Stuart. I share your dislike of being forced into this marriage. I swore never to marry again. However, this hospital is Miss Emma's home, and her standing in the community is very important to her. It should be to you as well," he said firmly. "As long as you and I reside here, we will respect that." He rose from the chair and loomed over her menacingly. "You will marry me, and as soon as possible."

"This is ridiculous. I will not," she replied stubbornly. They stared at each other. His face was calm despite her anger, confusion, and anxiety.

"You will," he said slowly, not releasing her from his gaze.

Savannah hesitated. Was it a threat she saw there? The intensity of his look cut right through her soul. "I will not, and you cannot force me to do so."

Jacob took a deep breath. "Miss Stuart, listen to me carefully. I am not interested in you as a wife. I need your medical skills desperately. However, if you will not marry me, I will put you out on the street. Your reputation will be ruined. There will be nowhere for you to go."

"What about you? It was your fault, after all."

Jacob shrugged. "I am needed as a doctor, so my actions will be overlooked. The important consideration is that Miss Emma will not be scandalized by her friends."

Hesitation must have shown in her eyes as Jacob smiled softly. Surprisingly, it wasn't a victorious smile, but a compassionate one. "I promise you, Miss Stuart. It will be purely a convenient arrangement. I do this for the sake of honor. Yours, Miss Emma's, and mine. I also cannot allow the hospital to be destroyed. That makes this decision the best for all of us." He rose and headed for the door; his stance indicated he considered the issue resolved.

Savannah realized his mind was made up; there was no use arguing with him now. Surely in the morning, this whole misunderstanding could be worked out. There was no reason to keep arguing while he was in such a mood. Resignation settled over her. After all, she was pretty much stuck.

Opening the door, he turned back to her. "Your answer?"

"I'll think about it," she replied stubbornly, not wanting to give in at once.

"You have until morning," he replied as he shut the door.

Savannah hoped he hadn't seen her face betray the fact that she had nothing to lose anyway.

Chapter Three

Savannah awoke to absolute silence. No cars speeding by in rush-hour traffic, no buses squealing their air brakes, no street sounds calling to her as they did every morning about this time. In her drowsiness, she snuggled deeper under the covers to enjoy the rare peace and quiet. It must be Saturday, she thought to herself with a lazy smile. She could sleep late.

A rooster crowed in the distance. Savannah opened her eyes. A rooster? Reality struck her hard. She wasn't in the city anymore, or rather she wasn't in her city. Looking around at the sparsely furnished room with foggy eyes, she realized it wasn't her condo in Memphis. She still wasn't in her own time, and dammit, she didn't even have a bathroom.

The events of last night were as fresh as the minute she finally drifted off to sleep. Like it or not, it looked like she was going to marry Jacob Cross. Less than six weeks ago, her fiance of five years had left her practically standing at the altar. In the middle of the night, she had practically become betrothed to a man she had known for only a few hours. Unbelievable.

It was crazy to think she could marry this man in the name of honor. She knew the "Old South" had peculiar ways, but these people didn't really take all this honor stuff *that* seriously, did they? Besides, if they were to marry, wouldn't she be altering history or something? Surely that was against some sort of universal rules.

Her smile faded a little. Who said there were rules in a situation like this? All she knew for sure was that she was dependent on these people, this town, while she figured out what was going on. And that meant not rocking the boat. Savannah tossed off the covers, grimacing when her bare feet touched the cold floor. She smoothed her hand over her rumpled clothing and wrinkled her nose at the fact that she had nothing to change into.

I'd have packed if I knew I'd be traveling, she thought sourly.

Opening the top drawer of the small dresser, Savannah's eyes widened in surprise to see socks and ties neatly arranged in several piles. This really was his room! While she hadn't considered that he might be lying last night, seeing his belongings was a shock. She rummaged through the contents, searching for a brush or a comb. She felt a little naughty for going through his things, but, heck, they were going to be married anyway. Catching her nail on a sharp object underneath his shirts, Savannah pulled out a small photograph in a gilt frame. She didn't realize they had photographs in this time. Picking it up carefully, she walked to the window for better light. A solemn-faced brunette stared back at her, a look of contentment filling her dark eyes. A sudden flash of unexplained jealously gnawed at Savannah. Jacob Cross must have someone in his life somewhere. She gently replaced the framed image back in the drawer. If so, why would he insist on marrying her?

Curiosity getting the better of her, Savannah turned to the wardrobe on the far wall. It was also filled with male clothing arranged neatly on wooden hangers. She touched the sleeve of a gray wool jacket, running her hand slowly across the material, lifting the soft fabric to brush against her cheek. It smelled like it had been hung on a line to dry. Savannah hadn't thought of that fresh smell since her mother bought an electric clothes dryer years ago. Or would it be years from now? She frowned at the irony and sniffed again. The coat smelled like him, too. Manly with the slight scent of a sweet cigar. Closing the wardrobe door with a soft click, she smiled. Maybe the situation wasn't so bad after all.

For the fourth time that morning, Savannah walked briskly through the main room filled with patients. And, for the fourth time, conversations ceased. Countless pairs of eyes followed her every movement, some leering, some amused, some sympathetic, but all watching. As much as she hated to admit it, Jacob Cross might possibly be right. Their encounter was going to be the topic of conversation for quite a while. You'd think people would have more to talk about than idle gossip. There was a war going on, after all.

It was still early. The smell of fresh coffee and baking biscuits filtered from the kitchen. She was probably needed to help serve breakfast, but her nerves couldn't stand it. Savannah fled to the sanctity of the veranda to escape the interested stares. Rounding the corner, she found her husband-to-be sound asleep on the porch, his long body contorted to fit a wooden swing meant for two.

Savannah laughed softly at the picture before her. Deep in sleep, his face was relaxed and youthful. Although his look was more rugged than Alan's polished appearance, he was definitely a handsome man.

"Image is everything," Alan used to say as he tucked his name-brand shirt into his designer pants. He had thought he could buy respect. Jacob Cross had a look that commanded it even in his sleep.

The man on the swing coughed slightly, as if vaguely aware he was being watched. He lifted his head quickly, banging it on the swing's armrest with a loud thud, then dropped it back down. Irritation shadowed his features. Slowly, he turned to face Savannah.

"Good morning, Nurse Stuart. I take it you had a restful sleep in *my* bed?" This time he sat up gradually, rubbing his forehead with his fingers.

"Other than being accosted and proposed to in the middle of the night, I most certainly did," she threw back at him in her sweetest voice. "What about you?"

He glared at her. "Not only do I have a possible head injury, I am now betrothed to an irritating fiancee."

She shook her head in frustration and spoke with much more self-assurance than she felt. "Perhaps you're right about getting married. Out of decency, I will let you have a cup of coffee before we argue about the details." She smiled magnanimously at him. "In fact, I'll get it for you. Do you take one lump or two?"

Jacob groaned. "Black, Miss Stuart. I want it black. And then we have a wedding to discuss."

Jacob and Savannah had just begun to see to the soldiers' wounds when a huge wagon arrived. Before coming to a complete halt, the driver was out of his seat, preparing to unload wounded men. Without hesitation, Jacob was out the door. Figuring it must be what she would consider an ambulance, Savannah quickly followed. Two frothing horses had been reined up out front; the wide wagon they pulled had men lying side by side on the wooden floor. Even though big springs had been installed to try and steady the vehicle, she knew it hadn't been an easy ride for the wounded soldiers.

"Where are they from?" Jacob demanded of the driver.

"A skirmish outside of Henderson," the man said hurriedly, out of breath. He reached for the first stretcher. "We had five when we started, Doc, but those two didn't make it." He nodded toward two lifeless forms covered with oilcloth as he lifted a groaning man. "We did what we could for the other three, but they're all pretty bad, this one especially."

The three wounded men were carried into a smaller room off the large main one. Savannah followed Jacob and the stretchers, her triage instincts taking over.

She reached the first man. "Who's the most serious?" She helped move one of the soldiers onto a bed, quickly glancing at his bandaged head and broken arm. The arm hung awkwardly, indicating that it was probably out of joint. He wasn't bleeding to death, so she turned to the next. Gunshot wound to the leg. Priority, she labeled him, moving to the third.

Jacob was already examining the semiconscious man. Savannah reached to touch his pallid skin. Cold. Bloody rags circled his forehead and his shoulder. His arm and leg were also bandaged and soaked with red. This man had lost a lot of blood.

"Artillery hit near him, Doc," the ambulance driver said. "He can't see, and he's been mumbling like a crazy man."

"Shock," she said, looking at the man's bluish fingernails and lips. She reached to check his pulse. It was weak. "His blood pressure is dropping. We have to get fluids into him."

Jacob briefly looked at Savannah in surprise, then focused his attention back to the wounded man. "How long has he been like this?" Jacob snapped, not taking his eyes off his patient.

"He's been shivering with cold since last night. I covered him with every blanket we had, but it wasn't enough. I couldn't get him warm."

"Get me some blankets and water," Jacob ordered.

Savannah moved quickly, although she knew they had nothing to prevent the man's death. The water would ease his thirst and the blankets might make him warm for his final hour, but he was almost unconscious. He wouldn't last much longer.

Handing the water to Jacob, Savannah covered the pitiful man with a wool blanket. He needed internal fluids, lots of them. Even then, survival would be a gamble. Sodium bicarbonate or a blood transfusion would give him more of a fighting chance, but since both practices were yet to be developed, he had little hope of survival.

"Jacob," she said softly, pulling him away to prevent anyone from overhearing. "He's in shock. He's not going to make it."

Jacob stared at her only for a second. In an instant, a tremor of emotional understanding passed through them. "I know, I've seen it before," he said. "I can make him comfortable, but that's about all." The anguish on his face spoke volumes.

The tragedy of the situation struck her hard. Working in this hospital wasn't going to be as easy as she thought, especially if she knew enough to diagnose the wounded, but had no way of properly treating them. Perhaps she could figure out how to perform a makeshift transfusion with . . .

Before her thoughts could go any further, the soldier on the bed gasped for breath. His body arched slightly in one last spasm of agony and then was still. The air of death filled the room.

Standing over the now lifeless body, Jacob closed the man's eyes and pulled the blanket to cover him. "God have mercy."

Savannah felt her eyes grow moist and quickly dabbed at them with a clean cloth. Rarely had she cried when a patient died; a nurse learned early to steel herself against the inevitable. It was just that the soldier's death might have been prevented if only she could have properly treated him for shock. If she was going to bring modern medicine to this hospital, Savannah knew she needed more than just modern diagnosis. She would have to figure out how to treat the wounded with the resources available.

Knowing there were two other wounded men waiting, Jacob wasted no time. He called the medics to make preparations for the dead man. "Give his personal effects to Miss Emma. She and I will write a letter to his family this evening."

He turned to the soldier with the gunshot wound. The damage was serious, although not life-threatening. Savannah headed to Jacob's office to gather up the necessary supplies to clean and bandage the man's leg. It wasn't going to be easy on him, but he would survive.

She knew that there wasn't much medicine to go around, and Jacob kept what painkillers, anesthetics, and whiskey he had in a locked cabinet. The significance of his handing her the key instead of unlocking it himself didn't escape her notice. It was a small start perhaps, but still a start.

As she looked through Jacob's limited store of medicines, she remembered from nursing school how common amputation was during the Civil War, and hoped that was not Jacob's intent. The wound was bad, but it was not yet infected. If she could keep it clean while it was healing, the man might have a chance to leave this place walking. She hurried back to the surgery room.

Jacob was examining the wound when she entered. His dark hair fell across his forehead. He was getting a haircut, she decided. Today.

Using a bullet probe and tweezers, he began to remove the embedded fragments of metal from the gash. No amputation at least. She breathed a sigh of relief. While the process was deliberate and painstaking for Jacob, it was clearly slow and excruciating for the soldier. The doctor looked up from his task to the man's ashen face.

"Savannah, give him a little whiskey, would you? He looks as if he might need it."

Quickly, she complied, allowing the man a swig from a half-empty bottle. Handing Jacob a clean bandage, she glanced around the room for the first time since entering. It must have been Miss

Emma's dining room at one time. Unlike the dark, deeply paneled main room, this area was bright with plenty of windows. Lace curtains still hung over each one. The walls were mostly white except where blood had splattered on the plaster and dried in dark spots. Miss Emma had courage to give up her beautiful home.

"Nurse," Jacob said, looking up from his work, "please take a look at his arm and let me know what you find." He nodded toward the first patient.

"Yes, Doctor." Savannah smiled at the fellow to offer encouragement, noting that he was almost as young as the boy from yesterday.

"Red didn't make it, did he?" he asked about his dead friend, pain filling his eyes. Savannah shook her head but remained silent. It was best to let him grieve in his own way. "He was a good soldier, Doc," the boy called out. "Tell his ma for me, will you?"

Savannah was on a mission. She bustled through the hospital, gathering every piece of medical and surgical equipment she could find, including all of Jacob's instruments. The folks of 1862 were about to have their first lesson about controlling infection. There was no reason for any of these men to die from infection, especially since sterilization was a relatively easy thing to do. She may not be able to give a blood transfusion, but she could make sure this place was as germ-free as possible.

She found several buckets and a bar of lye soap

in the storage room. It wasn't as good as the germicide in the hospital back home, but it would do. Now all she needed was hot water and she could begin. Filling a bucket with water from the pump outside, Savannah headed toward the kitchen located in a smaller building attached to the rear of the house.

The enormity of the task overwhelmed her. Once the medical instruments were sterile, she had to figure out how to keep them that way. Then she needed to convince Jacob of the importance of sterilizing them after each use. As stubborn as he seemed to be, that might not be easy.

Savannah also had to figure out how to disinfect the entire house. As a home, Miss Emma kept the place spotless. Since it was a hospital, though, it needed to be more than spotless. Immaculate was the word, especially in areas where Jacob treated patients. Jacob's instincts were on target when he separated the infectious patients, especially where gangrene had set in, from those in less serious situations. But more had to be done—and immediately. Without penicillin or other antibiotics, Savannah realized the only way to stop the spread of disease was to prevent it from happening in the first place. That would take some work. Knowing it would deeply offend Miss Emma to be blunt about her plans, Savannah sensed she would have to be delicate and approach the situation with care.

She started toward the kitchen in search of Miss Emma. The thoughts of changing history still nagged at her. If her plans were successful and she was able to do some good for the hospital, to save a man who would have otherwise died, what repercussions would there be? What if she helped save a general who might influence the outcome of the war? What if another lived to father a child who would dramatically alter the history of the United States twenty years from now? Someone who might never have existed had she not intervened?

The questions were overwhelming on the surface. But underneath they were quite simple. Despite her amazement at being thrust into this time, she was still a nurse with an oath to heal. Surely that counted for something. She sensed that she had to trust that instinct and whatever force that brought her here.

Savannah found the spry lady working in the kitchen shelling beans for the evening meal. A large black woman, dressed in red gingham, sat beside her, doing the same. Wonderful smells wafted through the room as stew simmered in a huge iron kettle on the stove. The scent of freshly baked bread drifted enticingly from the oven. Miss Emma's eyes brightened as Savannah walked through the door.

"Good morning, Miss Stuart," she said with delight. "May I call you Savannah? That's such a beautiful name, so full of grace. Don't you agree, Deltry?" Miss Emma asked the black woman beside her.

"Yessum. Fine name." She nodded, giving Savannah a wink.

"Jacob told me the wonderful news!" Miss

Emma went on without waiting for Savannah's reply. "I'm so pleased you've agreed to marry him. He's needed someone in his life since . . . Well, never you mind. I'm happy for you." She patted the chair next to her for Savannah to join them. "This is Deltry. Jacob told you that I run the place, but it's really not true. Deltry takes care of everything for me."

Deltry grinned, clearly pleased by Miss Emma's compliment. "Aw, go on, Miss Emma. This is your house, not mine. You do mighty fine, I say." She dusted a heavy iron pan with flour.

Putting her bucket on the floor, Savannah smiled at the two women. "I came in to heat some water. I want to sterilize the surgical instruments." She pleasantly avoided the topic of her impending marriage.

"Sterilize?" Miss Emma looked up from her beans. "What do you mean, dear?"

"I want to give them a good washing and make sure they're clean," she replied lightly. "I found one bar, but I could use some more lye soap if you have any."

Miss Emma nodded. "Certainly. There's already hot water on the stove, and Deltry will get you more soap. Cleanliness is next to godliness, the Good Book says. Help yourself."

Savannah breathed a sigh of relief. Perhaps recruiting Miss Emma to help wouldn't be difficult after all. The huge black woman rose to fetch the soap.

"Deltry's such a dear," Miss Emma confided warmly. "She's been with me for almost twenty-five years. Never have to worry about her, no sir. She's a gem, my Deltry." The old woman resumed shelling beans.

Savannah blinked in quiet disbelief at Miss Emma's words. Deltry was an honest-to-goodness slave. How naive she was not to have realized the several black people she met in the hospital were slaves, too. The reality of her situation again lashed out. Slavery was something you read about in history books, not something you saw in everyday life. She instinctively opened her mouth to voice an indignant opinion but thought better of it. The war was being fought to bring about change anyway. Would it do any good to alienate her new friend? Before Savannah could make up her mind what to do, Deltry returned with the soap.

"You know, dear," Miss Emma continued, not glancing up to see Savannah's shocked expression, "being a Cross has responsibilities around these parts. You are taking one of the few eligible bachelors off the marriageable list. Quite an accomplishment for someone new to St. George."

Savannah opened her mouth to object. Miss Emma made it sound as if she had wooed the man, and their marriage would be a real one. If Jacob had told her the truth during their conversation in the hall last night, Miss Emma was choosing to ignore it.

"It's important that you present the image they expect," she went right on, paying no mind to Savannah's attempt to interrupt. "Once word is out that Jacob is betrothed, people will be curious to see the future Mrs. Cross. It will be to your advantage to dress accordingly." She looked knowingly at Savannah and then at her rumpled clothing.

Savannah's faced flushed. She looked down at her wrinkled skirt and blouse, embarrassed. She would love a hot bath and a clean dress. The only problem was, she hadn't had a chance for a bath and didn't have a single clean dress to her name. Miss Emma probably thought she arrived with several travel bags, just like any other Southern woman. She had to think fast to offer a reasonable explanation as to why someone would travel without luggage. Only if she were fleeing from danger or running away from something like . . . like war. Remembering her fib from the day before, an idea spawned in Savannah's mind and quickly took root.

Assuming a look of shame, Savannah hung her head and spoke softly, "Miss Emma, I know fighting has been terrible here in Tennessee, but it's been much worse in Georgia, especially Atlanta." Savannah felt like a heel for lying to the old woman, but sent up a silent prayer of thanks for having seen *Gone with the Wind* eighteen times. "My cousin, Melanie, was about to have her first child, so my sister, Scarlett, and I waited until the last possible minute to flee. The city began to burn just after Melanie had her baby. We had to steal a wagon and an old, broken-down horse, but we managed to get them into it and fled with literally the clothes on our—"

"Oh, my dear!" Miss Emma exclaimed. "How

inconsiderate of me! You've been through so much! Why, I swear I don't recall hearing anything about Atlanta burning. Mercy, but messages are so garbled these days. How unkind of me to make you relive such horrid memories!" She patted Savannah's hand, offering comfort. "I have several lovely dresses that Deltry can alter to fit you until Jacob can get you a proper wardrobe. When he does, don't you skimp on it, either. The war has taken a lot from him, but thankfully not his fortune. His father was wise enough to invest in several European banks long before war was declared. We'll go to the sundry after dinner and get you the other things you may need. And, Savannah"—she looked humbled—"I am so sorry."

"Please, Miss Emma," Savannah said, placing her hand on the gentle woman's shoulder. "We've all suffered tremendously since the war began, and I appreciate your kindness. I do need a presentable dress." Self-consciously, she smoothed her hand over her skirt.

The sound of the door scraping open and boots wiping off mud interrupted their discussion. Savannah's heart jumped as her future husband entered the room. He had changed since this morning. His deeply tanned skin struck an attractive contrast to the crisp white fabric of his shirt. Immediately, her skin grew warm as something electric filled the air. Her heart pounded in a nervous rhythm as he sat down at the table with them.

"You fled Atlanta as it burned, Miss Stuart?" His blue eyes were cool.

Savannah nodded, not saying a word. He must have been standing at the door.

"Jacob," Miss Emma said, "I must take Savannah into town this afternoon to help carry packages. She will also need fabric for a proper wedding dress."

Savannah was thankful Miss Emma delicately avoided the fact that what she wore was all she had.

Jacob stared sharply at Savannah's peasant skirt and riding boots. Her white shirt was now dotted with red from this morning. Her own blood raced through her body, causing every nerve to stand on end as his icy eyes took in her appearance.

"Of course, Miss Emma," he said, glancing from her to the older woman. "I would appreciate it, too, if you saw to it that Miss Stuart has a proper wardrobe while you are there." His tone suggested he was not pleased.

Shame burned from his words. How dare he be so arrogant! The understanding she thought they had developed earlier was now replaced with confusion. This morning they shared a connection as they worked feverishly to save the dying man. Now he was cold and angry. A stubborn indignation began to take root and spread through her soul. She may not have the means right this moment to afford new clothes, but she would. Surely she'd be compensated for her work at the hospital in some way. The clothes she wore now were fine back in her world; they'd just have to do in this one. She opened her mouth to tell Jacob Cross just what she thought of his phony generosity when Miss Emma kicked her shin sharply under the table. Her warning look made Savannah bite her tongue. Miss Emma knew her soon-to-be husband far better than Savannah probably ever would. Perhaps a little humility was in order, if only for the sake of the hospital. If cleanliness was going to be next to a religion around here, clean clothing was a priority. No fresh blood stains allowed. She had no choice but to swallow her pride and lead the way.

"That's very kind of you, *Dr.* Cross." Sarcasm dripped from her words. Miss Emma had made her point in a single glance; the clothes on her back were the only ones she had. As much as she hated it, for the time being she was reliant on the generosity of the stony M.D. whose ice-blue eyes stared a hole straight through her heart.

"St. George was once a very beautiful town," Miss Emma mentioned as she and Savannah walked along the sidewalk toward the mercantile. "Now that we're at war, the bloom has left the city."

Staring at the faded gray buildings lining the street, Savannah realized they were just like she had seen in history books. Mostly women strolled along the planked sidewalks while horses, wagons, and buggies filled the hard-packed dirt road. St. George may not be a big town, but it was a busy one. The Confederate soldiers ambling along the streets on foot or on horseback were a constant reminder to the townsfolk that they were at war. Miss Emma and she returned the nod of an officer clad in gray wool riding by on a striking bay horse. His uniform's brass buttons glinted in glinted in the sun as his scabbard rattled against the saddle.

"Rumor has it," Miss Emma continued, "that the Yanks are headed this way. That's why so many soldiers are in town—"

"Miss Emma!" interrupted a shrill voice coming from behind them. "How are you?" A tall, middle-aged woman reached for the older one's hand. "It's so good to see you!" She turned toward Savannah, curiosity expressed in her face. "And who do we have here?"

"Ruth Ann Cox, I'd like to you to meet Miss Savannah Stuart from Atlanta." Ruth Ann held out her hand with a smile, and Miss Emma continued, "Savannah and Jacob are to be married this Sunday." Almost imperceptibly, Ruth Ann's smile froze as she coolly withdrew her gloved hand from Savannah's grasp.

"Yes, I heard." She looked down her nose at Savannah, making it a point to notice her bloodstained clothing.

"Of course," Miss Emma continued gleefully, "we do hope you will be able to join us for the ceremony. Even though it's short notice, we're hoping Rose can prepare a wonderful evening meal for us afterward. Do come."

"What? Oh, well . . . yes . . . of course," Ruth Ann stammered. The news of Jacob's impending marriage had spread as quickly as he and Miss Emma had assumed, Savannah noted.

Miss Emma chuckled as Ruth Ann made a hasty departure back up the sidewalk. "I've known Ruth Ann since she was a child, and I've never truly enjoyed her company," she said companionably. "Don't you fret about her reaction, either. She's been trying to marry her daughter, Edith, to Jacob since Anna died. She's been trying to marry that girl to every available man in town. The child is not blessed with a gracious face or a sunny disposition." Miss Emma grinned, patting her arm. "She'll be back to normal once she finds another eligible bachelor for Edith."

"Who is Anna?" Savannah asked, wondering if it was the beautiful brunette in the photograph. She mentally braced herself for the answer. Maybe she really didn't want to know if Jacob had anyone else in his life.

Miss Emma stopped walking and looked at her carefully. "I forget that you and Jacob have not known each other very long, child. Anna was Jacob's first wife, dear. She was killed before the war began. I'm certain Jacob will tell you all about it."

Savannah felt like someone had hit her in the stomach. While she mourned dreadfully the desertion of a stubborn fiance, poor Jacob mourned the death of his wife. No wonder he was so distant.

Once in the store, Miss Emma helped Savannah pick out the items she would need. Nothing was said about the new nurse not having the basic necessities like a chemise and corset. If Miss Emma thought anything was amiss, she remained silent as Savannah stared at the undergarments. How in the world would she get into these contraptions?

"Wouldn't this make a lovely day dress?" Miss Emma ran her wrinkled hand along a length of cream-colored muslin. A pattern of delicate pink roses added a feminine touch. "What do you think, dear?" She turned to see Savannah holding a corset, inspecting it at eye level. "Savannah, please, those are private items! The muslin, dear, do you like it?"

"What? Oh, yes, that is nice. But isn't there anything already made?" She glanced around, hoping for something she could wear right away. Her heart sank to see bolt after bolt of fabrics, but no dresses.

The older woman stared at her with a puzzled expression. "Of course not. We sometimes got such fashions from Paris before the war, but certainly not now." Her chin lifted slightly in offense. She obviously thought the Georgia peach considered herself above wearing home-sewn garments. Regret instantly filled Savannah.

"Oh, Miss Emma, I apologize for how that sounded." She rushed to her side by the fabrics. "I was only hoping to prevent Deltry from having to sew something for me. I hate to be a burden."

Instantly, the wizened face softened. "Savannah, dear, I do declare! Is that what's worrying you? Deltry loves to sew and will be pleased to make you a few dresses. Now, do you like the cream muslin or the blue?" Although her words were kind, the wise eyes still held concern.

"The blue," Savannah replied meekly. "It would look better with my hair." She turned to the ready-made shoes in the corner. The selection was meager so she opted to keep her riding boots rather than struggling with the tedious button-up versions. Miss Emma insisted on a pair of black slippers for evening wear and a pair of pale ivory satin slippers for her wedding.

"These are a perfect match with the silk dress Deltry's going to alter for you!" her friend exclaimed. "We are so fortunate to find them, too," she said sharply. "You do have the biggest feet I believe I've ever seen!" the older woman teased.

"Can't help it!" Savannah laughed, lifting her chin in mock indignation. "I come from a family of giants!"

Thinking of her late parents, it struck Savannah that there was no one back home who would so much as notice her absence. She had no relatives to speak of living nearby, her friends at work would simply think she was pulling a different shift, and thanks to her long hours at the hospital, her landlady was accustomed to not seeing her for weeks. Even Alan's obnoxious cat had moved in with her neighbors. There was no one who would really miss her, she thought sadly.

"Did your cousin have a boy or a girl?" Miss Emma interrupted Savannah's musing.

"My cousin?" Savannah looked confused.

"Yes, the one you mentioned this morning. Did she have a boy or a girl?"

"Oh! Melanie." Savannah knew she would have to be more attentive. Miss Emma may have faultless manners, but her mind was far too sharp not to catch inaccuracies. She smiled brightly, placing her slippers on the counter. "Melanie had a little boy. She named him Beau." She thought that was the baby's name in the movie, but she wasn't sure. A twinge of worry flashed through her as she struggled to remember.

"I'm sure you miss them all." Miss Emma touched her arm with compassion. "I've lost most of my family because of this war, too."

Savannah felt a sharp twinge of guilt for lying to her precious new friend, but she knew the alternative was just as unacceptable. No one would believe she was from the future. Not a single soul. She was alone in this strange time, this whole new world.

"No, dear, those are for men," Miss Emma said to Savannah as she looked over a selection of white cotton shirts.

Knowing she had to set an example for the rest of the hospital, Savannah was determined. She assumed a tone that implied Miss Emma would understand completely. "I really need several of these to wear over my clothes while I'm working with the patients. That way I can wash one every day and won't spread infection among them. What do you think?" She held the shirt in front of her so Miss Emma could offer an opinion.

"I understand, Savannah, but it's still a man's shirt," the older woman replied stubbornly. "How about something a bit more ladylike, like a nice apron?"

Sensing that Miss Emma wasn't going to back down on this issue, Savannah settled on several full-sized aprons. The aprons were large enough that she could wrap them around her front and back and still tie them securely. She'd have to be careful about her sleeves, but it was a fair compromise.

"Here, Savannah, you must have this, especially on your wedding night." Miss Emma held up a bottle of sweet-smelling magnolia blossom perfume. Considering the nature of her relationship with Jacob, Savannah doubted the need for such enticements. But she hated to disappoint Miss Emma's romantic expectations and put the bottle on the counter with her mounting purchases.

Only a few things were missing—modern conveniences that she'd always taken for granted, like tampons, makeup, deodorant, toothpaste, and hair spray. There were going to be some definite problems with being stuck in time.

"Before we were at war with the North, we were able to buy anything." Miss Emma walked up behind her. "Compared to then, most of our stores are now practically empty, and what they do have is outrageously expensive. Once Jacob bought a barrel of flour for twelve dollars."

Savannah raised her eyebrows. Twelve dollars didn't seem like much to her, but she could imagine what Miss Emma and Jacob must have had to go through for their hospital.

"I have to hand it to Jacob," she continued. "He's always found a way to keep the hospital running. The townsfolk generally keep us supplied in bandages, but rarely do we have enough medicines. He somehow manages to treat the wounded anyway. Jacob's a wonderful doctor." Pride lifted her head.

"That's exactly why we're glad he's in charge of our hospital, Miss Emma. He's an excellent physician." The startling clear baritone voice came from behind them.

Looking back, Savannah felt her heart rise to her throat. Behind her stood a man almost identical to her former fiance. If not identical to Alan, then definitely close enough to be his brother. Her heart lurched at his familiar smile.

"Colonel Sanger." Miss Emma nodded, coldly looking over her glasses at the striking officer. It was obvious she preferred better company. Savannah's eyebrow tilted with interest at her friend's tone.

"Might I ask for a proper introduction to your lovely companion, Miss Emma?" The colonel offered a brilliant smile, never once taking his eyes from Savannah's.

"That's Miss Long to you, young man," Miss Emma responded, pointing her finger at his chest. "Your kind may be in charge thanks to this terrible war, but I am still your elder. You will address me with respect." She lifted her chin, squared her shoulders, and narrowed her eyes.

Caught off guard by Miss Emma's reaction, Savannah's smile was replaced by a look of concern. No matter how handsome he was, or that he was a fellow Southerner, this man represented marshal law in this city.

Colonel Sanger drew his eyes from Savannah to glance at the old woman. "I do beg your pardon, Miss Long," he said with seemingly genuine remorse. "Everyone in town fondly refers to you by your given name. I'm afraid I've picked up the habit. I have the utmost respect for you and Dr. Cross."

"Yes . . . well, see that it does not happen again," Miss Emma said, softening a bit. She was obviously not expecting his apology, and her voice still had an edge. She started to turn away, a selection of colorful threads conveniently catching her eye.

"Miss Long?" The tall man stopped her. "You were about to make introductions." This time his voice was polite, but firm.

She returned to Savannah's side. "Miss Savannah Stuart, I would like you to have the acquaintance of Colonel Jordan Sanger, the officer in command of St. George." The emphasis on "command," Savannah was sure, meant to defer anything more than an introduction.

"How do you do, Colonel Sanger?" Savannah asked, offering her hand. Miss Emma may not approve, but this man was too much like Alan for her simply to ignore. His tall build and blond good looks were dashing in his neatly pressed uniform. Even his light brown eyes staring down at her were the same unusual color as Alan's. Although she was taken aback, her heart pounded with delight. Maybe there was a reason for her journey after all. In spite of Miss Emma's disapproving stare, her blood began to race.

Never taking his eyes from Savannah's, the colonel brought her hand to his lips brushing it softly. "The pleasure is mine, Miss Stuart."

"Miss Stuart is betrothed to Dr. Cross," Miss Emma interjected pointedly before Savannah could regain control of her senses. "The wedding is this Sunday," she added firmly, obviously not liking what she was seeing.

A glimmer of recognition briefly crossed Colonel Sanger's face and was quickly masked by a polite smile. "Oh, yes, I did hear something along those lines. You are indeed as lovely as I had imagined, Miss Stuart. I truly regret we met only today. Fate has played a cruel trick on me." He released her hand with a light squeeze. "Good afternoon, ladies." With a last heated glance at Savannah, he touched his gloved finger to the brim of his hat and turned for the door.

Savannah's hand was in the same position as when Colonel Sanger released it. The corners of her mouth lifted in a dreamy sigh. He may look like Alan, but the resemblance stopped there. It wasn't in Alan's soul to be that charming or polite.

"Savannah!" Miss Emma snapped. "Do not stand there gawking! Help me find thread to alter your dress."

Miss Emma remained quiet for most of the walk back to the hospital, no doubt disturbed by their encounter with Colonel Sanger. Maybe it wasn't such a good time to approach her about helping to sterilize the hospital and all the surgical instruments.

Savannah was sure she had mooned over Colonel Sanger just enough to offend Miss Emma's sense of propriety. She couldn't help it, though.

87

He was so much like Alan. Surely it was no coincidence. What if she was there because of him instead of the soldiers? It was all so confusing. Still, the hospital was important.

"Miss Emma," she hesitated, "I apologize for my reaction to Colonel Sanger. He looks so much like someone I once deeply cared for, someone who no longer exists."

The older woman's expression instantly softened. "I understand, dear. We've all lost a love or two by this war. What was his name, your lost love?"

"Alan," Savannah replied, thankful she could be truthful about that at least. "He was a doctor, too. In fact. . ." she began carefully as they strolled along the sidewalk. This was the opportunity she needed. "He believed that more soldiers died from infection than from their wounds."

Miss Emma lifted a thin eyebrow. Savannah took a deep breath and plunged ahead. "He thought it was possible to reduce the rate of infection and began showing me how." She grew quiet, sensing that Miss Emma's curiosity would surely prompt her for more. A soldier passed them on the sidewalk, and both nodded as he tipped his hat.

"What do you mean, dear?"

Savannah smiled inwardly. She had her hooked; now to reel her in. "There are things called germs that actually cause most of the infections. When a doctor or nurse moves from patient to patient using the same instruments or cloth pads, what we called sponges, the germs spread right along with them. If we could disinfect everything we use before it's needed again, I'd bet we'd see an improvement."

Savannah bit her lip nervously, hoping Miss Emma would understand. It was obvious how much importance Jacob placed on the older woman's opinion. Once she was convinced, Miss Emma herself would see to it that every scalpel, saw, probe, bucket, and bowl was sanitized.

"Are you saying that we can prevent these boys from getting infections if we wash Jacob's instruments each time he uses them?"

"Pretty much, and that includes infections that can lead to gangrene and traumatic fever."

Miss Emma's eyes gleamed. For someone who had never so much as heard about germs, she was sharp. They walked along in silence for a minute or two, Miss Emma considering Savannah's words.

"Savannah." She stopped suddenly, taking Savannah's hands into her own. "Does this mean that if we keep our boys from getting these . . . germs, more of them might live?" She looked intently at Savannah's face as if trying to determine if this was too good to be true.

"There's a definite chance of it, Miss Emma," Savannah replied honestly.

"Oh, child, you are a blessing!" Miss Emma smiled with genuine fondness. "I've sensed what you are saying for some time, although this is the first I've heard about germs." Her tone grew serious. "Have you discussed this with Jacob?"

"Well, no, we haven't really had a chance, but I intend to do so right away. Actually, I didn't think he would get angry if I used my own initiative to keep things clean, especially with your guidance."

"Good thinking." She patted Savannah's arm as they walked on. "He's stubborn, though, just like his father. You might get him to try it for a few days, but if he sees no change in the patients, he'll go right back to his old habits."

"Then it's up to us to make sure he sees an improvement." Savannah was confident he would see results. She just had to make sure they were dramatic. As they approached Miss Emma's beautiful home, she gave a quick prayer of thanks for the lady walking beside her.

The afternoon had gone well, Savannah thought as she eyed her image in the looking glass on Jacob's dresser. Back home, she had always been too busy to dawdle long in front of a mirror. Today she carefully considered her reflection. Wearing her brand-new chemise and petticoats, she leaned forward for a closer look. Her figure was thin, not unattractively so, but her pale hair was in desperate need of styling. She reached for her new brush to sort the tangled knots. Later she'd see about washing it.

Suddenly, a movement to the right caught her eye. Savannah turned quickly to see Jacob leaning against the door, watching her intently. His expression was unreadable. For a long moment, she did not move. The air grew warm.

"I . . . I was just fixing my hair," she finally stammered, nervously aware of the tight confines of the room. Her chin lifted as she struggled to maintain her composure. His glance stole downward to her new chemise. Savannah was suddenly quite conscious of the flimsy garment. Her knuckles turned white as she tightly gripped the wooden handle of the brush. As if drawing from a strong internal force, Jacob's eyes rose back to hers. This time, though, they were controlled. Any spark of interest she might have imagined had disappeared like a vapor.

He walked toward her and grabbed her hand. Excitement flirted across her skin when his fingers surrounded her own. She jerked at the intensity and quickly released the brush, breaking the connection between them.

"Can I not enter my room without finding you in it?" Jacob demanded, his voice low and disconcerting. He seemed intent to draw her into yet another argument. Remembering her promise to make the best of things, Savannah refused to rise to his challenge. Grabbing the brush from his grasp, she turned back to the mirror and resumed her task, trying to ignore his presence.

"Since no one told me any different, I assumed this is where I should stay until the wedding," Savannah spoke, struggling to control her temper. "Which, by the way, I've heard is to be this Sunday. You would think someone might let the bride know." She tossed a strand of her hair over her shoulder in a way that dared him to argue.

"Our wedding does not head my list of topics for pleasant conversation," he drawled with distinct mockery.

"Why is it then you insist on this marriage?"

Her attempts to hold her temper failed as she defiantly challenged him. Catching his eye in the mirror, she continued the steady rhythm with the brush. "I understand this code of honor you have, but surely . . ." Her voice trailed off in exasperation. Surely she could make one last stand.

"As I explained before, even though this is a hospital, it is still Miss Emma's home." He rubbed his hand along his jaw in frustration. "Many people know about the indiscretion that occurred in this house last night. That reflects on Miss Emma as well as you and me. I will see to it that Miss Emma does not suffer embarrassment because you were found in my room well after midnight," he added, his voice low, calm.

"Don't be unreasonable," Savannah countered. "I'm certain we can explain—"

"Madam, I assure you, the word unreasonable has crossed my mind," he interrupted. "But I am indebted to Miss Emma for allowing me to use her home as a hospital, and I am indebted to her as my late mother's dearest friend. We will do whatever is necessary for her sake. There is also the matter of the army closing the hospital."

"Why would they do that? According to Miss Emma, there is no other hospital within one hundred miles, and no other doctor within fifty. It would be foolish to close a much-needed hospital because of something like this, Jacob. It just doesn't make sense."

Jacob stiffened. "You're right. It wouldn't make sense to close the hospital." He ran his hand through his hair. "I've learned that rational men are not always the ones in charge during a war, especially this one."

Savannah walked to the bed and sat on the edge, facing him. Her hands nervously plucked the chenille spread. Her body tensed as she tried to think of a convincing alternative.

"If you object this strongly to our marriage, Savannah, you could leave and go back to where you came from."

Seconds ticked by like hours. "I have nowhere to go," she finally replied, dropping her gaze. "My home does not exist now."

"Then I guess you'd best be planning your wedding." With that, he rose from the chair and crossed the room in two strides. "I will ask Miss Emma to set up a cot in my office until after we are married," he added sharply. "Then I expect to sleep in my room and in my bed."

"Where will I sleep after that? You said there are no other available rooms."

"You seem to be a smart woman, Savannah. You figure it out." Jacob reached into the wardrobe, grabbed a clean shirt, and without so much as a glance at her, swung around and strode out the door.

Walking down the hall holding his shirt, Jacob smiled softly. That hadn't been so bad. He hadn't known Savannah and Miss Emma had returned from town as he headed to his room for a change of clothing. Opening the door to find Savannah standing there practically naked caught him off-guard. He probably should have excused himself and given her privacy, but he stood frozen. The afternoon sun streaming through the window behind her had caused her hair to glisten, and the thin material of her chemise had created an inviting silhouette, one that had almost beckoned him to come closer. It would have been so easy to reach out and answer the call, to touch her soft locks, to feel for himself her creamy skin, and to lose himself in her curves. He had taken a step forward, then had stopped as the vision swung around to see him standing in the doorway. Her eyes had been wary and uncertain. He inwardly sighed. After everything that had happened between them, he supposed she had reason.

Even as the words came from his mouth earlier, Jacob hoped she would not call his bluff and flee. He needed a nurse and, as distracting as this one was proving to be, the woman was quite competent in that regard. There were other reasons, too. Reasons he was afraid to contemplate.

Truth was, his future bride was getting under his skin. The last thing he needed was to get emotionally involved with another woman, no matter how attractive she was and no matter that she was about to become his bride. It would only mean heartache, and he was determined not to go through that again. Taking the stairs two at a time, he resolved to put one Miss Savannah Stuart out of his mind.

Damn! Savannah never dreamed any man could make her angrier than Alan, but Jacob Cross came mighty close. Tears welled in her eyes as she thought of their charade of a marriage. If only she could leave as he had suggested. As quickly as that thought sparked, it flickered out. The bottom line was that she had nowhere else to go. Even if she were brave enough to leave the hospital, it would be foolish for a solitary woman to travel through a war-torn country, not to mention that she was more than one hundred years out of her element. Besides, she had no money for travel and no idea where to go if she did.

She threw herself face down on the bed and let the tears come. Why had this happened to her? Of all the people in the world, why had she been chosen to come back in time? If she were supposed to use her medical skills to heal these soldiers, why was everything else proving to be so difficult?

A tentative knock came from the closed door. "Savannah?" Miss Emma gently opened the door. "On his way downstairs, Jacob asked me to inquire if you'd like to join him for supper at Rose's." Her faded blue eyes offered unspoken sympathy. "He can be a lout sometimes, dear, but his heart is good."

Savannah rolled her eyes as she dabbed them with the edge of an embroidered pillowcase. She strongly doubted that Jacob had actually asked for her company. More than likely, Miss Emma overheard the door slam and cornered the impossible man as he stormed back downstairs. Jacob was right about one thing: Miss Emma was special, and Savannah's only friend in this misadventure. That made her decision a little easier.

Even though her heart was heavy, she put on a smile.

"Of course, Miss Emma. Please tell Jacob I would be delighted."

Promptly at eight, Savannah stood nervously waiting in the foyer, her palms clammy underneath her lacy white gloves. Gazing at her image in the vanity mirror, she was pleased with the effect, even if her stomach was churning. Her gown was a lovely green silk with a low, rounded neckline that dropped off her shoulders. Miss Emma had called it a dress for romance as she and Deltry painstakingly altered it that afternoon. Considering her image in the mirror, Savannah understood what she meant. She felt very pretty and more feminine than she ever had.

Smoothing her hair, she touched the beautiful pearl comb holding it in a chignon. It was another present from Miss Emma, as were the gloves and a dainty lace handkerchief stuffed in a hidden pocket.

"Good evening, Miss Stuart," Jacob said formally as he walked through the hall into the foyer.

Startled, she spun at the sound of his drawling voice, holding her breath as he approached. He was dressed for supper in a gray broadcloth coat that hung almost to his knees. A starched white cotton shirt and a black tie accented his newly barbered hair while pressed, tan trousers emphasized his lean thighs.

"You look lovely this evening." His gaze roved over her with an intensity that startled her.

"Why thank you, Dr. Cross. You also look quite dashing." Recovering her composure, she returned the look with one as insolent as his own. Two could play this game. "I see you made a trip to the barber." She flashed him a saccharine smile.

"I'm glad it pleases you," he returned in the same tone. "Shall we go?"

Taking the wrap from her hands, he placed it around her shoulders, his fingers lingering a bit too long to be an accidental brush. His eyes gave no indication of his thoughts as he opened the polished door, allowing her to precede him over the threshold and into the night air.

Taking her by the elbow, Jacob guided Savannah through the streets of St. George toward Rose's Restaurant. Had times been different, he might have whisked her away in a fine carriage to dine in a more stylish establishment. Tonight, supper at Rose's and his charming personality would have to do.

The woman walking at his side was a mystery. Each time he looked into her eyes, he read something new. This afternoon she had been an irritating spitfire, and tonight she seemed, well, demure . . . almost charming. This might prove to be an enjoyable evening after all.

A companionable silence settled between them as they strolled along the sidewalk. He glanced sideways at the woman in rustling green, noticing how curious she was about the city's activities. She watched with childlike wonder as a formation of soldiers rode by on matching horses. It was almost as if she saw everything for the first time. She was a competent, experienced nurse and could match him wit for wit in an argument, yet she seemed so innocently fragile now.

In spite of his promise not to get involved, Jacob struggled not to look forward to their evening out. He hadn't dined with a woman in this manner since he was courting Anna. Guilt at impugning his late wife's memory was never far off, especially when it came to other women. Marriage was something he hadn't considered once since her death. Not only was he about to have supper with this beautiful woman, he intended to marry her, too. Surprisingly, it didn't bother him. He felt a reluctant sense of excitement when it came to Savannah Stuart, a sense that his life was about to begin again.

Rose's Restaurant proved to be a delightfully charming place, with dozens of small white-clothed tables filling the room. Each table was graced with a vase of wildflowers and small candles that cast a sultry glow, creating a comfortable and inviting atmosphere. A small crystal chandelier hung in the center of the large dining area, the last remnant of glorious prewar days.

They were seated in a quiet corner near the back of the room. Savannah looked around with interest, stealing a glance at Jacob as he gave their order to an elegantly tall redhead. The woman's smile at Jacob suggested he frequented the restaurant often. She cast a disapproving look at Savannah as she walked off. A nervous giggle formed at the back of Savannah's throat. Her reputation was definitely spreading.

Suddenly Jacob spoke, causing her to jump, "I was impressed with your skills this morning, Savannah. You quickly determined who needed the most attention, then saw to it."

Savannah shrugged at the compliment. "Triage is what we all do naturally. It comes with the profession."

"Triage?"

"That's what we call it where I come from," she explained. "It means sorting out the casualties." At his interested expression, she continued, "When wounded arrive in a group, the first thing you do is determine a priority of need. You know, who's the most serious and who needs attention the fastest."

Jacob was silent. "I didn't know it had a name, though. How did you?"

"I learned it in nursing school."

"There's a nursing school in Atlanta? I thought most nurses learned their skills from a doctor," he pressed.

Savannah sensed he was uncertain she was telling the truth but didn't want to call her on it. She hadn't considered how nurses were trained before the Civil War. Did they even have nursing school in this time? It really didn't matter. She had already put her foot in her mouth, and she couldn't back down now.

"In Atlanta," she repeated firmly, staring him right in the eye.

"Miss Stuart!" A male voice interrupted their gaze. Savannah looked up to see Colonel Sanger still in full dress uniform. "How delightful to see you again." He nodded at Jacob. "Dr. Cross."

Jacob rose to his feet, looking from her to the colonel. "You two know each other?" Confusion crossed his face as the gallant officer reached for Savannah's offered hand.

"Of course," Colonel Sanger replied before Savannah could speak. "Miss Emma introduced us earlier today." His lips brushed her gloved hand as he searched her face. Desire illuminated his eyes. If only Alan could have looked at me that way, she mused, a small sigh escaping her lips.

"Did she also tell you, Colonel," Jacob spoke sharply, "that Miss Stuart is my fiancee?" He glared at both of them, politeness turning to irritation.

"That she did, Dr. Cross. Allow me to offer my best wishes. You have found the most beautiful woman in St. George, so you must forgive me for being a little jealous." He smiled at Jacob, flashing his brilliant white teeth.

Savannah's lips lifted. The colonel was indeed charming, even though Miss Emma, and now Jacob, were outraged by his presence.

"I'll leave you to your supper." Colonel Sanger nodded and strode off.

Nothing short of fury marked Jacob's face as he sat back down. "Remind me to thank Miss Emma for her helpfulness," he said cynically.

"Jacob, please don't get angry." Savannah wanted to soothe his ruffled nerves, although she really didn't know why. "Whether I like it or not, this Sunday you and I are to be married. I intend to follow through with that no matter how charming Colonel Sanger might be."

Jacob didn't appear to hear her words. He was lost in his own dark thoughts. Savannah sighed. So much for a pleasant evening.

The redhead returned to the table a few minutes later with two plates of wonderfully aromatic fried chicken, mashed potatoes and gravy, snap beans, and fluffy biscuits with butter. Calories, fat, and cholesterol had yet to be discovered, either, Savannah thought with a satisfied grin, lifting her fork happily to her mouth.

Jacob sat moody and withdrawn, and Savannah wondered why Colonel Sanger had prompted his mood change. Judging from his reaction and that of Miss Emma, Colonel Sanger must not be as charming as he appeared. "How's your supper?" she asked in an effort to break the silence.

"What?" He looked up, startled she had spoken.

"Your supper." She glanced down at his plate. "How is it?"

"Fine, fine. Rose has outdone herself as usual." Dismissing her, he reached inside his vest pocket and pulled out his pocket watch. After glancing at the time, he slowly began to wind the gold stem.

"Nice watch," Savannah said politely in an effort to get the conversation going. Her husband-to-be was not a talkative man—that was certain. "My father collected watches. He had one in particular that has been in our family since . . ." She stopped. Since when, she thought, the Civil War? "Since my great-great-great-aunt. It's quite an heirloom," she finished lamely.

Jacob rubbed his fingers across the shiny gold. "This one is very special to me. It was my father's."

"May I?" Savannah held out her hand.

Jacob stared at her, then shrugged, and placed the watch in her palm, gently closing her fingers around it.

She looked down at the watch nestled in her hands. "How nice. Did he . . ." Savannah stopped, speechless. Clasped in her fingers lay the very watch that had been in her family for years!

"This watch?" she sputtered, almost choking. "It's yours?"

"Of course. Why else would it be in my pocket?" he demanded, grabbing it before it fell to the floor. "What's gotten into you?"

She ignored his question. "Will you excuse me? I need to go to the rest room." She rose, knocking over a glass of water on the table.

He stood as she did, reaching for his napkin to soak up the spill. "What, pray tell, is a *rest* room?" he asked, concern lacing his words, confusion in his eyes.

"You know, a *ladies'* room," she answered, stressing the term in hopes he'd catch on. "A powder room, a place for me to freshen up." She had to get away from him before he saw her cry. That would be too much to bear.

Fleeing his presence, Savannah headed toward a small empty parlor she had seen when they arrived. Sinking down onto a velvet settee, she felt the room began to circle her. It was as if her life were flashing before her eyes and she had no idea how to stop it.

Her father's watch once belonged to Jacob Cross!

Savannah reached to brush a tendril of her hair, her hands shaking nervously. It was all somehow linked. It was the prized piece of a valuable collection. Valuable enough that selling it would help pay the first-year expenses of medical school.

At her father's recommendation, she had taken the collection to one particular antique shop to sell. Now she was about to marry the original owner of the same watch. And walking the streets was a man who bore an uncanny resemblance to her ex-fiance. What did it all mean?

"You've seen the watch then." A vaguely familiar voice spoke beside her in the dark.

With a start, Savannah reached for a softly glowing oil lamp. She turned up the wick and the room glowed brighter.

"You!" She stared incredulously at the figure before her. "What are you doing here?" She stopped suddenly. "Were you sent back in time, too?"

The woman from the antique store stood squarely facing her. "I came back in time, but not the way you did," she replied. "I came of my own accord. You came to fulfill your destiny."

"What do you mean I came to fulfill my destiny?"

"The watch and the hat brought you back. The watch was already yours, and then you found the hat. Together, the two antiques brought you back here. Back to your destiny," she explained patiently, a bit of reproach in her voice. "I told you they were special."

"You said those hats belonged to people who came in and claimed them," Savannah said, not understanding the woman's words. "I didn't claim the nurse's hat as mine. I didn't even believe you."

"Don't get caught up in semantics. You claimed the hat, the hat claimed you. Who cares? What matters is that you're here." The rotund figure sat down in a tapestry-covered chair. She drummed her fingers on the armrest, carefully examining the fabric.

"What about the watch? Is Jacob one of my ancestors? If so, you might as well send me home now, because this isn't going to work. We're supposed to be married next Sunday!" Shock and disbelief only scratched the surface of her soul.

"No," the woman said. "The handsome Dr. Cross is definitely not related to you. It's true that the watch has been in your family, but back in this time, it, too, has its own destiny. Several things must happen before it becomes a part of your inheritance."

"Like what?" Savannah snapped.

"Don't worry about the minor details now," she admonished. "It will all come together."

"What about the hat?"

The woman shrugged impatiently. "You chose it as your destiny. Probably because of the watch,

104

you had a connection with that hat and this particular time, or your traveling here would have never happened."

"Can I go home?" Savannah demanded.

"Not until you fulfill your destiny. Then you'll find out if you were meant to return to your time or to stay in this one." The heavy woman looked around the room with interest, a glimmer in her eyes as her hands gently picked up a tiny figurine. "Just lovely." She sighed. "By the way, dear, my name is Mathilde. I'm an antique dealer, as you know."

"What exactly is my destiny?" Savannah snapped, irritated by Mathilde's obvious lack of concern about her dilemma. You'd think people went back in time every day from her distinct lack of interest.

She put the figurine back on the table. "Don't know. That's for you to determine. My family has been the conservator of these hats for many, many years. We've learned it is best not to interfere."

"So who would know why I'm here?" she asked. "Unless . . ." she hesitated, then continued in a small voice, "unless it's to help these soldiers. But, even though I know what needs to be done for them, I don't always have the means to do it. I've got the knowledge, but not the technology. How can this be my destiny?" She looked again to Mathilde for answers, as she nervously plucked at the green fabric of her dress.

"I can help you with that," Mathilde replied smugly. "As I said, I try not to interfere, but I might make an exception." She held up her stubby finger in warning. "But you must be willing to accept my help."

"How?"

The old woman leaned closer to Savannah. "I am willing to bring you some of the things you need if you are willing to help me in return," she answered, her voice low.

"Help you how?" Savannah repeated, annoyed the woman was being so evasive.

Mathilde arched her eyebrow. "I own a profitable antique shop," she urged, then sighed with impatience. "You are in a century full of antiques. . . ."

"You mean you want me to steal things for your antique shop?" Savannah gasped, appalled at the idea taking shape in her head. Why, this woman was nothing but a century-hopping thief!

"Don't think of it as stealing," the antique dealer exclaimed indignantly. "I am not dishonest! I think of it as . . . well, as trading. Trading things from this time for . . . certain things more abundant in our time."

"I can't believe you would even suggest such a thing! These people have taken me under their roof when I have nowhere else to go. I can't steal from them."

"Ah . . ." She sighed, sitting back in the chair. "Most everyone says that at first." She shrugged before she said, her voice firm: "The fact remains that your hospital needs vital medicines. You can either trade with me or stand by helplessly and watch your soldiers die."

"Savannah?" Jacob called from the doorway. "Who are you talking to?" He quickly covered the distance between them. "Are you not feeling well?" He touched her forehead with the back of his hand.

"I'm fine, Jacob." She leaned back against the cushion of the chair. "Just a bit shaky, that's all," she mumbled.

Her eyes darted around the room for the strange woman. Oddly enough, Savannah was not surprised to see she was gone.

Chapter Four

"With this ring, I thee wed . . ." Savannah could scarcely believe it was her voice numbly repeating the minister's words. She stood before the altar of St. George's tiny white church getting married to a man straight from the pages of a history book. How could this have happened to her normal and generally dull life?

"To love, honor, and cherish . . ." Reciting the words, she glanced up at the expressionless man standing beside her, then smiled in ironic amusement. *Love!* He certainly didn't love her! If she weren't a nurse, he probably would have sent her packing the very first day. As for the honor and cherish part, well . . . She couldn't help the nervous giggle that formed in the back of her throat. This was all too crazy.

Holding her ring hand in his, Jacob squeezed her fingers as a silent reminder to control herself. His hands held a warning, not the soft touch of a man smitten by his bride. She met his glare cynically, then dropped her gaze. She supposed it wouldn't do to make a spectacle of herself in front of the small gathering of townsfolk. Not a soul in the pews had attended this farce for her benefit; they were all Jacob's friends. Even her stunning ivory-and-white wedding dress belonged to Miss Emma. Together, they had dug it out from the bottom of an old trunk in the attic. Miss Emma had grown very quiet when she saw it, causing Savannah to wonder if the cheerful spinster had once intended to wear it herself.

"I now pronounce you man and wife," the minister said happily, his words slowly bringing Savannah out of her reverie. "Jacob, you may kiss your bride."

The smile on her face froze as her eyes widened to stare in disbelief at the beaming minister. A slight panic seized her. Like all happy couples, they were expected to seal their vows with a kiss. But this marriage was a business arrangement, nothing more. Kissing was not part of the bargain. She shot her new husband a sidelong glance and saw the surprise on his face, too. His body stiffened.

"Jacob"—the squat minister nudged him with a wink—"you may kiss your bride."

The tall doctor looked from the clergyman to Savannah, giving her a bewildered shrug. She supposed there was no getting around it. A kiss was inevitable. The surprise written on his face suddenly began to dissolve in obvious amusement. He turned to face her, a sly grin starting at the corners of his mouth.

"Of course," he responded. Moving his hands slowly, he lifted her ivory veil. His fingers softly brushed against her cheeks as his eyes swept across her face.

Savannah stared at him nervously, her heart pounding in anticipation. Her hands raised to his chest of their own volition. An unanticipated tremor of excitement zipped through her as her white satin gloves made contact with the heat of his body. In spite of her misgivings about this marriage, she suddenly lost her nervousness. Touching him felt natural, as if she were meant to be in his arms.

He brought his head close to her face, his breath flirting with her ear. "Thank you for marrying me, Savannah. I'll do my best for you."

Her eyes widened in surprise. The words were so soft, she wasn't sure she had heard correctly. She had been forced into this marriage. Why in the world would he now be concerned about her? He had been adamant that she was nothing but trouble since she walked into the hospital. She silently questioned his blue eyes for a long, still moment.

A slight cough from the minister urged Jacob to hurry, but he clearly had no intention of doing so. The air in the quiet church was charged as every guest in the small sanctuary watched with interest, the warm afternoon and uncomfortable wooden pews suddenly forgotten.

Savannah felt his warm breath move across her cheeks, stopping within a fraction of her lips. He brought his hands up to cup her face, his eyes never once leaving hers. His mouth began its descent, and she felt her legs weaken and her knees tremble. Her lids fluttered closed as she lifted her chin in anticipation of his touch. Short, pulsating bursts of raw voltage shot through her when their lips finally brushed. Without lifting his head, Jacob gently pulled her warm body to his, forcing her to accept more than a mere meeting of lips. Startled at her own breathless response, she parted her mouth to allow the soft tip of his tongue freedom to dance across her teeth, then settle deeper, savoring every second.

Never in her life had Savannah been so thoroughly kissed. Instinctively, she answered him as her lips widened to drink in the intensity of the moment. Her heart was pounding so loudly she vaguely wondered if everyone in the room could hear it. The flaming heat coursing through her began to settle deep inside, stirring age-old needs. There was something about this man that awakened every need she possessed.

Another cough doused her with reality. Jacob lifted his head only slightly, hesitated, then kissed her again in another long, slow moment.

The throat cleared again, this time louder. Unexplained disappointment filtered through Savannah as Jacob lessened his hold. She willed her eyes to open and meet his gaze. His expression was unreadable, but his eyes were like blue fire.

A small bead of perspiration dotted his forehead. It was obvious how the kiss had affected him, she thought with pleasure.

"Ladies and gentlemen, I'm pleased to present Dr. and Mrs. Jacob Cross," the minister rushed, seizing the opportunity. Jacob held his arm firmly around Savannah, refusing to break their bond. Her body fit perfectly next to his.

A crowd of well-wishers swarmed around them, offering congratulations. Although calm on the outside, her nerves were a jangled mess. First, there was the silliness of the whole marriage charade, and now she had a confusing feeling that something serious had just happened between them. She glanced up at her new husband's handsome profile, then looked away to fight an unexplained surge of despair. Even if there was something between them, it could never be permanent. He would never believe who she was or where she came from.

Savannah sat alone in front of a small dresser, removing the net veil from her hair. A huge four-poster bed occupied most of the room, a blatant reminder she would not be sleeping alone tonight. Apprehension grew with each dropping hairpin. She looked nervously around the room; Rose had prepared it for a happy newlywed couple. The bed was covered in embroidered white sheets with two fluffy feather pillows. A small vase of black-eyed suzies stood on the nightstand beside the bed along with a pair of wax candles in two brass holders. It didn't escape her that the candles were meant to illuminate the fire of wedding-night passion. The corners of her lips lifted ironically as she imagined Rose's surprise when she found the wicks still new in the morning.

Jacob was still downstairs in the restaurant with the last of the wedding guests. Miss Emma had planned a simple yet lovely dinner to celebrate their nuptials. The fact that the dinner party had been mostly made up of envious women did not escape Savannah. Their husbands were all off at war; some would not return. She had a husband in her bed this very night.

Bed, she thought, with a nervous pull at the veiled headpiece. She expected Jacob to follow shortly and what would happen then, she had no idea. The newlyweds were to stay at Rose's for the evening, supposedly to celebrate their new life together. Although they had both objected to the plan, Miss Emma was insistent. Her new friend pretended they were in love, not forced into a marriage of convenience.

Her own heated response to Jacob's kiss had frightened her, and now the thought of spending the night alone with him worried her more. Their marriage was not to be intimate, but she questioned the validity of his promise. After the intensity of their kiss this afternoon, she really wasn't sure what he would do, or how she would respond. Now that they were married, perhaps he had different intentions. In the mirror, her eyes brightened at the memory of his lips pressed against her own. Perhaps she liked this new turn of events. Perhaps she wanted him to have different intentions.

Truth was, while such thoughts made her a little nervous, they also caused a growing ache inside her. Jacob Cross thrilled her all the way down to her toes. Savannah doubted she could withstand him very long if he were to pursue a true marital relationship.

Gazing at her image in the mirror, she propped her chin in one hand and drummed the fingers of the other on the dresser. Things just didn't make sense. If she were there to fulfill some unknown destiny, it would be foolish to get involved with anyone of this century. She stopped the rhythm of her fingers as a thought struck her hard. If she were to trade objects for medicines, she'd have to steal. If she were caught as a thief, it was unlikely anyone would believe her true reasons or explanations. Then where would she be? In jail most likely.

Carefully removing Miss Emma's borrowed blue topaz necklace, Savannah considered her options. If her destiny was to provide as much modern medical care as she could for the wounded soldiers, then her attraction to Jacob Cross would only interfere with her efforts. And, as much as she might like it to be more, it could never happen. Never.

Lifting her nightgown from the dresser drawer, Savannah promised herself to be cool toward Jacob. It was better that way.

* * *

A soft knock sounded at the door. The room glowed from the low light of an oil lamp. It was very late, and Savannah had given up waiting for her new husband long ago. She lay on top of the fluffy feather bed, covered with a light blanket. Determined to keep distance between them, she had refused to get under the covers and settle into the warmth of the bed. She knew that she would need all her senses when he walked through the door.

"Savannah?" Jacob called in a low voice. Without waiting for her answer, he stepped inside. Her blood began a jittery race as she steadied her breathing and feigned sleep.

"I know you're not asleep," he said softly. "I saw you move when I opened the door."

Savannah opened one eye to peer at him, thankful the poor light prevented him from seeing her face flush. Her embarrassment turned to irritation. "No, I'm not asleep!" she snapped. "I'm too nervous waiting to see if you're going to accost me like you did in the church." She glared at him accusingly.

"I had the impression you enjoyed our first kiss," he said tightly, a muscle clenching in his jaw. "I regret I was mistaken."

"Perhaps I did," she admitted grudgingly. "But it doesn't change the fact that we have a deal." Dropping her lashes, she anxiously tugged at the blanket, trying to maintain her dignity. The nearness of her new husband was already causing her body to betray her. "We have a marriage for appearances' sake, nothing more. I kept my end of the bargain. You have to do the same." She stared up at him with all the indignation she could muster.

She felt more than saw his body stiffen. What he had expected tonight was unclear, and the odd haze of the room made his pending reaction even more alarming. She felt awkward lying on the bed as he stood over her, but she locked his gaze in a test of wills. Without dropping her eyes, her body again reminded her of the warmth and ease of their earlier embrace. His stare moved from her face down the length of her body, causing an unwanted desire to sift through her.

"I am a man of my word, *Mrs.* Cross," he stated. "Surely you know that by now." Jacob stepped away, turning his back to her.

Was that a twinge of regret in his voice? She exhaled a silent sigh of relief. It really didn't matter. She was doing what was best for both of them. Rolling over on her side, Savannah closed her eyes to escape the confines of the room. If she was doing what was best for both of them, why did she feel so terrible?

A moment later, her eyes flew open as a sudden weight dropped on the bed beside her. Surely he wasn't going to sleep in the same bed! The masculine body got under the covers and stretched out beside her. Near, but not touching. The heat was electrifying.

"What are you doing?" she demanded, turning to face him. "I thought you understood. Our marriage is a business arrangement, nothing more."

"You made yourself clear, Savannah," Jacob

muttered, his lids lowered. "But this is our wedding night. Eyebrows would certainly raise if I were to sleep in a different room." A twinge of regretful amusement sounded in his voice.

"I see," she said coldly. "We certainly can't have people wondering about such things." Sarcasm dripped from her words. "Will this be a permanent arrangement?"

"Of course," he replied shortly. "Every available room in the hospital is being used." Opening one eye, he considered her. "Besides"—he shrugged—"it would be difficult to explain to Miss Emma why we are not behaving as husband and wife. An explanation I'm not willing to provide her."

"You didn't tell her our marriage is only an arrangement? Surely, she knows . . ." Her voice dropped off in question.

He looked at her in surprise. "She does, but she's also a romantic." He laughed sourly. "She has a silly notion that we're meant for each other."

With a huff, Savannah plopped back down, crossing her arms over her chest. *Wonderful. Meant for each other, indeed!*

Minutes ticked by as they lay quietly, each staring at the ceiling, Jacob under the covers, Savannah still on top. In spite of her determination to resist, her thoughts unwillingly drifted to the hot body only inches away. She instinctively recognized what Jacob ignited inside her. How could this man affect her this way?

"Tell me about yourself," she finally said, hoping to break the uncomfortable silence. They had to reach some sort of truce, if only for the hospital's sake.

Jacob didn't answer. When no movement came from his side of the bed, Savannah began to think he was already asleep. She covertly dropped a sidelong glance in his direction. His arms were folded behind his head as he continued to stare at the ceiling.

"Not much to me, I guess," came his reply, accepting the offered olive branch of peace. "I'm trying to patch up the boys out fighting."

"What about your family?" Another long pause. "I overheard people talking about Riverlawn."

"What did you hear?"

"Not much. Just that it was your family's plantation, one of the biggest around, and that it burned to the ground."

"That about sums it up," he said, presenting his back to her. He obviously wanted to discourage more questions.

"What about Anna?"

His back stiffened. "What about her?" he asked slowly, rolling over to face her. The look in his eyes was treacherous. Savannah considered she might have pushed him too far as they warily stared at each other in the darkened room.

"She was my wife," he finally said. "She died in the fire."

Instantly, Savannah reached for his shoulder to offer comfort. "Oh, Jacob, I had no idea. I'm so sorry." She looked into his eyes, reading the bitterness mixed with sorrow.

"I might as well tell you so you don't hear it

from Ruth Ann and the other gossips in town." He took a deep breath as if he knew this was going to be difficult. "My father was murdered," he said quietly.

Savannah stared at him in shock. "Murdered?" she whispered in disbelief. At his pained expression, she touched his arm with compassion. "You don't have to tell me, I understand."

"No, it's been almost two years. I don't mind."

Slowly, he began the painful story, hesitating at times as if he couldn't bring himself to share the ugly details. Her heart went out to him. At the gentle stroke of her hand and the tender urging in her voice, he continued. Silently, she listened, and her anger, outrage, and pain surfaced as he purged himself of the horror.

"You know the name of the officer who ordered the raid?" Savannah asked in angry surprise. "Can't you just turn him in?"

"It's not as simple as that," he replied, shaking his head. "As the commanding officer, he made sure the men were brought to justice before his name was connected. All of the men were hanged except for the youngest, a boy of thirteen. He went to prison in Memphis instead. Another one of the cowards did name the officer before he was sent to the gallows, but the boy in prison won't corroborate it. He's afraid he'll be hanged, too."

She reached to touch his cheek. "Oh, Jacob, I am truly sorry. I shouldn't have pressed you to answer my questions."

He reached up to cover her hand with his own, then brushed it out along her bare arm. "No, don't be," he countered. "I've carried this inside me for a long time, afraid to think of it, much less talk about it. I'm actually glad you asked."

Not speaking, they lay facing each other on the small bed. Slowly, the air began to change as she became fully aware of his touch, of his hand tracing a glowing path. Before she could protest, Jacob leaned over until his face was only inches from hers. Her heart raced as a feeling of warmth spread over her entire body, while butterflies fluttered in her stomach in anxious anticipation. Jacob Cross was about to kiss her, and in spite of her previous words, in spite of her determination to remain aloof, she had never wanted anything more.

When their lips finally met, his kiss was soft and sweet and as intimate as the discussion they had just had. Clearly, this man had told no one his deepest feelings about the fire, and she was moved he had shared them with her.

Her husband continued to rub his hand up and down the soft skin of her arm, kissing her gently. Shocked by her own eager response, Savannah moved closer to him with each stroke, afraid of what it would bring, but afraid of what she would miss if she didn't. He encircled her with his arms and held her tight, his body brushing against the full length of hers. The covers separating them did nothing to hide his growing desire as she felt his hard shaft against her thigh. Her breath quickened as she realized she wanted more. It was either stop now, or lose herself in passionate desire.

Before she could regain control, Jacob pushed Savannah onto her back and deepened their kiss. His hand reached up to tickle against her neck, causing shivers to ripple through her. He released her lips and dropped tiny kisses on her eyelids with a feather touch more erotic than raw passion. As his firm lips softly swept down to the hollow of her neck, his hand moved to tantalize her breast through the thin fabric of her gown, her nipple instantly taut at his touch. Entangling her fingers in his dark hair, she softly moaned as his mouth slid to her shoulders. Her resolve to maintain a safe distance from this man faded into a hazy fog.

"Jacob," she said breathlessly.

He lifted his head to look at her, his eyes passionate with need. She returned his steady gaze as each silently asked the other the unspoken question.

How long they had stayed like that, she didn't know. She saw his features change as a slow reserve built on his face. He released her tenderly, then pulled the twisted blanket up to her neck. A disappointing hurt stole through Savannah's heart as he placed a light kiss on her swollen lips.

"It's not right, Savannah," he said, kissing her once again, then slowly backing away from her body. "Too many things stand in our way right now." He disentangled himself from their embrace. "If we consummate this marriage, I want it to be because of love, not because you want to comfort me."

"Jacob . . ."

"Shhh." He placed his finger on her lips. "I don't have much strength right now." He smiled gently at her. "You were right before. This marriage is a business arrangement, and until I can offer you more, I will keep that promise."

Returning to his side of the bed, he pulled the covers up to his chest. "Now turn over and go to sleep."

"Jacob . . . " Savannah said again.

"Go to sleep, Savannah." His voice took on a ragged edge.

Realizing he was serious, she sighed, rolling over on her side. Every aspect of this man was confusing, especially his ability to bring her to the frustrating brink of passion then abruptly turning away. Equally bothersome was her response to him. His touch stirred desires she had only dreamed of. So much for her promise to ignore him.

Savannah closed her eyes and listened for the sound of Jacob's breathing. He was silent, although the unsteady rhythm of his lungs proved he was not resting. She buried her head in her pillow. It was going to be a long night.

Savannah awoke to the cheerful chirping of a robin. Although it was still early, Jacob was already gone, his place cold. The tousled covers and indentation in his pillow were the only indications he had actually shared her bed. Just as well, she thought, knowing it would be difficult to face him. A hot flush reminded her how close she came to losing control last night.

Stretching her body like a relaxed feline, she was surprised to find herself under the covers rather than on top of them. Vaguely, she remembered the chill of the early-morning hours and snuggling near the warm body beside her. Her husband must have pulled the blankets over her. Smiling now, she shook her head. In spite of everything, Savannah doubted she could have resisted her new husband last night. She wasn't sure she wanted to, either.

Since their marriage was based on honor, it pleased her to know Jacob respected hers as much as his own. He had said he wanted their first time to be for love. Could it be that he felt something for her, too? Or was his hesitation due to the memory of his dead wife?

She threw off the covers with a sudden irritation. It really didn't matter what he felt, or what she felt for that matter. Even after her strange conversation with Mathilde, she had no guarantee that fate wouldn't return her back to the twentieth century, and it would be unfair to let him fall in love with another woman who might one day be ripped away with no word or explanation. Once again, she was falling for a man who would never belong to her. The only thing she could do was to try once again to keep her emotional distance. She knew it would be best for him, but for her she wasn't certain.

"A watched pot never boils, Miz Vanna." Deltry's pleasant face stared into the huge iron pot of water on the wood-burning stove.

Savannah stood beside her, also peering into the black pot. Steam rose in white puffs as tiny bubbles hesitantly began to form on the surface. She smiled at the friendly black woman. "I do believe you're right, Deltry."

They were in the airy kitchen waiting for the container of water to boil. Neatly arranged on the nearby table were all of Jacob's surgical instruments, which had been scrubbed clean with lye soap and were now waiting to be sterilized.

Jacob had yet to put in an appearance. After checking on the soldiers early this morning, he left the hospital, telling one of the medics he had several appointments in town. Mixed feelings of both disappointment and relief nagged at Savannah. She came close to abandoning all of her self-made promises last night, and she needed this time away from him to strengthen her determination. The antique dealer said she had to find her own destiny, and until she could figure out if it indeed involved bringing modern medicine to the wounded, or if she would ever return to her own time, she couldn't risk falling in love. The consequences would be too great for either of them.

"It's boiling now, Miz Vanna." Deltry picked up a pair of forceps with two fingers, holding them out from her body as she walked from the table to the steaming water.

Carefully lifting several scalpels, Savannah dropped them one by one into the pot, each rattling as it struck the bottom. She surveyed the miscellaneous assortment of saws, scalpels, needles, knives, and forceps on the table. His collection was relatively small and limited, but there was enough equipment to resterilize them between patients, especially since Miss Emma agreed to keep water boiling throughout the day.

"This is the easy part," she thought out loud. "Now to get Jacob and the others to wash their hands between each patient."

Staring intently into the pan, Savannah didn't hear the kitchen door open.

"Get me to do what?" he asked.

Adrenaline surged through her veins as she recognized the drawling masculine voice.

Internally steeling herself, she slowly turned to face him, her heart lurching to see how attractive he looked with his mahogany hair slightly ruffled. Remembering the sensuous feel of his lips on her neck, she felt the heat rise as she tried to remain cool.

"Thank you for letting me sleep this morning," she stammered, deliberating changing the subject. "I didn't realize I was so tired." She was lying, of course—she didn't get any sleep last night. From the dark circles under his eyes, neither did the man standing before her.

Jacob casually strolled across the room, grabbed a cup from the cabinet, and poured coffee into it from the blue-speckled kettle on the stove. He nodded to Deltry as she wisely excused herself. "I thought you might need a little privacy after . . . last night." He looked into the pot of boiling water, his eyebrows lifting at the sight of his surgical knives at the bottom. He cleared his throat just as Savannah began to speak.

"Jacob," she rushed, while she still had the nerve. "I appreciate your integrity last night. I allowed myself to get carried away, and I'm, ah, thankful you were able to maintain your control." She spoke quickly before she could change her mind. "I think it's best if we make every effort to prevent such things from occurring again." She twisted the string of her new apron apprehensively.

His face remained guarded as he watched her. She swallowed hard, knowing she had to do what was best for both of them, to save them from hurt later on. Nervously, she fidgeted with the nursing cap on her head.

"We married without considering that each of us may care for someone else." She saw a glimmer of surprise on his face before he quickly masked it. She hoped that was just enough to stimulate his integrity and keep him at bay.

"I see," he said, giving away nothing of what was going on inside his head. "I'm glad you made that clear. However, I—"

"Good morning, you two!" Miss Emma interrupted in a cheerful singsong voice as she burst through the kitchen door. "Isn't it a lovely morning?" If the apron-clad woman noticed the strained air in the room, she gave no sign.

Savannah was relieved her friend unknowingly put an effective end to their conversation. She had been afraid, and hopeful, of what Jacob had intended to say. Smiling warmly to Miss Emma, Savannah turned back to the boiling pot on the stove.

Jacob grunted his greeting as he stared into his coffee cup.

The motherly woman patted his hand. "You never were a morning person, Jacob," she said, smiling. "Is the water boiling, dear?" she asked, turning to Savannah.

Nodding, she reached for a pair of long tongs to remove the sterilized scalpels. She nudged Miss Emma and tilted her head toward Jacob. "Germs," she whispered at the older woman's confused face.

Miss Emma winked in understanding. "We're sterilizing your surgical instruments, Jacob," she said. "Cleaning them to kill germs and reduce infection."

"You're doing what?" he asked, skeptically amused. "Killing germs?"

Sparks of irritation flew at his casual manner. Savannah bit her tongue to keep from giving him a severe lashing over something so serious. This was too important. Besides, she couldn't really blame him for being dismissive of something that was yet to be proven. Resuming her most professional demeanor, she began to explain the facts about germs, bacteria, and infection. At first, disbelief replaced the amusement in his eyes. Then interest. He listened closely, but it was obvious he was not convinced that such simple measures could help prevent men from dying.

"In certain cases, it won't prevent them from dying," Savannah added, sensing his cautiousness. "But if you can keep one man's germs from another, you can prevent the spread of disease and reduce infection. Even the infection that leads to gangrene." She paused to see if her words were sinking in. One by one, she removed the newly sterilized scalpels from the boiling water while Miss Emma tightly wrapped each in fresh linen.

He watched their work silently. Minutes ticked by as he considered her comments. "Before the war, I attended a lecture in Nashville about germs," he finally said, sitting down at the kitchen table. "The professor spoke about bacteria and infections, too. As I recall, no one seemed to take him very seriously."

He glanced between her and Miss Emma, then continued, "Frankly, I still need to be convinced about sterilizing." He held up his hand as Savannah began to protest. "However, I don't see how cleaning my scalpels could cause any harm."

Stretching his lean form, Jacob rose from the table and walked to the stove. "I should have known it was dangerous to get you two together!" He dropped a quick kiss on their cheeks. "I'm interested to see what you come up with next." Whistling, he walked out the door.

Listening to the fading sound, Savannah smiled at Miss Emma, her cheeks blushed from Jacob's kiss. "You did it!"

"No, dear," she said. "I may have gotten it started, but the credit belongs to you."

It was early afternoon by the time Savannah finished sterilizing all of Jacob's surgical knives. Leaving the hot, humid kitchen, she took a deep breath of fragrant afternoon air. Deltry had made a comment about the beautiful spring flowers in Miss Emma's garden, and she wanted to see for herself. Thankfully, the air hadn't yet become unbearably hot. She vaguely wondered if she'd still be there during the summer. The thought of life without air conditioning was not inviting.

Savannah paused to smell Miss Emma's roses and several giant white magnolia blossoms. The sweet camellias were still in bloom, and the trees were full of tender new leaves. Again she was reminded how rarely she had taken time to enjoy such things in her own time.

Leisurely, she rounded the corner of the porch only to see several horse-drawn ambulances outside the hospital. Quickening her pace almost to a run, Savannah rushed through the hospital door. Jacob and a lanky medic were already bent over a bleeding soldier as she rushed into the surgery room. She cautiously approached the injured man and saw he was bleeding profusely from a grotesque gunshot wound on his lower leg. While the field surgeons had patched him up, the trip to the hospital on the rutted roads had caused the bleeding to begin again.

"Nurse! Get me a tourniquet!" Jacob issued orders in a tone that indicated he expected no objections. "Looks like we'll have to remove it."

Savannah quickly reached into a nearby cabinet, then handed him a long cloth and a stick to twist it tight. He began to cut the worn fabric of the man's pant leg with a newly sterilized knife.

"No, Doc! Not my leg! It's not hurt that bad!"

Horror spread across the man's face as he protested from the bed. He tried to rise, but a strong steward placed his hands on the man's shoulders to subdue him.

Savannah's heart wrenched at the man's agony. As Jacob hurriedly removed the pant leg of the uniform, her eyes widened. Never before had she questioned a doctor's actions, but this was different. This man's leg did not need to be amputated. It was serious all right. The leg had several significant fractures, the bleeding had to be stopped, and the severe wound needed immediate and certainly long-term attention, but the leg didn't need to come off.

She knew it was common in this time to remove any injured limb mainly because there were no other treatments and infection was such a danger. Even after it was removed, the threat of gangrene was always a serious gamble. She understood why Jacob thought he had to remove the leg, but she knew it was wrong. Drawing on every ounce of strength she had, she made her decision.

"Jacob!" she said loudly. He interrupted his preparations to look up at her in surprise. Savannah took a quick breath to gather her courage. "The artery is not extensively lacerated, and the wound is not to the knee joint. You don't need to amputate. If we can stop the bleeding, we can treat the wound."

"How do you plan to stop the bleeding without a tourniquet?" he snapped, startled and angry. "And how do you plan to save the leg once we tie the tourniquet tight enough to stop the bleeding?

Look at the damage, Savannah. It's the only way."

The room was noisy with the scramble to treat the other newly arrived wounded. The noise added to the sense of urgency. For an emotionally charged instant, they stared at each other.

"Don't use a tourniquet," she said firmly. "Stop the bleeding at the pressure point." Quickly, she moved to the man and reached for his thigh, placing her hand at the top of his leg.

"She's right, Doc," the man pleaded. "She's right! Just don't cut off my leg. I've got a farm to work, a family to raise." Jacob glanced at the man on the bed, his face reflecting his indecisiveness. "Please, Doc," the man begged. "Give it a try, at least."

"Trust me on this," she implored, pulling Jacob away from the injured man. "I know you may not have heard of pressure points, but it's common practice where I'm from." She searched his face for understanding. "Trust me," she whispered. "Please."

"No," he replied stubbornly. "Even if you can stop the bleeding, there's shrapnel and bone fragments still in the muscle. If we don't remove the leg, gangrene will kill him within a week."

"If you amputate, he may still die of infection," she argued. She placed her hand on his arm. "We can remove the debris once we stop the bleeding," she said, her voice softening to a plea. She tightened her grip on his arm as he started to object. "He may die either way, Jacob. At least give him a chance to keep his leg."

For what seemed like an extra long moment,

Jacob studied her face. "Show me this pressure point," he relented, the decision made. "But if I can't stop the bleeding your way, I go back to mine."

She smiled at him gratefully, pulling him back to the bleeding man. "With your whole hand, apply pressure here, as strong as you can," she instructed, then lifted her hand from the top of the man's thigh and replaced it with Jacob's. "Wrap your other hand around the base of your wrist for extra force, and press. You," she said, pointing to the medic, "hold pressure on the wound. Don't let up until I tell you."

Turning back to Jacob, Savannah put her hands on top of his. "You know the blood to the leg runs through the femoral artery here. If you stop the rush of blood before it gets to the wound, the blood already there will clot and stop the bleeding."

Savannah held her hands over Jacob's, not allowing them to move. She felt the power and strength in his hands as they stood together. Several long minutes passed as they stayed still, holding the man's thigh. Looking around the room, she realized Jacob had been snapping orders to several medics since the wounded had arrived. This patient was the most serious, although others were in need of immediate attention, also. There were two who already had bloody bandaged stumps where their legs had been amputated. Another with a head wound. She'd have to see to them next. She hadn't thought to ask where these men had been fighting, but it must have been close. Apprehension stiffened her spine. She never once imagined herself facing the realities of war.

She stood straight, releasing her hold on Jacob's hands and pulling them off the man's thigh.

"Try it now," she said to the medic.

The medic lifted the bandage and stared at the wound in amazement. "It's stopped," he said, not looking up.

Savannah breathed a silent prayer of gratitude. The soldier on the bed caught her hand, squeezing it to convey his thanks. He was still in pain and needed immediate surgery to remove the offending bone and metal, but he would probably keep his leg. Slowly, she looked up at Jacob and saw a new respect in his eyes.

"Where did you come from?" he asked softly as she brushed by in a hurry to get to the next man.

Less than an hour later, Jacob and Savannah had doctored the eight patients from the ambulance. Each of them already had some type of quick treatment from the field surgeons. It was up to them to clean up what had been done in a hurry.

"Savannah, I still need to clean the fragments from the fellow's leg." Jacob nodded toward their first patient. "Will you get him ready for surgery while I finish up here? You'll find what you need in the cabinet in my office."

"Certainly, but no amputation, right?"

He shook his head and smiled. "No, you proved your point. No amputation."

Pleased, Savannah headed for the cabinet. She stopped by the kitchen to return several contaminated scalpels for sterilized ones.

"That's the last we have for now, Miz Vanna." Deltry nodded to the linen-wrapped instruments on the table. "We'll have more as soon as them boys bring me the dirty ones."

"Thanks, Deltry. These should be all we need for a while. I'll gather up the used ones myself and bring them to you." She turned back toward the surgery room, then stopped short. "Deltry." The huge woman looked up. "Thank you. We couldn't have done it without your help."

The black woman smiled. "You're welcome, Miz Vanna, you're welcome."

Savannah heard a happy little whistle begin just as she reached the door. Deltry deserved the credit for her help for the past few hours. She repeatedly sterilized the few instruments they had. No doubt the eight soldiers would live, thanks to the quick and constant action of a slave. Sadly, probably not one of them would even thank her for it.

Savannah unlocked the cabinet where Jacob stored the hospital's medicine supply. The contents proved frugal. Laudanum, quinine, arsenic, a little morphine and ether, sulfur, poultices, dressings, salves. Not much in the way of serious medications. No wonder Jacob was so stingy with administering them. There was plenty of fine silk thread for stitches, no doubt thanks to Miss Emma, but that wouldn't help without proper

134

drugs to treat the wounds.

She lifted her eyes to the next shelf. Blue Mass? Calomel? Powdered rhubarb? Sulphate of magnesia? The way Jacob had them stored, they must be purgatives to empty the stomach or such. Savannah wrinkled her nose. Antique ipecac, just what everyone needed. Too bad he had plenty of that and barely enough painkillers.

What in the world was Dover's powder? She lifted the lid and smelled the pungent aroma. Since the jar was sitting by nitrate of potassa, it might be some type of diuretic, she thought. She'd have to ask Jacob about that one. He obviously got by with the medicines of this time, but, boy, what she'd give for simple penicillin and alcohol. There just had to be something she could do.

"Mathilde?" Savannah called from a hidden spot behind the barn. No answer. She called again to the woman from the future, this time a little louder. "Mathilde? Please come. I need to speak with you. I have questions."

It was dusk; the sun had set, leaving the crickets and katydids to sing a crooning good evening. She leaned against the back of the barn in discouragement. It's no use, she thought. The old woman might never come back. How could she help these soldiers without proper medicines?

Her frustration had been growing since her arrival. The hospital had a terrible shortage of supplies, and Savannah knew the precious little inventory on the shelves would not last long, even though Jacob was sparing in their use. They needed everything from his time like more laudanum, morphine, quinine, chloroform, ether, even whiskey. And everything from hers, too. The penicillin and antibiotics to kill infections. Vaccines to prevent them. Painkillers to bring relief to the suffering men. Germicides and alcohol to eliminate deadly germs. Even aspirin and ibuprofen would help. And, oh, what she'd give for a thermometer!

According to Jacob, the shipments of new supplies had been promised, but never materialized. He had merely shaken his head when she had asked at supper about their arrival.

There had to be something she could do, Savannah thought, especially if this was to be her destiny. Mathilde's proposal called to her every time a patient cried out in pain. It called to her again much more strongly every time one died. It was tempting. She could do so much good by trading a few of Miss Emma's everyday objects. If only she could to do it without getting caught. For that matter, if Miss Emma knew the truth of the situation, she would probably give any object in her house without question. The problem was that Savannah doubted Miss Emma would believe her ludicrous story of being from the future. Savannah almost didn't believe it herself.

She gazed up at the stars coming out of hiding in the darkening sky. Her mind wandered to the aspects of her profession she had always taken for granted. Even something as natural as pure oxygen was not available in a medical capacity.

The thought brought her back to reality. The only way she could get things like that would be to steal for them, and that had repercussions she wasn't ready to deal with. There had to be some other way.

She watched a shooting star dart across the sky and disappear into a small speck. An idea suddenly came to her as the star flashed its brilliance. The army! She would ask the charming Colonel Sanger! If anyone in this town could get the needed medicines, surely Jordan Sanger could. Not only was he the officer in command of St. George, he seemed like the type of man who could get anything he wanted without much trouble at all.

She would pay a call to Colonel Sanger as soon as possible. And she would do it without Jacob or Miss Emma knowing. For reasons she didn't understand, they seemed to dislike him intensely. Perhaps they wouldn't, but she could certainly ask for his help. He was the commanding officer, after all. It was his duty to help these men. Pleased with herself for coming up with such a plan, Savannah left her spot behind the barn.

The dashing Colonel Sanger was her last hope. If he couldn't help, then she would have to try reaching Mathilde again. The thought of actually stealing from Miss Emma did not sit well with her, but she had no choice in the matter. Anything had to be better than letting the soldiers suffer.

"Where have you been?" Jacob asked as Savannah started up the porch steps. "I was about to come look for you." He kept his voice cordial. She would not hear the anxiety that had been eating at his insides for the last hour.

Jacob stifled a yawn and stretched his body, filling the entire porch swing as it rocked back and forth in the moonlight. He forced his hand to relax as it rested along the back of the swing. He hoped she could not see the apprehension caused by her sudden disappearance.

Truth was, for almost an hour he had sat in the swing, glancing repeatedly at his pocket watch as he anxiously awaited her return. A unit of soldiers had ridden by, reminding him this was no time for a woman to be unaccompanied on the streets. The Yanks had taken a nearby town to the north, and while they were in no immediate danger, one couldn't be too careful. Even knowing the dangers, she had mysteriously slipped out of the hospital without a word to anyone. What could she have been thinking?

His reluctant wife worried him more than he cared to admit and for reasons other than her brief absence. She was unlike any female he had ever known. Not only was she a tremendously skilled healer, she had disagreed with him and confronted his wrath. No matter who she was or where she came from, a nurse simply didn't do that to a doctor. Her courage intrigued him.

He ran his hand through his tousled hair and watched her draw closer. An oil lamp shone through the front windows, the light outlining her lithe form like a sensuous and mysterious shroud.

"I was out walking," she replied, her voice soft.

"I needed to think, to clear my head." She stopped on a polished marble step and bent to pick a gardenia from a bush covered with blooms. Its fragrance drifted toward Jacob like an intoxicating perfume. "How's the fellow with the wounded leg?"

"Still in a lot of pain, but resting," he answered briefly. He had much to say to his beautiful wife tonight, but her cool reserve held him back. Jacob rose from the wooden swing as she reached the top step of the porch, the delicate white blossom still in her hand.

"I was worried about you," he continued. "No one knew where you were." He reached for Savannah's hand and pulled her to the railing. Their bodies stood close, her small hand engulfed in his, as they gazed at the rising moon. The woman beside him was guarded, as if she protected a valuable secret. Quiet fell as neither wanted to break the spell of the calm night air.

With a quick glance, Jacob saw she had changed from the dull gray muslin dress to a deep green gown of soft brushed cotton. Although it was dark, he was certain it was the same color as her eyes. A lace shawl was wrapped delicately around her shoulders to ward off the evening chill. The tresses of her pale hair had fallen free from her loose chignon and feathered her face, creating a moonlit image of a mythical beauty.

Jacob couldn't shake the memory of her in his bed last night. His nerves remained jagged from having her so close. Gentle compassion had filled her face as she had listened intently to his story.

While he had relived the pain of the murders, she had opened her heart to share his grief. When he had shared his vow to avenge, she had understood. In one night, this small woman with gossamer hair had awakened a stirring deep inside him, something he had long ago buried and tried to forget. For the briefest of moments, Jacob considered it possible that he could love again.

In the light of dawn, however, things were different. Last night had been an illusion, a sweet nightmare. Every hope he had for the future crashed when she had calmly recited a speech thanking him for his self-control.

Self-control? Hell, that had been the last thing on his mind as she had lain nestled in his arms.

While she worked by his side throughout the day, Jacob had realized how wrong it would be to ignore what he felt. He recalled reading once about the bonds of affinity, a belief that two strangers could meet and instantly know their lives were entwined. He sensed a connection between him and Savannah and instinctively knew she did as well. It was greater than a mere love of healing. Much greater.

He struggled for the right words as his gaze returned to the stars twinkling in the night sky. There was so much he longed to say, but she wasn't ready to hear. Medicine was the only thing they could talk about without the warmth of her body dousing his senses.

Turning slightly, Jacob peered down at his wife. "I was prepared to amputate that soldier's leg this afternoon. It's a difficult decision we face, whether to amputate or not. If we don't, the patient may lose so much blood that he goes into shock and dies. If we do amputate and he makes it through the surgery without the shock, gangrene can still kill him. Even then, there's really no way to know how much internal bleeding is involved. Sometimes I feel I'm playing a deadly game of poker and the stake is someone else's life."

Savannah nodded silently, then withdrew her hand.

"You convinced me not to remove the leg. I admire that," he said, taking her hand back. "Tell me about these pressure points," he encouraged. "Are there others? How did you know exactly where to apply pressure to stop the bleeding?"

"Like we talked this afternoon," she replied, clearly relieved he had chosen a neutral topic of conversation. "I learned the procedure at nursing school. It's one of the fastest ways to control bleeding. It doesn't always work, but it's always worth a try." Savannah considered him through her long lashes and finally lowered her eyes to the buttons of his shirt. The corners of her mouth lifted to form a tentative smile. "Would you like me to show you all of them?"

To learn the technique correctly, Jacob knew Savannah should demonstrate on a patient, but the anticipation was almost unbearable. At his nod, she reached for his hand.

"You have pressure points on both sides of your body," she began with the voice of a teacher. "I'm sure you know that this is called the radial-ulna artery. If you hold it like this and apply pressure here, you can lessen the flow of blood to your hand." She wrapped her middle finger and thumb around the base of his right wrist, then held it tightly. "You'll feel a tingle begin from the lack of blood."

At his nod, she released his wrist, then lifted a trembling hand to trace a path lightly from his elbow to his forearm. The contact shot a sudden chill down his rigid backbone.

Savannah hesitated at his movement, obviously uncertain about continuing. Jacob shrugged with a grin, then looked at her expectantly. Of course he knew of the arteries, but not about how to stop profuse bleeding at these pressure points. He used a tourniquet and that usually meant eventual amputation. He definitely wanted to learn more—and he craved her touch.

"The brachial artery is here, as you know," she indicated, pressing her fingers tightly on the artery just above the bend in his arm. "If you press hard enough, you can lessen the flow of blood to the lower arm." She dropped her hand in hesitation, clearly uncertain if she should continue.

"No," Jacob protested, his arm suddenly cold. "I want you to show me. Are there others?"

Indecision crossed her worried face as she paused another moment. At his encouraging nod, Savannah reached to his shoulder and placed a hand above his collarbone. He inwardly smiled. This was most interesting.

"This point affects the subclavian," she continued quietly. "By pressing like this"—she placed her thumb on the top of his artery and her fingers around his shoulder—"you can control hemorrhaging from the hand all the way down the chest on this side."

Using her free hand, Savannah slowly drew an oval line along his white cotton shirt from his shoulder past his chest. Her fingers rounded the middle of his torso and moved down to his side. The motion was hot and silky, as if she had taken a candle and quickly run it over his entire body. His skin scorched underneath the cool fabric.

Jacob's hand came up to catch Savannah's roving one. He stared intensely at the spark smoldering in her hazel eyes and leaned his head closer.

"Any others?" His throat was tight, his voice husky.

"Yes. Three more," she said slowly, deliberately drawing out each word on a long breath. Jacob knew they played a dangerous game, but he didn't care.

"The pressure point for the temporal artery is right here," she said. Savannah reached just below his left ear and touched it gently with her thumb. "The carotid artery has one here." Her hand dragged downward, pulling his neck toward her as she applied pressure to the artery. Jacob's face came closer to hers each second. "And finally, there's the facial artery." Her fingers touched under his jaw just before her mouth raised to meet his.

The instant their lips met, Jacob knew he was

right. This woman was his. She belonged in his arms.

"That's all of seven of them," she whispered against his lips. "Do you need another demonstration?"

Jacob laughed softly. "Can we review that last part?" He encircled her in his arms, then stepped forward to catch her between the porch railing and his chest. "I've wanted to do this all day." Determined to savor the moment, he lowered his head slowly.

"Excuse me . . . Dr. Cross?" The quick footsteps and slight cough of the night medic interrupted their kiss. "Private Wells is calling for you. You might want to take a look at him, sir."

In frustration, Jacob raised his face from Savannah's. Her eyes were still closed from their kiss, her lips gently full, demanding to be caressed.

The perils of being a doctor, he thought, letting out a deep sigh.

Chapter Five

Just as she had done the previous night, Savannah lay in bed waiting for Jacob to join her. Once again, her nerves were overwrought as she anticipated what might happen when he arrived. Her skin was flushed, and her lips gently ached from his kiss on the porch. Or was it actually her kiss? It didn't matter who initiated it, she supposed. Getting involved with him was not what she planned, yet the minute he looked her way, she blossomed like a flower long deprived of water.

She stared at the ceiling, contemplating the situation. She wanted her husband; that was obvious. He wanted her, too; that was just as apparent. But it wasn't right. Her presence in this century was based on something she didn't understand, and without knowing what the future

145

held, it was not wise to fall in love.

Surprising even herself, Savannah realized she actually enjoyed life in this time. Back home, she had worked in a huge hospital and had punched a time clock just like a hundred other nurses. Here, she stood between life and death for many wounded soldiers. For the first time in her life, she knew she could make a difference, and while she had always loved her profession, a yearning for more had nagged her. She always wanted to become a doctor, but until recently had never quite had the courage to quit nursing and go back to medical school. A small laugh emerged at the irony. Although she never fulfilled her childhood dream of becoming a doctor in her own time, in this life she pretty much was.

According to Miss Emma, Jacob Cross was the best doctor around St. George, even before the war. People would send for him from two counties away, and he would go quickly. He was a caring, compassionate man who was truly dedicated to his patients. Healing was his motivation in life, and he was willing to try new, sometimes unusual, methods in order to do that. His acceptance of Savannah's seemingly strange ways proved that. He didn't have to trust her, but he did.

Yes, Jacob Cross was a good doctor; he was just limited by the knowledge of his day. Medical technology would not begin to make advances until the turn of the century. The differences between 1862 and the future were tremendous. If Jacob had so much as an inkling about the power of a tetanus vaccine, he'd help steal treasures for

Mathilde himself. Her lips lifted in a slight smile.

She toyed with telling him the truth. Maybe she wasn't being fair by not allowing him to decide for himself. But would he believe her? Probably not, she supposed. If the situation were reversed, would she believe him? A trip to the nearest psychologist would be her suggestion.

Savannah rose and pulled a blanket off the bed, then walked to the open window. The breeze ruffling the white lacy curtains was cool and refreshing. Picking up her nurse's cap from the dresser, she dragged the rocking chair over, bundled herself up in the blanket, and sat contemplating the stars. At least *they* were the same in both centuries. She ran her finger along the delicate lace of the cap. Even though the nation was in the midst of the bloodiest war in history, she felt revived living in this era. If she were meant to stay, she would relive history, watch life unfold, and know the outcome before it happened—the thought was overwhelming.

If she couldn't stay . . . Well, she'd think about that tomorrow, just like her "sister," Scarlett.

If she were to remain, the first thing she'd do is insist Jacob and Miss Emma leave the South as soon as possible. Neither would dream of moving while their boys were at war, but after it was over, she'd have them on the first train west. Any schoolgirl in Savannah's time knew that unspeakable troubles were ahead when the South finally surrendered. The atrocities after the war were almost as bad as the bloodshed during it. Unscrupulous carpetbaggers would arrive to make their fortunes off the South's misery. Exorbitant taxes would steal homes, farms, and businesses from helpless citizens. A severe depression would cause children to go hungry. The ridicule these proud people would face would be flagrant. Their honor would be gone, deprecated by those who didn't understand it and had no respect for it anyway. Savannah closed her eyes against the grim sadness. She couldn't prevent it from happening, but she could insist Jacob and Miss Emma move away from it.

Wrapped in her thoughts and still watching the stars, she jumped when a warm hand reached for her shoulder, then relaxed as her husband drew near. The room was dark except for the moon's gentle illumination.

"Jacob," she said softly, her hand reaching up to cover his. "Have you ever considered going to California?"

He looked astonished as his free hand moved toward his coat pocket. Reaching inside, he pulled out a small book. "As a matter of fact, I have. This is a book about the state. It belonged to a young soldier who was here about six months ago. He was pretty bad off, so every night I'd sit and read to him. Then we'd talk about California. I shouldn't have, I know, but I grew pretty fond of him." He turned to sit on the wide window ledge, facing his wife, and handed her the book. "He gave it to me before he died." His shoulders dropped almost imperceptibly, his voice soft with introspection. "Ever since then, I've promised myself I'd go west after this blasted war is settled.

I want to go. Maybe to fulfill his dream, and maybe mine. And now for you," he added quietly.

She opened the book, discerning pictures of San Francisco and Sacramento in the dull light. The caption under one picture boasted the coming railroad. Nothing was said as the night air released a calming effect on both of them.

"What makes you ask that?" he finally asked.

She lifted her shoulders slightly. "California's supposed to be the land of opportunity. It pleases me to know you've considered it." That wasn't quite the truth, but what else could she say? Unable to meet his eyes, she nervously cleared her throat.

"Savannah," he admonished gently, "I haven't known you very long, but I can tell something is bothering you. What is it?"

His genuine concern lodged in her heart almost like a beacon of trust. She opened her mouth to speak, stammered, then closed it again.

"Savannah," he repeated, "what is it?"

"Suppose you knew something that affected the people you cared about . . ." She spoke quickly before she lost her nerve. "Something so far-fetched that probably no one would believe it anyway. For some of those people, it's a life-and-death situation. For the others, it would just make their lives so much easier." She leaned forward in the rocker and continued earnestly, "Would you tell them even if it meant you might lose them? Would you insist they follow your advice?"

He stared at her in bewilderment. "Savannah, what are you talking about?"

Sitting back in the chair, she exhaled slowly, disappointed. He had avoided the question.

A shooting star gave her another surge of courage. In a determined rush of fortitude, she decided to go for broke, to tell him everything. To tell him she was from the future, to tell him that he and Miss Emma must leave the South, to tell him that she could get medicines that would help the agonized men downstairs, medicines far better than any he could imagine. She'd tell him that all he had to do was help her steal.

Then she looked into his eyes. Although they were questioning, they held a glimmer of admiration she hadn't seen before, undoubtedly due to his growing respect for her medical skills. While that made her happy, it also made her sad. Her story, no matter how truthful, was unbelievable. The respect she had earned would be instantly abandoned if she breathed words like time travel. He would think she was touched in the head. Closing her mouth tight, she felt a tear slide down her cheek. She couldn't do it, to him or to herself.

"Why are you crying?" he asked tenderly. "Tell me what's wrong. Maybe I can help."

Another tear worked its way from her lashes, dropping to the thin cotton of her gown. It was a silent tear, a quiet cry of despair.

Gently, her husband leaned forward, bringing her head to his warm neck with a comforting hand. For a few minutes they stayed like that, wrapped in a moment all their own. An owl hooted a mournful song. He picked her up from the rocking chair, blanket, hat and all, then placed her on the bed. Quickly undressing, he slipped in beside her, bundling her into his arms. Without saying a word, he brushed a tendril of hair from her face and held her until her tears subsided. As she drifted off into a fitful sleep, she heard his words.

"I don't know what burden you're carrying inside, my love," he said softly. "But I intend to find out."

"Mrs. Cross!" Jordan Sanger stood from behind his desk, surprise and delight showing on his face. He reached for her gloved hand and lifted it to his lips. "How delightful to see you again! I was disheartened to learn you actually married the good doctor last Sunday." He flashed her a brilliant smile, clutching his hand to his chest in mock disappointment.

Savannah beamed, amused. "You are indeed charming, Colonel Sanger. I am quite sure many women are pleased your heart is not spoken for." The blond man chuckled at her teasing.

St. George was not a large town, but she was still slightly out of breath from her walk. Not only was she unused to hiking in a floor-length dress, but the army offices were located at the opposite end of town in a house commandeered for the duration of the war. As she'd approached the house a few moments before, Savannah had been apprehensive. Colonel Sanger was her only chance for the medical supplies. If he said no, she'd be forced to find Mathilde and steal what the woman wanted.

Several days had passed since she hid behind the barn and decided to pay a visit to the dashing colonel. The hospital swarmed with injured soldiers sent in from a distant battlefield. Jacob and she had been working around the clock to tend them all. Each night he had sent her to bed alone, while he tended the last few patients and completed any necessary correspondence. She was already sound asleep by the time he finally crawled into bed. She did want the emotional distance between them, but she wondered if Jacob might be avoiding her.

Standing now in the colonel's office, she wasn't sure of what to expect from their meeting. His office was exactly what a military man should have during the middle of a war. A large selection of firearms were mounted on one paneled wall, two sabers hung crossed over the fireplace mantle, unfolded maps lay on a table near an open window, and a huge wooden desk sat covered with stacks of correspondence. Behind the desk an unusually large overstuffed leather chair beckoned like a throne.

Colonel Sanger himself was the epitome of a military officer. He was dressed in an immaculate gray wool uniform with brass buttons polished to a gleam. His double-breasted frock coat was perfectly pressed with the edging, collar, and cuffs handstitched in a contrasting red. The insignia on his coat and the braids on his sleeve were gold, which Jacob had told her indicated an officer's status. Savannah's eyes dropped to the floor, unsurprised to see highly polished black leather shoes. Even with no military experience, she knew it had to be his dress uniform and wondered why he would wear it when everyone else dressed in the more traditional Confederate gray.

Sanger's stance and demeanor held strength. Strength and cunning.

"To what do I owe the pleasure of your visit, Mrs. Cross?" Colonel Sanger offered her a chair, then sat on the edge of his desk slightly turned so that one leg rested higher than the other. As he gazed at Savannah with interest, it was obvious the position was practiced to emphasize his muscular form. His words pulled her back to the matter at hand.

Lifting her chin, she began, "Colonel Sanger—"

"Please, call me Jordan," he said, holding up his hand.

She smiled. "Jordan, then. I need your help," she said, her voice serious. "We have a hospital full of wounded men and an urgent need for medical supplies." She hoped for a glimmer of understanding in his eyes, and was disappointed.

"Yes, I'm aware of the unfortunate shortages." He shook his head regretfully.

"Then I imagine you know why I'm here. We desperately need medicines."

Without acknowledging her plea, the colonel moved from the desk and picked up a small silver bell, a gentle sound ringing out as he shook it. A young private entered the room from a small door to the right, carrying several silver-covered platters on a large tray.

"I was just about to have my noontime meal,

Mrs. Cross. Would you care to join me?" He made a grand gesture of offering her one of two high-backed chairs covered with red velvet.

Without looking up, the private proceeded to cover a small table between the chairs with a white linen tablecloth, the intricately crocheted corners draping over the edges. He placed three silver platters in the center, then arranged two place settings with fine china, silver, and crystal. Lifting the silver covers, the young man glanced at the colonel for a nod of approval, then left through the door he'd entered.

Savannah was overwhelmed by the food on the table. A large succulent roast beef, neatly carved, was surrounded by sweet early peas and mashed potatoes. Wonderfully smelling rolls and an entire pecan pie completed the meal. While not as scarce as the medical supplies, food was also carefully watched at Miss Emma's hospital. The roast beef alone would make a pot of stew large enough to feed the entire hospital.

"My, Colonel, you certainly know how to impress a lady."

"That's my aim, Mrs. Cross." Grinning, he sat her opposite him, then reached for a bottle of wine also left on the table.

"You haven't answered my question, though," Savannah reminded him as she placed her napkin in her lap, took the glass he offered, and lifted the crystal to her lips.

"Please. It's so rare I dine with a beautiful woman, I would prefer to discuss your situation after we're through. That is, of course, if you don't find it offensive to dine with me?"

"Don't be silly, Colonel. This is a wonderful meal."

"St. George is a supply town for the fighting men," he said companionably. "Goods come into town and I oversee shipping them to the lines. While we're not close to the major fighting, skirmishes do occur nearby, especially when Yankee scouts want to take a look-see over the area.

"As the commanding officer, it's my job to be ready for battle at all times," he continued. "I'm here to make sure the troops get the ammunition and other things they need. Even uniforms and boots are my responsibility. If somebody wants something, he has to come to me," he said with pride and a touch of arrogance.

While she absorbed his words calmly, inwardly Savannah was delighted. Surely he was telling her all this so she would truly appreciate what he was about to do for the hospital. If stroking his ego was all that was needed to get the medicines, she'd be first in line.

"Does Jacob know you are here?" he asked suddenly, his eyes narrowing.

Surprised at the quick change of topic, she put down her fork and studied him intently. "Does it matter?"

He shrugged noncommittally.

"No, Colonel, he does not. I came on my own."

Smiling then, the colonel reached for another roll. "You came to see me just because you wanted to?" A look of satisfied smugness settled on his face.

Without really knowing why, his expression sent a jolt of edginess through Savannah. There was definitely something odd going on. Perhaps he wasn't going to be as cooperative as she thought.

"Jacob came to see me a few days ago about this same matter, and I'm afraid the answer is still the same." Colonel Sanger placed his fork delicately on the edge of his plate and considered Savannah carefully. "Medical supplies are limited all over the South. What we do receive must go directly to the field hospitals."

"Surely you could spare several jars of morphine at least."

He looked at her down his long thin nose. "Savannah," he started. "I assume I may call you that?" Without waiting for her approval, he went on. "Even your husband agreed the soldiers on the battle lines need it first. Surely you can understand that as well."

She was quiet for a minute, the sense that something more was going on thick around her. Jacob and Sanger had an obvious dislike for each other, and she wasn't sure why. "What is between you and my husband, Colonel Sanger?" she asked quietly.

Surprised, the colonel looked up at her, his face hard. "Forgive me for being blunt, Mrs. Cross, but the troops here consider your husband a coward," he said levelly, a nasty smirk forming at his mouth. "He is needed to treat the wounded out on the battlefield, not in a relief hospital well away from the guns. He refuses to join our efforts."

Through the window, Savannah saw an old man in a tattered uniform walk by, leading a string of horses. Jacob had lost so much over what had begun as a requisition for horses. She didn't doubt he had refused to fight for the South, and she understood why.

"My husband is a brave man, Colonel Sanger. He has extremely valid reasons for refusing to join your efforts." Savannah fought to control the almost uncontrollable anger that grew inside her as she lifted her chin and set her shoulders. Don't let him rile you, she chided herself. Focus on your reasons for coming here. "Let me get this straight. You're refusing to give us medicines, to help your own soldiers, because you personally dislike my husband?"

Sanger grinned again. "One of the perks of the job, you might say."

Savannah bit her tongue hard to fight her outrage. No wonder Jacob and Miss Emma despised this man. She stared Sanger right in the eye, meeting his challenge. "I can tell you for a fact that the South is going to lose this war in part due to officers like you who hoard necessary supplies and dole them out to whoever suits your own personal ambitions. It's in the history books."

Colonel Sanger quickly glanced up from his meal. "Do not speak foolishly, Mrs. Cross. You have come to me for help." The veiled threat hung heavily in the air.

"Perhaps, like my husband, I have wasted my

time," she said, barely hiding her anger. "We have dying soldiers in our hospital, Colonel Sanger. They may not be out on the field, but they are your soldiers, and they are dying just the same. I don't see how your conscience allows you to ignore the situation."

Flinging her napkin on her plate, she pushed away from the table and rose to her feet without dropping her eyes. This man infuriated her, and his stare was meant to intimidate her, but she refused to break his gaze. She now realized the slight differences between his face and Alan's. Colonel Sanger had a hard dangerous look about him, a look that frightened her.

Finally, he rose and stepped toward her, meeting her resistance with a charming smile. "I regret I have been harsh. I apologize for being the one to tell you such truths about your new husband. Let's discuss your situation further."

He suavely guided her back to her chair. After she was seated, he walked to his liquor cabinet. Opening the door and pulling out a bottle of whiskey, he poured it into a sparkling crystal tumbler. A dozen more bottles, all unopened, filled the cabinet. He grabbed two of the unopened bottles and placed them on his desk, then crossed the room to stand close behind her chair.

"Savannah." Her name rested on his lips. "Such a beautiful name." He sighed. "As I said before, I don't have much in the way of medical supplies, but I am, though you may not believe it, sympathetic to your plight. You may take these bottles with you."

Before she could respond, he dropped his hands to rest lightly on her shoulders. A shudder instantly ran through her, but she didn't move. He was playing a game, testing her to see how far she would go. Using all her inner strength, Savannah ignored his touch and stared at the two bottles. It wasn't morphine, but Jacob could use it.

His hands began to knead her shoulder blades in a slow, irritating motion. Savannah tried to pull away, but his grip became like a painful vise. The colonel bent forward, his warm breath close to her ear. "I am also willing to provide you with whatever you need," he said softly, "on one condition." His hands lifted to stroke her hair, twirling the ends between his long fingers.

"And what might that be, Colonel Sanger?" she asked in clipped tones, averting her head as far away as possible. She wanted the whiskey, but she refused to let him see how much.

"Simple. Spend an evening with me." He placed a wet kiss on her neck, nuzzling her skin with his tongue.

"How dare you!" In one quick motion, she jumped to her feet, turned, and slapped the insolence from his face. A trickle of blood escaped from the corner of his lip.

"Damn! Look what you've done!" He reached for a crisply starched white handkerchief to pat the blood.

She lifted her chin. "I'm a married woman, Colonel Sanger, and I do not appreciate your advances."

"I realize you are married, Savannah," he said

159

through gritted teeth. He glared at her with menacing eyes. He quickly masked his anger, then regained his composure as he wiped his bleeding mouth. "However, I would enjoy the company of a soft yet intelligent woman." Savannah stared at him angrily, but he boldly continued, "Of course, we would take precautions to prevent any unforeseen gossip, but I am, as you say, able to dole out supplies when and to whom I want. If you want medicines for your husband's hospital, you must spend the *entire* evening with me."

Even without the emphasis on "entire," Savannah knew exactly what he meant.

"I know it's blackmail," he said, sighing in mock regret, "but I am truly forlorn that I did not have an opportunity to get to know you before you were married. You arrived in town rather suddenly, I understand." When she didn't respond, he pressed further, "I am a lonely man, Savannah. I long for a night with a woman of such beauty."

Savannah was flabbergasted. It was either steal from Miss Emma or sleep with this man.

"If I agree, and I haven't yet," she interjected, figuring she could toy with him just as he was doing to her, "what's to keep you from breaking your promise and not give me what we need?"

"Why, Savannah, I'm hurt that you do not trust me." He sighed, rolling his eyes heavenward. "You may take these bottles now and send me a list of what your, shall we say, time, will cost. Your items will be here the night you arrive."

Slowly, she began to smile. Savannah walked forward and picked up the whiskey, gently cradling the bottles as if they held liquid gold. "You, Colonel Sanger, are a low-life, belly-crawling rat snake."

Colonel Sanger, sure of his victory, opened his mouth with a loud laugh. "Perhaps I am," he agreed with pleasure.

Savannah walked toward the door, opened it, and stood poised to exit. "Then I'm sure you know that a rat snake is overlooked on the farm because it's of no consequence. It doesn't demand the respect or fear one gives a rattler.

"The answer is no, *Colonel* Sanger."

Pleased to see the superior smile drop instantly from his face, she turned and strode out the door.

Where was she? Jacob wondered. Miss Emma told him earlier that Savannah had gone to the mercantile to purchase linen for bandages. That was midmorning. Dinner had been served and cleared, and there was still no sign of her. While he wasn't worried, it did concern him. He still had no idea what secrets she held, and her absence nagged at him.

"There you go, Ely," he said to the man in the bed. "Your leg is showing signs of improvement. I'm pleased we didn't have to amputate." Kneeling beside the bed, Jacob completed his inspection of the deep gashes on the man's leg, then reached for a fresh bandage.

"No more pleased than me, Doc." Private Ely Wells grinned, although his face was ashen from pain. "I'm glad Miss Savannah knew how to stop the bleeding so you didn't have to cut it off. I've got a field to plow when I get home and four kids to raise. I don't know what we would have done. I know I'll probably limp the rest of my life," he went on before Jacob could tactfully remind him of the difficult recovery still ahead, "but I can get around good enough to chase boys away from my little girl!"

"Things to be grateful for!" Jacob returned with a chuckle. He patted the man's shoulder as he finished. "When she returns, I'll send Savannah to see if you need anything. I'm hoping for a shipment of morphine today, so maybe we can ease your pain a bit."

"The morphine didn't come in, but I managed to get this," Savannah said, walking toward them with a bottle of whiskey in each hand. She joined Jacob and his patient.

Reaching for a bottle, Jacob looked at her, amazed. He broke the seal, popped the cork, and held it out to Ely, who promptly took a deep swig.

"Jacob! What about germs? He needs a glass." Savannah was clearly mortified, thinking her instructions on germs was all for naught.

"Whatever germs are on that bottle will soon be gone, I'm sure." Jacob laughed, although his eyes held uncertainty. Where had she been, and where did she get the whiskey?

"How's the leg?" Savannah asked.

"Better," Jacob replied. "Ely's gonna make it." He smiled again at his patient. "Thank God, it was your leg. A .58 caliber can rot your gut."

Seeing the man nod in agreement, Savannah questioned, "What do you mean?"

Jacob stared at her, incredulous. "Surely you've seen a .58 wound to the chest?" This woman knew far too much about medicine not to know the tragic consequences of being shot with a .58 caliber weapon. He couldn't believe it when her pale head shook and her soft shoulders shrugged.

"A .58 caliber will kill you slowly, Mrs. Cross," Ely explained as Jacob considered her carefully. "The bullet shatters when it hits, causing tremendous damage. If it's to the leg or arm, a man knows he'll probably lose it, but he should be able to get help. If it's to the chest, and especially to the gut, he knows there's nothing he can do. He's gonna bleed to death."

"When you see a dead man arrive with his uniform ripped to shreds," Jacob interjected impassively, his arms folded over his chest, "it usually means he tore at it himself to see if he had a gut wound. If so, he knew he was a dead man."

Jacob could see the horror in her eyes as she looked back and forth between him and Ely. For some reason, he was no longer surprised by her reaction. She wasn't telling the complete truth about herself, and she was aware he realized it. She knew less than she pretended and more than she was telling. He meant to find out about what.

Chapter Six

"Mathilde?" Savannah called from her place behind the barn. "I'm ready now. I want to trade." She looked around, hoping the woman would answer her this time. Just as before, it was late in the day before she could escape Jacob's watchful eye.

About sixty wounded men still filled the hospital, all needing some type of attention. The ones who were more seriously injured were kept apart, including those who had succumbed to gangrene in spite of efforts to prevent it. Fortunately, there had been a noticeable drop in the number of severe cases, and thanks to Savannah's determination, the patients were quickly isolated. The care she, Miss Emma, and the medics could render was limited without antibiotics, and there wasn't much she could do except to keep them comfortable and try to break the fever.

After her unpleasant encounter with Colonel Sanger, Savannah had spent most of the afternoon wrapping wounds, cleaning infections, and prudently administering what little morphine and laudanum they had to those who needed it the most. The new bottles of whiskey were carefully stored for amputations. If worse came to worse and they ran out of morphine or ether, they could get the patient drunk before the horrendous act occurred.

Jacob was different, too. A resolve was set about him. He was pleasant enough; in fact, he made several comments on the improvement he'd seen from what she called "aseptic" techniques.

Several times this afternoon, he had again pressed her about her medical training. Holding firm to her story about nursing school in Atlanta, she had racked her brain trying to think of what she might have said that would make him doubt her story. Guilt from lying weighed heavily on her mind, but what else could she do?

Once, while handing him a pair of scissors to remove stitches, their fingers had brushed, sending a thrill through her body. Even though she was wary, he still could make her blood boil. A few minutes later, she had covered his hand with her own to steady a small glass of water. As they counted out the five precious drops of laudanum falling into the water, their eyes had met and held. The noise of the room around them had faded until they seemed to be alone. Only when the sleeping concoction almost spilled to the floor had they regained their senses.

"Mathilde?" she called again, this time a tremor of concern filtering through her voice. Savannah had no way of knowing if she was being heard across time. She had no guarantee the woman would come back, although her greedy proposition made it certain she'd return to badger Savannah into trading. Now that she had made the decision to help the hospital, she was anxious to trade and get it over with. These men were suffering terribly, not to mention that her encounter with Sanger and this afternoon's gripping story of the .58 caliber only reinforced her desire to help.

Leaning back against the weathered wood, she sighed. People always wanted to go back to the "good old days." If they only knew that the old days weren't so good. Take the colonel, for instance. In a time and place where honor was revered above all, this man blatantly used the plight of his fellow soldiers in an attempt to fulfill his own desires. Her initial excitement of meeting another "Alan" had quickly fizzled as she realized that, like her ex-fiance, this man would do whatever it took and use whomever he could to get what he wanted. Now, his charming good looks made her sick to her stomach.

She made a fist with one hand and slapped it against the other. She was damned if she did, because it would be stealing, and damned if she didn't, because people would die. Underneath the turmoil of her internal struggle, she knew this had to be the right decision. For a few, practically invaluable objects, Savannah could help this hospital. Of that she was certain, and it was the only thing that eased her conscience.

"So, you're ready to trade?"

Savannah had been so wrapped up in her own musings, she hadn't heard anyone approach. But there was Mathilde, dressed in a flagrantly orange flowing kaftan. The loose folds of the material billowed gently in the breeze.

"I would have come sooner, except I was tied up with another client. Here, I brought you this as a gesture of my good will."

Savannah reached for a shiny stethoscope. "We already have one of these," she said, shocked by the shopkeeper's offering.

"Perhaps, but not of this quality."

Thanking her with a nod, Savannah put the instrument around her neck as she had all of her professional life. "What else can you bring me?" she asked, hurriedly looking around to ensure no one could see them from the house.

"What can you trade?" the woman answered slyly, her eyes following Savannah's toward the hospital.

"Look," Savannah said, irritated by the woman's coyness. "You know antiques, and you know what you want. Tell me what it is and I'll try to get it. I don't want to do this to begin with, so let's not waste each other's time."

"Agreed." The rotund woman smiled, then pulled out a list from the folds of her dress. Quickly glancing over it, she looked back at Savannah. "I want a Confederate saber, as much crisp Confederate money as you can find, a Confederate hat—"

"Fine, I can manage those," Savannah interrupted. She wasn't about to fill a grocery list for this strange person. "Now, in return I want a case of tetanus vaccines, syringes, and needles. I want—"

"That's not possible, I'm afraid," Mathilde objected this time, holding her fingers out to check her manicure.

"What do you mean it's not possible?" Savannah snapped. "You were the one offering to trade."

"I can only trade you what these people already have in some form." She held her palms out and shrugged. "Anything that has yet to be developed can't travel back."

"You didn't tell me this before."

"Of course not," she said impatiently. "You probably wouldn't have considered a trade if you realized you couldn't have things from your own time."

Shocked, Savannah stared at her. "That's incredibly cruel."

"Now, don't be silly. Your hospital is almost out of medicines. Do you or do you not need supplies?"

Savannah's eyes narrowed as she considered the woman's words. She had been tricked, that was true, but the crafty old woman was right. Did it really matter? They still needed painkillers and other drugs. She sighed, closing her eyes. Suddenly a wondrous thought dawned on her. A thought just as sneaky as Mathilde herself.

"I want aspirin," Savannah said firmly.

Mathilde gave an exaggerated sigh. "I told you . . ."

"Aspirin is acetylsalicylic acid." Savannah took on an indignant air, while giving thanks to God for Trivial Pursuit. "That was developed in France in 1853. It wasn't in widespread use as a pain-killer until the 1890s, but it still had been invented."

"Perhaps this is so, but it wasn't used for what you intend in this year."

She held up the stethoscope from around her neck. "The quality of this stethoscope has not been developed, yet it's here. I want the aspirin or no deal."

Mathilde sighed and rolled her eyes.

"I'm not through, either. I also want morphine. As much as you can get," Savannah demanded. If she was going to have to steal, she'd damn well trade for all she could.

"Where would I get that? I'm not a doctor!"

"I don't care where you get it. Hop to a Union hospital and steal it if you need to. Just get it."

"For that I want your doctor's watch."

Savannah stopped talking, instantly appalled by the woman's bartering. Surely she could not mean Jacob's watch; it was his most precious possession. She would not steal it, not for any reason. "Out of the question," she replied coldly.

"You know as well as I that it's already in the shop. If you want the morphine, get me the watch."

"I won't do it, Mathilde," she repeated. "Miss Emma has a beautiful hand-sewn quilt. When you carry it back to the future, it'll be worth more than the watch. Even I can imagine how much an 1862 museum-quality quilt is worth. I'll trade you that for the morphine."

Mathilde appeared to consider her words thoughtfully, then shrugged. "Okay, you've got a deal. I'll meet you here just before the sun rises in the morning. Don't be late."

"One other thing," Savannah pressed as the woman turned to leave. "I want a toothbrush. Even an old-fashioned one."

Mathilde smiled. "That's an easy one. I won't even make you trade for that."

Savannah accepted the tentative truce. "You said your family has been the conservator of the hats for generations. It seems to me you should already know the outcome of my journey. Tell me, will I ever get to go home? Am I to be here forever?"

"Have you determined your destiny yet?" the strange-looking woman answered with her own question.

"I'm not even sure what my destiny is," Savannah cried, frustrated. "How can I figure it out if I don't even know how long I'll be here?" She touched the pudgy orange-clad arm. "Help me, Mathilde. I'm so confused. What is my destiny? Am I supposed to stay here? How do I know?"

The old woman patted Savannah's hand with her own, a glimmer of compassion showing in her eyes. "I truly wish I could help, Savannah. But

170

the hat brought you here for a reason. It's up to you to determine why."

With that, the shopkeeper stepped away and vanished before Savannah could blink.

As it had so often since her arrival, sleep eluded Savannah. Tonight she was consumed with worry about her pending thievery. She was also worried about the man lying next to her. Since their talk by the window the other night, he hadn't so much as touched her. Instead of being thankful that he was maintaining his distance, the torture of being next to him grew worse each night.

Recognizing the real problem didn't make her feel any better, either. She was falling in love with Jacob Cross. To deny the truth was difficult, yet to admit it was getting harder and harder.

She rolled away from him on the narrow bed, acutely aware of how her body was betraying her, as if two fires burned side by side, waiting for the second they would be close enough to merge into one. Restlessly, she tossed back over and faced the man beside her, the tangled covers pulled tightly across both of them.

Motionless only for a minute, she squirmed onto her back, looking for a comfortable spot, then started to turn on her side. A hand suddenly shot out and dropped heavily on her stomach. She froze as her senses jumped to life.

"Savannah, go to sleep." The deep seductive voice did nothing to calm her tense nerves as his hand wrapped around her like a soothing blanket. Jacob's head rested on the pillow just above hers.

As he breathed, a continually warm puff of air in her ear sent shivers across her body. She wanted to turn toward his inviting mouth, but knew she couldn't.

She had a mission tonight: Mathilde's shopping list.

Once Jacob was asleep, she'd begin.

When his breathing was deep and even, she gently lifted his muscular arm and slipped from underneath it, groaning inwardly when her feet touched the cold wooden floor.

"I'm going for warm milk," she muttered quietly, knowing if Jacob was awake, he'd be more likely to believe that story and not follow.

Wrapping Miss Emma's borrowed thick robe over her modest nightgown, she opened the door and entered the darkened hallway. Tiptoeing lightly by Miss Emma's closed door, Savannah headed downstairs to perpetrate her crime.

Her bare feet padded softly down the stairs toward the main room. The best place to get a Confederate hat is from a Confederate soldier, she reasoned, heading toward the rows of sleeping men. Bending nonchalantly to touch a sleeping man's head for fever, Savannah used her other hand to reach for his hat under the small cot. In one smooth motion, she straightened, hat in hand, brushing the dirt from it as if the action was routine, then walked away nonchalantly. She put the gray hat on the vanity in the foyer.

Jacob had a sword in his office due to the recent death of an officer, so that wouldn't be a problem. He hadn't been able to find the man's family to return it. He was too observant not to miss it, but he would probably assume another soldier stole it for the battlefield.

Suddenly she stopped, then backed up her steps. The vanity. That very same piece of furniture was already in Mathilde's antique shop in the future. Would she have to steal that, too? Stricken, she wondered how she would be able to take the few remaining possessions Miss Emma held so dear.

"Mrs. Cross?"

Startled, Savannah jumped quietly, then quickly relaxed to see Ely leaning up in his bed, calling to her. Leaving the hat on the vanity, she quickly crossed the distance between them.

"I saw you checking patients. You can't sleep, can you?" he asked in a hushed whisper. "Me, either. Sometimes, my leg hurts so bad, I think I'm gonna die. Don't get me wrong. I'm grateful to you for not letting Doc Cross cut it off. It's just the pain won't let me sleep. Like tonight."

She smiled compassionately at him. "I understand, Ely, and you're right. I can't sleep, either. Actually, one of the reasons is that I worry we don't have medicine for your pain or for the others."

"You can't think like that, Mrs. Cross. This war's a terrible thing, but we all willingly signed up to defend our homes and families. We have to accept the consequences. You and your husband are good people, trying to help us the best way you can. I'll always be grateful to you for fighting for my leg," he added a bit shyly. "It took courage for you to stand up to Doc Cross, you being a nurse and a lady and all." He grimaced suddenly. "Know any good stories that might take my mind off this place?"

Savannah lifted her finger to her chin and thought for a minute. She'd never been much of a storyteller and, of course, she didn't know any popular stories of the day. She could tell him about Scarlett and Rhett, but that might need too many explanations. Every single story she could think of would be full of inventions he'd never dreamed of. All except one. She bent to adjust Ely's blanket as a thought came to mind. There was a tale about a shipwrecked crew without any modern conveniences. "Gilligan's Island" had been in reruns for so long, she was certain it could be considered a classic anyway. Pulling up a stool, she began in her most dramatic and sing-song voice,

"Just sit right back and you'll hear a tale, a tale of a fateful trip . . . "

Savannah spouted the words to the theme song as a way of setting the stage for Gilligan's antics. She began telling Ely some of the hapless adventures of the shipwrecked crew, about the professor who tries to invent things to take them off the island, but how Gilligan thwarts every effort. She carefully avoided mentioning the radio, describing in great detail the huts and hammock beds and constant source of coconut cream pies.

For almost an hour they sat together, laughing softly at her stories. When Ely's eyelids began to droop, she knew he felt a little better. So did she, in fact. Her conscience was soothed by the knowledge she could do more than just tell Ely stories, she could ease this man's suffering for the price of a Confederate sword. As she said her good nights and headed toward Jacob's office, Savannah recalled how much she had always loved "Gilligan's Island." Now she knew her dad had been wrong all those years. She had not wasted her time in front of the TV.

Jacob sat on the staircase, listening to Savannah's ingenious stories, smiling softly. He would never cease to be amazed by this woman. There was a streak of wildness and independence in her that intrigued him. Not only was she a healer wise beyond her years, his beautiful wife had enough compassion to sit and talk to a hurting, lonely man until the wee hours.

He hadn't been asleep when she rose from the bed. Determined to learn the mysterious secret she was hiding, he had followed her. He was still puzzled about the two bottles of whiskey she had brought, especially since she wouldn't say where they came from. And the new stethoscope. Where had that come from? It was far superior to any he had ever owned. That only tweaked his suspicion more.

After supper, Jacob had been writing letters to families of the deceased when he looked through an open window to see her slip outside and head toward the barn. When she had come back a short while later, a mixture of anger, fear, and worry had been on her face. His own trip behind the unused barn had proven fruitless in finding any indication of what was going on.

When they had retired for the night, Savannah had been agitated, restlessly tossing and turning in bed. She was up to something, all right. Jacob just had to figure out what it was. Not knowing what to expect, he had been surprised to see her check each man in the room, to pick up a man's hat, probably one that had been stepped on, dust it off, and place it on the vanity.

He didn't have his watch, but he was sure she had been talking to Ely for almost an hour. Not the habits of someone up to mischief. He raked his hand across his stubbly chin. Perhaps he was overreacting to this whole situation. This woman awakened a need in him he hadn't felt in a long time. He wanted to fight that attraction. He wanted to be suspicious. Ever since the murders, he had not trusted anyone, and now he suspected Savannah of . . . of what? Being a kind person? An excellent nurse? A warm wife? A tempting lover?

She was all those things, and more. Pushing doubts out of his mind, Jacob rose quickly. He suddenly wanted to see her. Following Savannah's direction, he walked by Ely, stopping only for a second to check him.

"She's a great lady, Doc. You take care of her," he mumbled, his voice thick with sleep.

Looking up, he stopped in his tracks as she came out his office and shut the door softly behind her. Another tremor of suspicion rumbled slightly, then settled when he saw a small glass of water in her hand.

"You caught me," Savannah stuttered nervously.

Jacob cocked his eyebrow, his heart beating heavily as he waited for an explanation.

"I'm sorry, Jacob. I know we need to be stringent with the laudanum, but poor Ely is in such pain. I wanted to give him a little to help him sleep. I mixed in eight drops."

Jacob considered her carefully, glancing from the glass in her shaking hands to the apprehension in her eyes. He took it from her and nodded toward the sleeping man with a slight smile. "Your stories must have been really dull because he's sound asleep," he whispered so as not to wake the other men nearby. "We'll save this for someone else."

Opening the door to his office, he stepped inside, and Savannah followed. He placed the glass on his desk and reached for a clean, empty bottle to store the mixture. A breeze through the open window rustled a stack of papers, knocking several to the floor. Quickly crossing the distance to the window, he shut it with a click.

"You're not angry?" she asked in a small voice.

"Of course not. You were doing what you thought best. I trust your judgment." Taking her hand, they walked back through the maze of beds. "Since neither of us can sleep, let's step outside and enjoy the stars."

"I don't know." Savannah hesitated. "Every time you and I stand on that porch together," she said nervously, "things happen."

"Exactly," he replied, grinning.

He opened the heavy mahogany door and led her toward the far corner of the porch to the wooden swing. The isolated swing, meant only for two, was almost hidden from view by a huge, fragrant camellia bush. Jacob sat her down, then turned to face the rail. He was just tall enough to see over the flowery bush as the white flowers glistened in the moonlight. Glancing back at Savannah, he was glad of the almost full moon in the sky. It allowed him to study this woman without her being completely aware of it. She was terribly nervous, and there was an air of sadness about her, almost as if the burden she carried was too much for her delicate shoulders to bear.

Turning back to his view of the street, he spoke softly. "I'm not a trusting soul, Savannah. Ever since I lost my family, I've withdrawn from the very people who care about me." He laughed slightly. "I'm afraid I've gone to extremes to avoid any type of involvement." He moved to sit beside her on the swing. "That is, until you came into my life." His hand reached for hers, closing around her fingers.

"There's something about you that calls to me, something I can't seem to define. It's almost as if you were always meant to be in my life. And the hospital"—he nodded toward the far window—"has seen drastic improvements since you arrived. But there's more to it than just that. I haven't figured it out yet, but I will."

Even in the dim glow of the moon, the growing

fire in him could not be hidden. The intensity with which he wanted this woman was more than he could bear. Very gently, he pulled her near as his head bent to hers. His mouth lightly touched hers, his eyes closed almost to a slit. The teasing tip of his tongue tried to convince her to forget her determination to remain distant.

"I know, Jacob," she muttered against his lips. "I feel it, too."

No matter what she was up to, he wanted to remember this moment, remember the taste of her, so warm and feminine. Her nearness caused his senses to whirl as her scent combined with the camellias to create an exotic perfume. A burst of pleasure shot through his soul as he started the swing in a slow rocking motion. His mouth was still on hers, gently playing her lips as the swing's seductive rhythm began.

When Jacob lifted his head inches to gaze into her eyes, Savannah suddenly became self-conscious of her own desire. Lifting her trembling hand to her hair, she ran her fingers through it, certain it was tousled. She had not brushed it after tossing and turning in bed. Jacob reached up, laying his hand over hers, bringing it to his lips. He opened her palm and kissed it tenderly.

"You're beautiful the way you are."

Drawing courage from his touch, she slowly lifted her arms and entwined her hands around his neck, drawing him closer as she leaned back against the swing. The night air was crisp through her robe and nightgown, but she felt giddy and hot. The contact of skin against skin only intensified the ache growing deep inside her.

Jacob's mouth began a slow demanding exploration of her neck and shoulders. The high neckline of the gown caused Savannah to long for her silk teddy back home.

Back home. Oh, how time stood still with this man! He made her forget her sensibilities. Forget about home.

As the swing continued its perpetual motion, his palm covered her breast. Her quick intake of breath brought a gentle smile to his lips. Even through the layers of fabric, his touch created an abrupt zing in her heart. With gentle pressure, he began a delightfully slow massage of her breast that sent an urgent throb down her entire body. His mouth played a romantic game with the delicate curve of her jawbone and intensely ticklish earlobe. He slipped his hand into the front of her robe, where her nipple was taut and anxious for him. Savannah knew she should stop him before she lost her reservations.

Then she realized she already had.

She wanted Jacob, and she couldn't deny her body's reaction any longer. He could do with her what he willed. Hidden by the camellia bush and the darkness of night, they were alone as his hand continued a masterful exploration.

Jacob lifted his head to gaze at her. The moonlight peeking between the bush and the roof caused a sensual shadow to outline them both. With a kiss as tender and sweet as the cool evening breeze, Jacob whispered in her ear, "Be mine, Savannah. Be my wife in every sense of the word."

In a second, her heart was torn in two. She wanted her husband. God, how she wanted him. In his eyes, she saw how much he wanted her, too. The enveloping breeze suddenly became cold as anguish seared her soul. Until she could resolve her reason for being there, she couldn't risk hurting this man.

"Jacob, no." She clung to him, barely able to breathe. "This isn't right. You said once that you don't have much to offer, but that's not true. I'm the one with nothing to offer."

He stopped the motion of the varnished swing, obviously surprised. "You're wrong, love. You've restored my hope, given me another chance to trust, another chance at happiness." He leaned forward to kiss her still-tingling lips again.

Her heart sank at his words. Less than an hour ago, she was betraying his trust by stealing from him. Now, he was wanting to love her because he trusted her. That was exactly why she couldn't betray him.

"No." She pushed him away. "I can't do this, Jacob. I care about you too much. If only . . . "

"If only what?" he asked coarsely, trying to mask the hurt in his eyes.

"If only things were different." Pushing him away, she ran quickly from the porch before he could see her cry.

Chapter Seven

Damn it all. Savannah stood wearily behind the barn and rubbed her eyes. She hadn't slept a wink since leaving Jacob on the porch hours ago. Pale streaks of pink and gray began to lighten the sky, casting an eerie tinge to the early-dawn mist. A rooster called his first morning alarm with an irritating urgency while she waited for Mathilde.

At her feet lay the stolen Confederate sword, soldier's hat, and ten dollars in Confederate notes. Miss Emma's beautiful quilt was wrapped around her shoulders to ward off the morning chill. Her conscience continued to gnaw at her with faint twinges of guilt. Briefly, she considered returning the objects before Mathilde arrived. The only thing stopping her was the vision of Ely's suffering last night.

No, stealing was the hard part, and she had done that. She was committed now. Whether or not this was her destiny, she wouldn't back out now.

She glanced back at Miss Emma's home, her gaze resting on the window to Jacob's office. Thankfully, he hadn't returned to their bed after the encounter on the swing. When she had retrieved the sword an hour ago, she had peeked through his office window and saw him asleep in a overstuffed chair, his long frame uncomfortably contorted to fit. The mere sight of him had caused her heart to tumble with emotion. With the gentlest of touches, her handsome doctor had stirred a deep longing in her soul. She had sworn off doctors once and for all, and now she'd fallen for another. She had jumped as the man in the chair lifted his hand to scratch his rough chin. She quickly ducked from the window, picked up the sword and the money, then wasted no time in darting to the barn. She'd managed to steal everything the creepy old woman wanted. The last thing she needed was to get caught before the secret trade was made.

Waiting for her accomplice in the misty air, Savannah took several deep breaths to calm her nerves. She pulled the quilt more tightly around her, unconsciously remembering the satisfying warmth of lying next to her husband in their narrow bed. She loved Jacob; of that there was no doubt. But with their bodies entwined on the swing, he had confided in her about his inability to trust, and yet last night he had offered his trust to her. How could she abuse the one thing he did not give lightly? Being caught as a thief was one thing, but how could she risk hurting him when the possibility existed that she might one day disappear without a word? She knew what the future held for the South and this war. If only she could determine what it held for her, then she would know what to do about her husband.

"Do you have everything?" a hushed voice asked through the fog.

Although Savannah expected the woman, she was startled at the whispered sound, then struggled to catch sight of the matronly figure. "Where are you? I can't see you."

The hairs on the back of Savannah's neck stood on end as an eerie feeling crept down her back. This time-travel stuff is getting just a little bit spooky, she thought as several long seconds ticked by. A large shape finally emerged from the mist and drew closer. In spite of the ghoulish atmosphere, she raised her eyebrow, amused to see Mathilde approaching in a loud yellow housecoat and fluffy slippers. Large pink curlers wound tightly around her hair like a helmet.

"It is early, you know. I haven't had my coffee yet." Mathilde lifted a defensive chin at Savannah's mirth.

"I found everything you wanted, including Miss Emma's quilt." Controlling her emotions, Savannah plunged ahead to get this over with as quickly as possible. What the woman wore was really of little concern as long as she kept her promises. She held up the quilt for the antique dealer's inspection.

Mathilde remained silent, but her satisfied smile indicated she was pleased. Stroking her thick fingers over the neatly sewn fabric, she sighed, glancing up at Savannah. "You were right, it is beautiful and worth much more than the watch. What else did you find?"

Reluctantly, she held out the Confederate sword with both hands.

"Yes! Oh, yes! This is exquisite and in mint condition! I know the perfect collector for it. He will treasure it, Savannah, I promise you." Mathilde gently lifted the sword from Savannah's hands and wrapped it lovingly in the quilt. "Did you get the hat and notes, too?" Her eyes began to sparkle at Savannah's answering nod.

"Wonderful! I'm so pleased." Her delight grew more apparent as she looked over the items. "You've done well."

Suddenly irritated by Mathilde's praise, Savannah cleared her throat to focus the woman's attention back to the matter at hand.

"Ah, yes." Mathilde held out a new toothbrush. "I have some things for you, too. And, to show my sincerity and good faith, I brought even more than we agreed upon," she said happily, pointing to two cardboard boxes sitting on the dew-covered ground. Beside the boxes sat a large cobalt-blue glass apothecary jar barely visible through the rising fog. "There's two cases of aspirin and a jar of crystalline morphine. I had to get it from an unwilling Yankee doctor. I had to—"

Savannah held up her hand to stop Mathilde's

chattering. "No. I don't want to know how you got it."

She walked to the cases and opened the first to see forty-eight bottles of good old aspirin. The aspirin wouldn't be of much help to the men in serious pain, but it would offer some relief without the addiction caused by morphine. Turning to the heavy blue jar, she lifted the lid to reveal a white powder the consistency of corn meal. Jacob would have to grind this down with his mortar, but it was wonderful. Behind the case of aspirin sat a small shipping crate of lemons and oranges.

"Vitamin C! What a great idea, Mathilde!"

"Just consider it my contribution to the cause," the garish woman replied.

"Thank you, Mathilde," she said softly. "We really need all of this."

A surprisingly soft hand touched her shoulder as the old woman bent slightly over her. "This was a difficult thing for you to do, Savannah, but you've helped this hospital far more than you know." Her face held an expression Savannah didn't quite understand. "Now, let's decide about our next trade."

"Are you certain you don't know the outcome of my journey?" Savannah asked, changing the subject, convinced this woman already knew what was to happen. As Mathilde objected, Savannah stopped her. "I know, I know. It's up to me to figure out my own destiny. It's just that things have gotten complicated." She began to pace a small circle around the woman. "You see, I've fallen in love with Jacob, and I think he feels the same about me. How can I follow that instinct if I don't know what my future holds?"

"I do see your problem." Mathilde studied her with a thoughtful look. "Have you carefully considered everything about your journey? Every possibility, not just the obvious. If you can figure out whose lives you have affected the most, then you'll discern why you are here."

"The obvious answer is Jacob." She continued to pace without looking up. "He's beginning to heal after the tragic murder of his family. On the other hand, it's the soldiers. How many of them are alive because I prevented the spread of infection? Because I was able to heal a wound or control an infection that would have probably killed them? And how many will be able to hang on now that we have some type of painkiller for them? Who knows, I may save the life of a man destined to die. I might save hundreds of them."

"That's hosh-posh logic, Savannah. Perhaps those men lived because they were supposed to. It seems to me that the truth has already revealed itself to you. You're allowing yourself to be confused by other things. Consider everything." Mathilde bent to retrieve her new possessions.

"So you do know the outcome!" Savannah accused, stopping directly in front of the yellow-clad figure. "Are you not telling me so I'll continue to steal for you?"

"No." The woman patted Savannah's arm. "I truly don't know the outcome, and I'm hurt you think I'd withhold that information from you. I suspect what will happen, but it would be unfair of me to distort your thinking. Think about yourself, your desires, and your situation carefully. After you do that, allow what's natural to happen. Your destiny will reveal itself, I promise. Now, what about our next trade?"

Realizing Mathilde had spoken her last word on the matter, Savannah dropped the subject. She would determine her own destiny, with or without the help of this supposed time-travel monitor or conservator or whatever she was.

"I want you to bring Jacob a set of surgical steel instruments. I've got to get rid of his wooden-handled knives." She continued to be amazed by the primitive conditions, knowing his instruments and the velvet-lined cases he insisted on storing them in were breeding grounds for infectious bacteria. "I also want laudanum and whatever medicines you can find to bring me."

"Fair enough," Mathilde replied. "In return, I want Miss Emma's crystal lustre." Savannah looked puzzled, and Mathilde gazed down her large nose at her. "A lustre is a small crystal oil lamp with prisms hanging from the glass top. I'm sure you saw one in my shop. Miss Emma has one in her attic."

"Her attic! How do you know what's in her attic"?

"Now don't get your feathers ruffled," Mathilde soothed her. "I have my ways." At Savannah's reluctant nod, she continued, "I also want a copper kettle from the kitchen and a Bible in good condition. Can you manage that?"

"Yes, I suppose so," she replied sadly. "When shall we meet?"

"Two days, same time. Now, if you'll excuse me, I must get back. It's Saturday, a busy day in the shop." The old woman gathered her new antiques and stepped back into the fog.

"Remember, just consider everything: whose life you've changed the most, what are your own desires, and whether you want to stay here. Things will become clear." With that, the mist swallowed the yellow-robed gypsy.

The sun began peeking its bright head above the horizon as Savannah got the blue jar, the citrus, and the two boxes into the barn. She put her new toothbrush and a bottle of aspirin in the pocket of her robe, then hid the remainder high in the dusty loft. She hadn't quite figured out how to get the new medicines into the hospital or the fruit in the kitchen without lengthy explanations to Jacob, Miss Emma, and Deltry, but she had gotten this far. She'd think of something. She could probably keep refilling the morphine in the jar locked in Jacob's office. That would be easy enough. The oranges and lemons, too. She could just add one or two to the kitchen as needed, or even sneak one to a particular soldier in need.

It was the aspirin that presented the real problem. Since Jacob had never heard of aspirin, she wouldn't be able to empty an occasional bottle into a jar in the supply cabinet. She'd have to figure out some way to get them to the men, even if it was covertly. Suddenly, all this wasn't as easy as she thought it would be. Many explanations would be in order once Jacob began to wonder where all these medicines were coming from.

No matter, she was glad it was done. Whether or not stealing was her destiny, she did have something to offer these men, and that made her happy.

It was still early when Jacob awoke, the rising sun slowly replacing the dim haze of night. He rose from the spine-crushing chair and stretched his body to unfold the kinks. The office chair was not made for slumbering, but it was far better than the swing on the porch. It wasn't only because of the chair's cushions, either. The swing held too many reminders of the evening before.

Groaning, he rubbed his hand over his tired eyes. He hadn't meant to let things go so far last night. Hell, he hadn't consciously meant for any of it to happen. When he had led Savannah outside to the swing, he had wanted to talk, to gain her trust and find out what she was hiding. He'd had no intention of baring his soul. Neither had he planned to touch her glorious hair, kiss her full lips, or seduce her. But, he had. He had done all of it. He had demanded too much, and she had run from him.

He wanted more from his nurse than just her medical expertise, and the mysterious air that surrounded her only added to his desire. She was hiding something; that he knew. What he didn't know was why his feelings for her were so strong.

Her body had responded to his. She had answered his every demand with one of her own. What had made her run from him? She had once suggested there was someone else in her life. Was it possible? Did her heart belong to another? An unexplained sick feeling gouged his stomach until he realized it didn't matter either way. She had married him, and that had to count for something.

A movement outside the window caught his eye. Although the early-morning fog hung in the air, he could make out a figure moving near the barn. Walking to the window, he pulled back the lace curtain for a closer look. The last thing they needed was for a hungry renegade soldier to raid their chicken coop. With one rooster and only half a dozen hens, eggs were scarce enough.

Quick recognition jolted him out of his sleepy state. Despite the thick robe, he knew the curves of that body instinctively, and the dampness of the air emphasized her femininity. Drawing back to the side of the window, he watched Savannah carry a blue jar into the barn. Two boxes waited nearby. Although he was a good distance away, he could see that the boxes seemed to be made out of some type of thick brown paper rather than wood. And were those oranges inside the wooden crate? She returned from the barn, picked up both boxes at once, and carried them into the barn. Another trip for the oranges.

Jacob waited by the window to see what would happen next. His glance stole around the area, but he could see no one else. After a few long minutes, the barn door opened slightly and Savannah peered out cautiously. He supposed her sly action was an attempt to make sure no one saw her. If only she knew, he thought as he dropped the curtain, smiling like a cat who just found a patch of catnip. As soon as she was safely back upstairs, he would venture out to the stables himself and find whatever she'd hidden. Savannah Stuart Cross's mysterious secret was about to be revealed.

The weathered door creaked loudly as Jacob entered the dark, musty barn. He'd had to wait while Savannah crept back to bed and slowly fell into a deep slumber. Now the smell of old hay was intensified by the humid morning air. Less than two years ago, the barn was busy with activity. Miss Emma had had a fine pair of carriage horses and several good brood mares. Now it stood lifeless. The horses had been confiscated for the war effort, and so the barn stood empty. It surprised him the army had not also commandeered the dusty black buggy in the far corner. Looking around, he wondered where Savannah had hidden her treasures. He wasn't expecting an easy hunt, for she was far too intelligent not to find a careful spot. But he would find what she was hiding. Then he would have answers.

It took him almost an hour of searching through the nooks and crannies of the barn before he spotted the bright blue apothecary jar up in the hayloft. It had been stuffed down into a small crevice between several bales of hay. The boxes were nearby under another unobtrusive pile of straw. He didn't see the oranges, but that didn't matter.

He knew they were there somewhere.

He carefully lifted the lid of the jar, not sure of what to expect. His jaw dropped in astonishment to see crystalline morphine. All he needed was his mortar and pestle to grind it down into a powder, and his soldiers would have the painkiller they needed so desperately. His amazement quickly fizzled as suspicion took hold. He practically had to beg the army to get even a fourth of this much morphine. Where had she gotten it? From whom? And what did she intend to do with it? A salty bile rose in his throat as he considered the possibility that she was addicted to the powerful drug. He'd seen it happen too many times, especially since the war began. No—he pushed the thought aside as quickly as it arose. She wasn't the type. It appeared that she had gotten the morphine for the hospital. But how? Why?

Gently replacing the lid, he turned to the two boxes, brushing the hay off as he drew them closer to his kneeling position. The boxes were unusual, unlike the wooden crates or tin containers he was accustomed to. These appeared to be made of a thick and rigid heavy paper. Stamped on the outside of the box in bold red letters read "ASPIRIN." Opening one, he found forty-eight large bottles of white pills. He lifted a bottle for a closer look, surprised by how light it was. The bottles were clear like glass, but not heavy. He needed more light to read the words printed on the bottle, so he walked to the hayloft doors. Lifting the latch, he opened them only aa inch, letting in a stream of morning light. "ASPIRIN," the yellow label read, "Contains 250 pills." A quick breath caught in his throat as he read the next statement, "For relief of headaches, pain and fever of colds and flu, minor pains of arthritis, rheumatism, menstrual discomfort, and toothaches." He swallowed hard.

Savannah had found a wonder drug!

My God, where had this come from? he wondered in amazement as he turned the bottle over and over in his hands. First the morphine, now this. And what in the world did "Exp. 3/98" mean? He tried to open the bottle, but the top wouldn't budge. It twisted as if it were coming off, but refused to open. Looking more closely at the white cap, he read "Child-proof cap. Line up arrows and push cap with thumb." Grinning sheepishly, he did so and watched the white cap pop right off and fall to the hay-covered floor.

Bringing the open bottle to his nose, he breathed deeply as a sharp pungent smell filled his lungs. Wrinkling his nose at the acidic aroma, Jacob dumped several white pills in his palm. Putting one on the tip of his tongue, he found a bitter yet tolerable taste. As he held it in his mouth, the taste grew sharper, causing a catch in the back of his throat. The longer it stayed, the worse it got until he spit it out with a cough. This must be a pill to grind or swallow he surmised, hoping it could do all it claimed it could. This aspirin had to be a new drug, but how did Savannah know about it? Where did she get it? Why was it delivered under such secrecy? Who was bringing it to her?

Instead of finding answers, Jacob realized he

now had even more questions, and there was only one person who could answer them. Grabbing both boxes and the jar, he headed up to see his sleeping beauty. This was one puzzle he was going to put together right now.

"Savannah. Wake up. I want to talk to you." Jacob tapped her arm impatiently.

Opening one eye, Savannah gazed up at her husband, irritated at having been jostled from her already-restless sleep. "No, I want to sleep."

Groggy, she rolled away from the man towering over the bed. She couldn't have had more than an hour of sleep and certainly wasn't ready to talk coherently with anyone. Unless an ambulance full of dying soldiers pulled up at the front door, he was going to have to wait.

"Savannah!" Jacob called again, this time louder. "Wake up. We need to talk."

"Not right now. I'm tired."

"I bet you're tired. You've been up all night." The deep voice was persistent. "What is aspirin?"

Her eyes flew open and moved around the room to focus on Jacob. Suddenly wide awake, she stared at him in horror. In his hands he held an instantly recognizable bottle containing 250 little white tablets.

She sat up in bed, raising the covers to her chin. "I don't know," she stammered, swallowing hard, fighting a sinking feeling. "Where'd you hear a word like that?"

He shrugged, raising his eyebrows as if he, too, were confused. "Oh, I don't know. How about from the boxes you hid in the barn?" Moving his hand closer, he lifted the bottle for her to read the conspicuous label.

What should she do now? She had been hoping for a way to tell him about the painkiller, but in her own way. Now he knew and waited for an explanation. Telling the entire truth again flashed through her mind. It was quickly squelched by the continuing thought that he would not, could not, believe her. Dejected, she leaned back against the headboard. While she wanted to help the soldiers, she hadn't really considered the full impact of bringing Jacob something he had never heard of. Now that he had found it, she would have to fess up to something. "They are for the hospital," she admitted in a small voice.

"I assumed that," he said, controlled irritation tracing through his words. "Where did you get them, and what do they do?"

Ignoring his tone and avoiding his first question, she replied, "Aspirin is a mild painkiller. It's good for headaches and other minor things. Not much use for serious injuries, but it may help some. We use it routinely where I come from. I thought you needed some here, too." There, at least that was true.

"Why have I never heard of it?" he asked with a skeptical tilt of his chin.

"I don't know. You're the doctor!" she snapped. The look on his face made her instantly sorry she had been so sarcastic. He didn't deserve that. She softened. "It's a new drug based on something called acetylsalicylic acid," she explained. "No one really knows why it's so effective. It just is. I knew the hospital needed painkillers. I was able to get some, so I did."

"And the morphine?"

"Same situation. The aspirin is not nearly as strong as the morphine, of course, but it's also not addictive. The oranges and lemons will provide the men with a treat and much needed nutrition."

He stood up from the chair and walked to her bed. "If you're doing all this to help the hospital, why didn't you just tell me about it? Why did you have to sneak around in the fog this morning?"

"Because I knew you wouldn't approve of where the medicines came from." Unable to meet the hurt in his eyes, she stared down at the delicate stitching on the bedspread.

"Ah, yes, you neatly avoided that question. Where did you get it?"

"I'm sorry, Jacob, I can't tell you. Can't you just be pleased that I was able to get medicine for the hospital? Can't you just trust me?"

"Trust? This is a Yankee product."

She looked surprised. "Who said that?"

Tiredly, he answered, "It's on the bottle."

He held it out for her to see. A tight smile formed on Savannah's lips as she read "Made in Cincinnati."

"I suppose it is." She sighed. This was not going to be easy.

"How, may I ask, did you get medicines from behind enemy lines? Who do you know who can do that? Are you a spy?"

She only stared up at him, struggling for an answer. He wasn't going to let this rest, and she didn't know what to say. Taking a deep breath to steady her nerves, she spoke softly. "I went to visit Colonel Sanger." It was partly the truth at least. Maybe it was enough for Jacob to draw his own conclusions.

"Sanger?" he asked with renewed anger. "He got this for you?"

"I went to see him about getting us medicines, but—"

"I should have known." Rage filled his face as he brought it inches from hers. "I've known him long enough to realize he didn't give it to you out of the goodness of his heart. What was his price? What did he want from you in return? Did you meet behind the barn? Is that where you went when you rushed from my arms last night?"

Without thinking, Savannah pulled back her hand and slapped him right across the face. "No, I didn't sleep with him! How dare you insinuate such a thing!"

Jacob drew away from her, a nasty red mark staining his cheek.

"I tried to do something good for this hospital, and you accuse me of being unfaithful to you, unfaithful to a marriage of convenience."

He stood silently looking at her, his expression bitter. Regaining her composure, Savannah stared right back, refusing to drop her gaze. Instinct told her he was sizing her up.

"I will repeat this one time, Jacob Cross. I did not sleep with Colonel Sanger. Furthermore, I will not allow you to speak to me that way. I saw a way to help these men, to help this hospital, and to help you, so I did. I cannot tell you where the aspirin or the morphine or the citrus came from. You wouldn't believe me, anyway. You say you trust me, now it's time to show it."

"Wrong, Savannah. I *trusted* you. Last night I thought we had the beginning of something special. I can see I was wrong." He turned and strode out the door, slamming it behind him. The walls rattled right along with the pitcher and basin on the dresser.

Suddenly, the door swung open again. "Tell me how this aspirin works," he said coldly. "I have men downstairs who need it."

She returned his glare. "Read the directions," she replied sarcastically, falling back on the bed and pulling the covers over her head.

Another slam was her answer.

Maybe it's for the best, Savannah thought as she closed her eyes against a pounding headache. She reached for the bottle of aspirin she had stuck under her pillow and swallowed two tablets. Thank goodness, she'd had the foresight to save a bottle for herself.

It was clear Jacob believed she was involved with the irksome Colonel Sanger, and maybe it was best to let him go on thinking so. While it sounded logical on the surface, the plan broke her heart. For the first time in her life, she was hopelessly in love. Instead of making her happy, the knowledge weighed on her heavily. Any chance of happiness with Jacob was now gone. He despised her for not being truthful with him and for meeting with Colonel Sanger. If she were to tell him where she actually got the medicines, he'd believe she was making up the incredible story to hide the truth. He'd hate her even more.

If only she could go home. Home. To her normally calm and peaceful existence, to her dull and boring life. She had tried to help the men as best she could, using the only way she knew—and look at the disastrous results. Maybe her destiny wasn't the hospital after all. She closed her eyes as the aspirin began to work. If Jacob didn't need surgical instruments so badly, she'd refuse to steal for Mathilde. The problem was that he did. And she could help, even though it meant sacrificing her love. As much as Jacob would hate to take the supplies, there were too many lives at stake. That was the very thing that would cause irreparable damage between them.

Savannah tossed restlessly as she lay amongst the fresh-smelling, line-dried sheets. Not only were things in a mess with Jacob, she had to get to Miss Emma's attic for the lustre Mathilde demanded. Tossing aside the bedclothes in irritated frustration, she padded across the floor to the wardrobe and selected a lovely cream-colored muslin dress. Holding it against her body, she considered her image in the mirror. The effect of the light-colored dress with her light hair was stunning. Deltry had done herself proud with this creation. The woman had just finished sewing it yesterday. She proudly presented it to Savannah complete with matching handkerchief.

As she pulled the fabric over her head, she realized she hadn't had a homemade dress since her grandmother made them for her many years ago. Even though her grandmother had died while Savannah was young, the tender memory made her long for her own home, for her own time.

Jacob had made it clear he would not forgive her, and once she presented his new surgical steel instruments to him, the situation between them would be even more tense. Reaching for the brush, she began to sort her tangled hair while she thought over the situation. She loved Jacob, and even though she felt fulfilled in this century, she didn't know if she could stay. And what about Jacob's feelings? He had made his hatred perfectly clear.

Since breakfast was being served downstairs, everyone would be occupied. Now was probably the best time for thievery. Peeking through the bedroom door, Savannah turned right toward another door at the far end of the hallway. It creaked as she opened it and peered up the dark steps. She wished she had brought a candle or an oil lamp. Dark attics had always frightened her, and it was definitely spooky up there.

She shut the door behind her, and the stairwell became dark. The humid smell only added to the eerie atmosphere. Within a few moments, Savannah's eyes grew accustomed to the dim room. A small window on the far wall offered some light. She took her first step up the attic stairs, her new muslin skirt swishing about her legs. Now to find the things Mathilde wanted before she lost her courage.

Quickly looking around the attic, Savannah spotted what must be the lustre sitting on a wooden shelf. It was dusty, but it was indeed as lovely as Mathilde described. The small crystal lamp stood only about twelve inches tall. A narrow stem sat on a wide base holding a ballooning shade of crystal. A dozen clear prisms hung from the shade. Lifting it carefully, Savannah blew the dust from it and held it up toward the single window. The sunshine immediately caught the rainbow of colors inside the crystal and cast colorful smiles on the walls of the attic. Miss Emma must treasure this very much. A dose of conscience struck Savannah as she carefully cradled the lustre in her arms. Ignoring it, she wrapped the lamp carefully in her apron and turned to head back down the attic stairs. On the first step, an open box caught her eye. Laying on top was a gilded frame containing a daguerreotype of a smiling Miss Emma and a handsome man. The look in their eyes was love. Miss Emma had never mentioned a sweetheart or a husband. It was sad that Savannah could never ask, either. To do so would reveal her secret visit to the attic. Reluctantly, she replaced the treasured image where she found it, then headed back down the stairs.

Once in her bedroom, Savannah painstakingly wrapped the crystal piece in a chemise and hid it in her dresser drawer. Now only the old Bible and the copper kettle were needed for the next trade. Those shouldn't prove to be too much trouble.

* * *

The hospital was unusually quiet as Savannah walked into the kitchen. They hadn't had any new arrivals in the past few days, which allowed her to devote time to the patients already there. Her efforts toward infection control were beginning to pay off. She had hadn't been able to stop all the cases of gangrene, but she had drastically reduced the number.

"Savannah! There you are, dear!" Miss Emma called from the hallway leading outside to the kitchen. "I've been wondering where you were."

Smiling, Savannah nodded and headed toward the motherly figure. After Jacob's cold stare from across the room, she could use a happy face.

"Here, come out and sit in the sun with me." Miss Emma tied on her bonnet and handed one to Savannah. "The men are still eating, and I need a break."

Deltry nodded her greeting as Savannah walked by. The cook was busily stirring simmering stew in an iron kettle. Savannah made a mental note to look through the kitchen for a copper one on her way back inside.

Miss Emma led Savannah to a group of several wooden whitewashed chairs grouped together under an ancient oak. Once settled, she said, wasting no time in getting to the point, "Jacob told me about the medicines."

"He did?" Savannah swallowed the growing lump in her throat.

"Of course." She waved a hand to indicate his confidence was expected. "I want to thank you." Surprised, Savannah glanced at her, and the elderly woman continued, "You knew we needed the medicines—although I must admit I had never heard of aspirin—and you figured out how to get them. For that, we are in your debt."

"Why, thank you, Miss Emma," she sputtered. "After Jacob's angry reaction, I appreciate your kind words more than you know."

The pleasant woman leaned forward to pat Savannah's hand. "Now, dear, it's really none of my business, but I have come to care for you a great deal over the past few weeks. I hate to see you and Jacob at odds. I insisted that he was foolish to believe you were having a . . . er, clandestine meeting with that rude Colonel Sanger. Why, anyone can see you're in love with Jacob."

Savannah felt her cheeks become hot. "Is it that obvious?"

"Of course, dear. I think it's wonderful. He needs you. You've put the spark back in his eyes, something that's been missing for a long time."

"Was it terrible for him, the fire I mean? He's told me a little about it, but not much."

Miss Emma was silent for a minute, considering her carefully. "Yes, it was," she said quietly. "His mother, Ruth, God rest her soul, was my dearest friend. She passed on less than six months before it happened. Six months before a group of overzealous men in uniform came to take the plantation's horses. Only, it wasn't just horses they were after." She looked away as tears filled her eyes. Savannah offered her the new handkerchief from her pocket, and Miss Emma dabbed her eyes. "We all knew the army was out to teach Nathaniel a lesson. They had already moved in to make St. George a garrison town. Most around these parts were happy St. George would be a vital part of the war effort. Not Nathaniel. He wasn't quick to want war like the others, and he made no bones about it to the army."

She calmed her tears and looked at Savannah. "It's not that he refused to defend our way of life. He just didn't want the bloodshed between our own countrymen. Tempers were hot, and when Nathaniel spoke, it was as a voice of reason. That infuriated some of the overly anxious army officers. An order was issued to confiscate the property he refused to give willingly. I believe you know the rest. Jacob—"

"Miz Vanna! Miz Vanna!" Deltry called urgently from the house. "Dr. Jacob needs you. Your friend is dying!"

"Who, Deltry? Who's dying?" Savannah jumped up from the chair and rushed toward the house.

"Your friend! The man you talk to all the time! Hurry, he needs you!"

Savannah rushed past the black woman toward the living room, just as Jacob began to pull the sheet over Ely's bluish face.

"No! It can't be. Not Ely! He has a family."

"They've all got families, Savannah." Jacob gave her a warning look not to upset the others in the room.

Undaunted, she rushed to the man's bed. "How long has he been like this? What happened?"

"He just now stopped breathing and passed

205

on." Jacob reached to pull her away from Ely's lifeless body.

"He was eating, then suddenly he started gagging and acting like he couldn't breathe," a patient in a nearby bed called. "He turned blue and fell over dead."

"No!" She jerked her arm away from Jacob's. "He's choked on something, but he's not dead yet. There's still time. Help me get him to the floor!" she commanded, reacting instinctively. She got behind Ely's head and began lifting his limp torso. Normally, she wouldn't have had such strength, but now adrenaline flowed through her veins. She had done the Heimlich Maneuver and cardiopulmonary resuscitation several times in her career. She could do it again.

"What are you doing?" Jacob made a move to stop her efforts by trying to grab her arms.

Not expecting an argument, she looked at Jacob, surprised. "Help me get him on the floor, so we can resuscitate him. He needs to be on a firm surface."

Irritated, she yanked her sleeve from his grasp before realizing that Jacob had no idea what she was doing. The basic lifesaving technique of the Heimlich Maneuver and CPR had yet to be discovered, and as usual, she had forgotten Jacob's lack of understanding in her effort to help. In a split second, she touched his arm, and looked into his eyes to plead for understanding.

"We may still have time, Jacob." She could see the hurt and anger still in his eyes from this morning. It was clear he wanted to believe her, despite the indignant voices in the background. Although confusion was written on his face, he lifted the man from the bed and lay him gently on the floor, straightening his body to lie flat. She smiled in relief.

"Turn his head to the side," she ordered as she straddled the man's hips.

"Jacob!" Miss Emma objected. "Savannah is distraught. Don't let her do this. The man has passed. Let him rest."

Clearly torn, Jacob looked from Miss Emma to Savannah.

"Listen to me," she said firmly. "He may still have a chance if we begin immediately."

Without waiting for Jacob's response, she quickly placed both hands on Ely's stomach just below the ribcage and gave a forceful upward thrust. Leaning forward, she checked his airway. Nothing. She sat back and repeated the procedure several more times.

Suddenly, a large piece of gristle came up from his throat and rolled to the floor. Step one. She checked her mental list of procedures.

Without wasting a second to acknowledge the murmur of the crowd, she moved to tilt his head back, bringing his chin up to open his now-clear airway. Ely wasn't breathing and she couldn't feel a pulse. CPR would be needed if they were going to save him. Acting on years of practice, she bent forward, her cheek above Ely's open mouth and nose to feel the slightest breath. None. She pinched his nose shut, then pressed her mouth against his and gave two full breaths.

A gasp went up from the crowd of medics and patients gathered around the confusion. From the corner of her eye, she saw Miss Emma's hand fly to her mouth in disbelief. As far as they were concerned, she was doing the unspeakable on the body of a dead man. There certainly wasn't enough time to explain the procedure. Ignoring their voices, she continued. She had performed the CPR procedure many times—sometimes it was successful, sometimes it wasn't, but she had to try. Ely was her friend, one of the few she had in this century. She couldn't let him die. Who would keep the boys away from his daughter?

Pinching Ely's nose closed again, Savannah repeated her actions, blowing in to fill his lungs with air, then releasing to allow them to empty. She again waited a second for Ely to take his own breath. No luck. She bent to try it again.

Jacob was stunned to see Savannah work furiously on Ely. She had obviously become so attached to the dead man that she couldn't think clearly. Ely had died, probably his heart just gave out. And the piece of gristle? Who knew? When death stared one in the face, it was best to accept it and let the soul rest in peace.

He stepped forward to pull her away, her body resisting his attempt to lift her. "Savannah, you're obviously upset. Come with me." He bent low to her ear, his voice deliberately low so only she could hear. "Ely is gone, love, there's nothing you can do."

"We can revive him, Jacob. Help me." She

rushed as if there was no time to waste.

Without waiting for an answer, Savannah shrugged free and quickly moved over Ely's chest. Placing her hands above his heart, Jacob watched speechlessly as she began a repetitive press with all her might. What was she doing? The man was dead, wasn't he?

"One, two, three, four, five, six . . ." She counted to fifteen before stopping to breathe twice into his mouth. Lifting her head slightly, he supposed she must be listening for Ely to breathe on his own. Was it possible? Could one bring a man back from the dead?

"Jacob, help me." She looked up at him before moving to begin the compression again. In between each push, she spoke, "We have . . . to keep . . . the heart . . . pumping blood . . . until he regains his breathing." She moved back to force more air into Ely's open mouth. It was obvious she knew what she was doing. He remembered her knowledge of pressure points, her knowledge about sterilizing to control infections, her knowledge of aspirin. Suddenly it was clear to him, and he was a fool not to believe sooner. This woman was gifted in healing. She knew what she was doing.

"Here, show me." Instantly, Jacob's hands came down to cover hers, picking up the motion. After showing him what degree of pressure was needed, she removed her hands.

"If you're going to help me, you need to press like this for five counts, stop, then start again after I breathe into his lungs. If we can mimic the actions of his body, keep air in his lungs and the blood circulating through his heart, he may begin breathing again."

"Jacob, not you, too!" Miss Emma was crying. "Please don't do this." Jacob didn't look up as he heard her retreating footsteps. He now understood what Savannah was trying to do. Silence filled the room as she pressed her fingers against Ely's carotid artery.

"There's a faint pulse. He might just make it, Jacob."

She bent her head to give another breath, and Ely suddenly coughed. Under Savannah's direction, Jacob continued until Ely sputtered several times and tried to push him away. A cheer went up from the crowd. Suddenly Jacob's mind was made up. No matter what his wife was involved in, no matter where she had gotten the medicines, he believed in her. She was a healer, and she had the courage to fight for a man's life, even when no one else would.

Jacob had never been so confused. Even the murder of his family had a reason, something he could grasp to explain things. Savannah Stuart was different. Her knowledge of medicine far outweighed his. That was something incredible for a nurse, and it wasn't the fact that this healer was a woman. He'd known many strong women in his life, his mother and Miss Emma, to name just two. It was that she was so mysterious.

He had been first in his class at medical school. Yet she practiced medicine with skills he had never heard of. She had an ease that almost frightened him. She knew of aspirin; he had never seen it. She knew about pressure points; he knew about amputations. She knew of this breathing life back into a man; he'd stood with his mouth agape just like every other onlooker in the hospital. Where did she get the knowledge? Why was she here?

He walked down the streets of St. George, going nowhere in particular, pondering his situation. The streets were usually busy on Saturday night. Tonight was no exception. After bumping into more than one passerby, he headed toward Rose's, where he could sit and think in peace.

With the briefest of acknowledgements, Rose lead him to the private sitting room near the front of the restaurant. Bringing him a tall glass of tea, she slipped away, leaving him with his thoughts. Invariably, they turned back to Savannah. Even though they were married, he hardly knew anything about her. What he did know was not flattering. The trumped-up story about Atlanta burning had not fooled him, especially since he had received a letter from a fellow doctor in Atlanta several days before her mysterious arrival. Her appearance in the foyer was another mystery. A hired coach would have had to bring her to the hospital, but his discreet inquiries had failed to find a driver who remembered the oddly dressed woman.

He had kept quiet about the circumstances, mainly because she had proven to be a good nurse, and he desperately needed help. He may not know how she arrived, but he knew Atlanta had not burned. In spite of all this, he felt drawn to her like a bear to honey. That's about what it amounted to, he thought sourly, a grizzly bear ready to frighten away anyone who got too close.

He felt remorse because of their argument this morning. It upset him that she didn't believe she could trust him enough to tell him where the aspirin and morphine had come from. There seemed to be no ulterior motive. She had got the medicines for the hospital. Had he not found them and confronted her, he was certain she would have brought the aspirin and morphine to him.

And today. Ely had stopped breathing. His skin had turned blue, and Jacob had been sure he was dead. Savannah, however, had refused to believe it. Every soul in the room had thought she was hysterical, but when she had looked into his eyes and pleaded for his help, he had known for certain she wasn't irrational. She possessed the knowledge to revive the man, and she had. This soft woman, this pale-haired nurse, this . . . doctor, had saved the man's life.

At that very moment, he knew without a doubt that he loved her. He had been attracted to her from the moment he saw her standing on the steps the very first day. He hadn't objected too strongly when Miss Emma insisted they marry, he admitted to himself. If he hadn't wanted the marriage, even Miss Emma could not have forced him to meet Savannah at the altar. No, the truth was suddenly clear as he recognized the connection between them. Each passing day drew them closer. The bond they shared as healers had developed into an unspoken trust. At first, he had tried to ignore it, to squelch his desire. Even though lying close to her in the bed had been sheer torture, he had resisted. When he had finally acted upon his urges, she had run from him, claiming it wasn't right.

She was correct, though. It wasn't right, at least not now. Not only did she have to work out her mysterious secret, he had his own to resolve. He could never be free from the past until the man responsible for the murders of his wife and father paid for their vicious crimes. If he could settle that and come to terms with it, then he would be free for Savannah. Free for their love to blossom. Then maybe she'd allow him into her world and share what she was hiding.

Coming to a decision, Jacob finished his glass of tea in one swallow. He'd leave first thing in the morning. The prison in Memphis would be a two-day ride there and back. He had visited the boy before, and the kid had always been too frightened to talk. Jacob hadn't been strong enough to force the issue. This time was different. He would convince the boy to admit Sanger ordered the raid. Too much was at stake.

Chapter Eight

The moon was nestled high amongst the bright stars as Jacob hurried back to the hospital. Pausing before he reached the steps, he looked up to see Savannah staring at the glorious night sky from the window of their room. She looked so lost, so forlorn, as if she somehow didn't belong. A faint glow, probably that of a small candle, flickered behind her, creating a halo around her luminous hair. Her gentle beauty stopped his heart.

An overwhelming urge surfaced in his mind, the urge to hold the vision in his arms, to whisper words of endearment in her ear, and, yes, to love her. All that mattered at that very moment was to make amends for this morning and convince her of his true feelings. He prayed that she, too, felt the bonding spark between them. He walked through the hospital without stopping to check on a single man. Someone else was in desperate need right now—him.

Jacob slowed at the top of the stairs to collect himself, took a deep breath to calm his racing nerves, then cautiously opened the door.

Savannah lifted her eyes at the sound of creaking hinges, trepidation filling her.

Jacob had returned.

A single candle lit the room from the table by the bed. He stood outside its small circle of light, the expression on his face unreadable. He had been furious at her this morning because of the fruit, morphine, and aspirin. When she had refused to reveal her source, anger had consumed him. The rift between them had grown deeper. After the situation with Ely, however, she had caught a guarded look in his eye. The emergency had caused a drastic change between them. Exactly what, she had no idea.

For a moment, he remained at the edge of the room, studying her intently. There was no way to imagine his thoughts, and the uncertainty in the air grew tense. She inhaled deeply, trying to relax as a little voice inside whispered a warning to remain calm. Another of Miss Emma's beautiful quilts covered her lap, her hands gripped together underneath.

"Savannah, we need to talk." The deep baritone of Jacob's voice broke the silence. He sat down on the bed, no more than an arm's length away from her chair by the window. Running his hand through his dark wavy hair, he searched her face.

"Yes," she agreed quietly. "I suppose we do." She broke his gaze to look back up at the stars, then forced her lips into a stiff smile. There was no sense in avoiding the matter; she might as well make it easy for him. "It's time for the truth, Jacob," she began. "I can promise that you won't believe me, though. In fact, I expect you'll become very angry and storm out of the room."

She shook her head as he opened his mouth to interrupt. "Everything I will tell you is the God's honest truth." She cast her eyes downward. She wished she had the courage to meet his stare, to let him see the sincerity on her face, but she couldn't risk the tears that threatened.

Jacob hesitated, obviously measuring her words. She knew this was what he wanted, what he had demanded, and now she had offered it all. Savannah expected him to push her immediately for answers. Her eyebrows drew together at his surprising silence.

"No, I don't need to know," he said finally, a calm strength in his voice. "I told you last night that I trusted you, and in spite of today, I meant it." He rose from the bed and kneeled beside Savannah, sliding a warm hand down the sensitive skin of her inner arm. His hand went further to catch her fidgeting fingers under the blanket. A sudden tremble spread across her body.

"I was angry when you refused to answer my questions." He lifted her chin. "The situation with Ely made me realize that you care about these men and the hospital just as much as I do. Whatever it is, it must be for the good of the hospital. I shouldn't have judged you so harshly." His big shoulders shrugged as he took a delicate strand of her hair and twirled it between his lean fingers.

"That doesn't mean I'm not worried," he added quietly, "and I hope you're not in danger, but I do trust you. I won't force you to tell me until you're ready." He ran the back of his long finger down her cheek, leaving a trail of tingling skin. "And Savannah, I *will* believe you."

Savannah stared at him in disbelief. Her mouth opened slightly as she nervously ran her tongue over her dry lips. This time, she didn't try to hide her tears of joy and relief. God, how she loved this man! She wanted to tell her tale, but Jacob stopped her. That could only mean one thing. He truly did trust her. The shadows binding her heart began to loosen.

Bringing her hand from under the quilt, she tenderly traced the line of his cheekbone and jaw, feeling the prickly stubble on his chin. As her fingers fluttered down to his neck, she felt the steady beat of his pulse. Their foreheads drew together for a long moment, relishing the words that had just passed between them. Silence filled the room as Jacob covered Savannah's hand with his own. His blue eyes met hers with the realization of what was destined to occur in the moonlit room. The knowing anticipation grew unbearable. In one silent look, Savannah knew that Jacob loved her. Whatever bound him, whatever it was that kept him from saying it, didn't matter. It was love that filled his eyes.

Still kneeling beside the rocker, Jacob brought her hand to his mouth, then leaned forward, his eyes intent on her lips. Her head retreated against the back of the chair to relish the coming joy, a smile parting her mouth as she felt the heat of his breath on her cheek. A sudden tremor of worry escaped her throat in a small moan. Even though he loved her, it was still too soon. There were still too many secrets. She should stop this craziness and send him away. Keep the promises she made last night. When his lips descended, she was powerless to do more than offer her own.

Ecstasy spiraled when his tongue traced the soft fullness of her lips and his hands wound through her disheveled hair. With a sanguine sigh, Savannah opened her mouth a bit wider, allowing their tongues to meet and entwine. He tasted heavenly, and she wondered if a soul could melt from desire. Jacob's dark head came up slightly to place tiny kisses on her face and neck, while his gentle hand skimmed over her body to her waist, then further down. He touched her thigh, then lifted his wandering fingers to gently massage her breast through the soft cotton of her dress. Ten pearl buttons blocked skin from touching skin. With frustrating patience, he opened each one, then slid his hot palm inside. She shivered with pleasure when his teeth lightly scrapped her throat and bare shoulders. Jacob spread the dress wider and let his tongue follow the path of his fingers around the delicate lace of her bra. His sudden hesitation conveyed that her modern lingerie momentarily startled him. She felt his smile as he quickly recovered with a tender kiss through her garment. Savannah caressed the curls at the back of his neck, pleased she had refused to wear the drab underthings of this century. She murmured his name with a pleasant sigh, relishing the inner excitement and strange aching that began at her core.

The thought that she should stop him before this went too far tormented her. His words of trust had left her stunned and shaken, but also had provided a new confidence. She might disappear tomorrow, but right now she was here, and her body longed for his touch. This man, so full of tenderness, compassion, and trust, was also full of reckless abandon. She wanted him never to stop.

Jacob lifted her from the rocking chair and carried her the few steps to the bed, gently easing her onto the sheets. The white candle beside the bed continued to burn; the bobbing flame matched the pounding of her heart.

He kissed her again, this time hard and demanding. The growing ache spread as a fire consumed her. She pressed her trembling arms around his back to bring him close enough to quench the burning. Hurriedly, he pulled the cotton dress over her head, then tossed it to the floor. A sensuous jolt of cool air was replaced by his body heat when he lay atop her again. A new warmth surged across her lacy bra and panties. A heady surprise registered again on Jacob's face at the wonder of the flimsy garments. He resisted a few agonizing seconds before running a hot tongue along the edge of her bra, causing her newly bared flesh to tingle. Her nipples thrust against the silky fabric with wild arousal when his dancing tongue pushed her closer and closer to the edge.

"How do you get this thing off?" he breathed with a husky whisper. "I want you. All of you. Nothing between your heart and mine."

She laughed. Where she was from, boys learned to unsnap a bra at an early age. "Here, watch." She grasped the white snap between her breasts, unhooking it with one hand. Jacob's grin turned serious as he lifted away the delicate lace. His eyes raked boldly over her.

"My God, Savannah, you're beautiful." His tongue caressed her already-sensitive nipples as his hand moved magically over her breasts, gently kneading one, then the other. His fingertips brushed over the rosy circles, making them draw even tighter. Tracing a path down her abdomen, he stroked her skin. Then his hand slipped to explore the intimate warmth of her femininity with soft caresses.

Inhaling Jacob's masculine scent, Savannah reached to unbutton his white shirt, impatient to rub the bare skin of his shoulders and back. His nipples were as hard and as taut as her own, and she savored each with her lips, fervently wanting to share the same joy he gave to her. She craved every part of him, to touch, taste, and love each inch. He gave a guttural moan as her lips cast their spell. Racing passion roared in her ears when his mouth slid up to hers.

He rose from the bed to take off his trousers, his eyes caressing her body's every detail. As he slowly returned to her arms, Savannah reached with seeking fingers to find his rigid length. He jumped at her touch, obviously startled by her action. She supposed a proper woman of this era had not yet discovered the joy of twentieth-century feminine boldness. A contented sigh escaped with his breath. She may not be proper, but she was certainly bold.

Meeting her gaze, Jacob groaned in pleasure as her fingers encircled his manhood and began an uninhibited massage. He lifted his head again to crush his mouth against hers, kissing her ardently, matching her rhythm with his powerful tongue. Her head spun, her body trembled, her pulse thundered, her breathing grew ragged.

The heat of his body seared and enveloped her as he caressed her ear with low whispers. She thought she heard the words "love" and "forever," but wasn't certain. Jacob's hands continued magically to stroke her intimate flesh. They were driven by a commanding need, one that made them abandon all sensibilities.

"Yes, my love," she breathed against his throat when he positioned himself carefully above her. For a brief eternity, he paused. Then it was instant. Powerful. Searing. "Wonderful," she sighed, and time stood still.

He pushed deeper. Briefly, unreadable emotion flickered on his face as he moved again inside her, only to be replaced by passion as the rhythm of love began its song.

His chest crushed her breasts when his hands slid underneath to lift her into his thrusts. She clung to him with trembling limbs, his heartbeat entwined with her own.

A sense of urgency drove them slowly, at first, then building until her body began to vibrate with burning sweetness. Savannah glowed with fire and passion, abandoning herself to the whirlwind of loving. Release came with uncontrollable joy. The passion of his ardor mounted steadily until he, too, shuddered.

They stayed unmoving for several long minutes. Finally Jacob turned on his side and cradled her head on his shoulder, his other arm wrapped possessively around her hips.

"Are you real, Savannah?" He caressed her ear with a whisper.

"I don't know," she replied honestly, lifting her finger to stroke gently the warm skin of his arm. Jacob had no idea the seriousness of her answer, and she had no plans to tell him. All she knew was that she felt happy. For the first time since her arrival in the foyer of the hospital, Savannah drifted off to a wonderfully restful sleep.

She came awake slowly, aware that Jacob still held her close, his arm tossed protectively over her own. His chest rose and fell with the even sound of contented slumber. A dim glow still emanated from the nub of the candle, the wick almost consumed by the slow burn. Through the still-open window floated a cool breeze, gently encouraging her to snuggle closer to his warm masculine body. She looked dreamily at his relaxed face, noting that his usual tension was gone. Amazement was the only way to describe what had happened between them, amazement to know that Jacob Cross needed her. Sighing contentedly, Savannah willed away nagging thoughts of the future. Lying next to him felt right, and whatever her destiny, she would always treasure this memory.

Jacob's heavy thigh was thrown across hers, the weight bearing down on her legs uncomfortably. She moved carefully, trying not to disturb him, and disentangled herself from his hold. She continued to stare at the sleeping man as her lips curved in happiness. The exhale of her warm breath caused him to open his eyes to a lazy slit.

Not a word was spoken as he brought her back into his arms. The world was theirs tonight, and neither wanted to waste it. He leaned forward to bury his mouth in the curve of her neck, his thighs pressed close against hers. No mistaking his intentions. Savannah returned his sweet kiss as the candle flickered its last flame, leaving the room in complete darkness. He took her again, this time slow and relaxed but with an urgency that could not be denied.

"Savannah," Jacob began hours later, kissing the top of her head. Dawn was not far off. Dozing only a little, they had spent most of the night talking softly, laughing quietly about this and that.

He had never felt so strongly about anyone before this woman breezed into his life and took over. His marriage to Anna Kent had not been like this. They had married because it was expected of them. She had been beautiful and charming, the epitome of gentility. Plus, her family's plantation had adjoined Riverlawn, making them the perfect match.

He had gone along with the marriage because he had indeed been fond of Anna. They had grown up together and had been comfortable with the familiarity. But something had been missing. In spite of Anna's beauty and charm, she had been unable to lose herself to passion. She had hated it, in fact. She had claimed it wasn't proper to behave in such a way, and they rarely had. After the first few months of marriage, their relationship had grown no further.

He looked tenderly at the woman now resting in his arms and sighed. Happiness was giving him a second chance. A chance to live again, to love again. He stroked the delicate face cradled in his arms and realized how much he cared for her. He loved her gentle and caring manner, her kindness toward others, her intelligence, her wit, and her annoying stubbornness. Most of all, he loved the fiery passion she had shown him last night.

"Savannah." Jacob tugged a strand of silken hair. His sleeping beauty stirred as he lowered his lips to meet hers. "As much as I would like to stay wrapped in your arms forever, I must leave you for a few days."

She pulled away, questions forming in her eyes

as she rubbed her hand across them. "Can I come with you?" she mumbled, still only half-awake.

He smiled, stroking her soft hair. "No, I'm afraid not. This is something I must do alone. Besides, I need you here to care for the soldiers." The sky outside the window had lightened a degree as dawn began to creep in.

"Are you going to see the boy in prison?" she asked softly, her hand lazily caressing his cheek. Stunned, he nodded slowly. She rolled away from him, slowly wiggling her back against his chest. "Good. It's time you bring justice to the man responsible."

In one simple sentence, this woman understood him far better than anyone else in the world. His heart swelled with tenderness as he turned her body to face his and loved her again.

The morning dawned bright as Savannah came awake, slowly stretching in comfort. If she entertained the thought that last night was a wonderful dream, the warm indentation on the pillow next to hers dispelled any doubt. She was happy. Jacob had not only given her his trust, but also his heart and soul. His body, too. Repeatedly. She grinned with satisfaction, her body pleasantly sore from their night of love.

She rolled toward the sun to feel its warmth streaming on her face. She had tried to stay distant from her doctor, but couldn't do it. It was impossible to be in the same room without feeling drawn to him, without wanting to make him forget the tragedies of his past. A terrible pang of guilt shot through her stomach. What if she was his next tragedy? What if the forces that dropped her in this hospital decided to return her to 1996? So many unanswered questions, and no one to turn to for answers. Her only connection with time travel was Mathilde, an odd woman who was being deliberately obtuse.

She sat up in bed as a thought struck her suddenly. Maybe Jacob Cross was actually her primary destiny, not the hospital. Mathilde said it wasn't necessarily obvious. Since Jacob and the hospital were so closely connected, it could be possible. She relaxed back against the pillows. If he were her destiny, would she be allowed to stay?

In truth, when her attempt at the vanity failed to take her back, she hadn't been terribly disappointed. She had thought that her adventure might even prove a bit exciting. Since then, she had become so busy in the hospital that she really had had no chance to miss her old life. After that, she had fallen in love with her doctor.

The realization that home was actually wherever Jacob Cross was soared from deep within her heart. Her place was here, and she would fight to remain. When she met Mathilde for their next trade, she would find out exactly what must be done to break her connection with the future.

Jacob looked up from his work to see his wife slowly descending the stairs. The light glimmered off her long hair, reminding him of how it felt wrapped around his body. Now it was neatly brushed and pulled into a chignon, with no sign of the passion that consumed them only hours before. Nothing to remind them except the expression on her face and the look in her eyes. He broke their gaze to nod at a nearby steward, who took the rolled bandage from Jacob's hand and bent to complete the job of changing a soldier's wound dressing.

She was breathtaking. Even more so now that their love had been sealed. Their eyes locked across the room, and the humming noise of the hospital ceased for him. All that registered was Savannah Stuart Cross coming near.

Last night had been wilder and sweeter than anything he could have imagined. She was as delicate as a man wanted his wife to be and as wildly passionate as a man wanted from his lover. The combination of the two was inexpressible.

He knew the only way to give himself freely to this woman was to settle the murders of Anna and his father. The need to do so was intense. As fate would have it, now was an opportune time to head to Memphis to see the boy in prison. There seemed to be a temporary ebb in nearby battles. The field hospitals usually sent their wounded to St. George. They hadn't had any new arrivals in several days. He hoped he could get to the prison and back before any new casualties were brought in. He had heard that forces were building to the southeast. Within a few weeks, one of the generals would get nervous and the battle would begin. Once that happened, they would be overrun with wounded. If he were going to go, he should do so immediately. Even if a few wounded arrived while he was away, he realized with pride that his wife could handle things on her own.

He hated to leave her, but it couldn't be helped. If he were to put the past to rest, he must go.

"Good morning, love." Jacob bent to kiss Savannah directly on the lips, oblivious to anyone watching—including Miss Emma, who smiled grandly as she served breakfast to the men. Even at a distance, he could see her wink at Savannah and his wife's returning blush.

"How did you sleep?" he murmured, pulling her into his office. Shutting the door for privacy, he lifted his arms around her neck and pulled her tight.

"Oh, Doctor." She sighed. "I couldn't sleep a wink last night. I had the trembles, terrible goose bumps, repeated hot flashes, rapid, shallow breathing, and a pounding heart rate. Whatever could be the matter with me?" she purred. "Do you think I've caught something?"

A hearty laugh burst from his throat. "Let me see," he replied with mock seriousness. "Does it hurt when I do this?" He lifted her arm and placed it around his neck. At the shake of her head, he lifted the other. "What about this?" He bent to kiss her lips. "And this?" She exhaled deeply.

"Why, Doctor, I guess I'm cured. I can't seem to remember anything right at this very moment." Savannah giggled playfully. "Maybe I need another treatment." She leaned forward, her lips teasing his with a smile.

"I could stay wrapped in your arms forever, Mrs. Cross, but I'm afraid I must take my leave shortly." Jacob reluctantly disentangled himself from her arms.

"I wish you didn't have to go, especially now that we've"—she looked up shyly—"found each other. But I understand. You've got to resolve this."

He stroked her hair. "I want us to have a fresh start." He spoke softly. "If all goes well, I'll be back late tomorrow evening. Memphis is only a day's ride. If I hurry, I can get there before dark, speak to the boy in the morning, and be back in your arms late tomorrow night."

"I'll wait up for you."

"I was hoping you would." He looked around on his desk, under papers, in boxes, in drawers. Then irritation flashed across his face. "I've misplaced my father's timepiece. Have you seen it?"

"No," she answered with concern. "How long has it been missing?"

He nodded with a worried frown. "I guess a day or two. I'm afraid someone has stolen it, perhaps one of the medics. It's the only thing I have left from my father other than 250 acres of scorched farmland. Would you and Miss Emma look for it while I'm gone? It would break my heart to lose it."

"Of course, Jacob," she assured him. "We'll turn this place upside down until we find it."

He nodded in thanks, then lifted a leather saddlebag to his shoulder. Opening the door of his office, he stood back to allow Savannah to pass

229

first, then followed her through the hospital.

"I'm hoping you won't have an influx of wounded while I'm gone. If you do—"

"Jacob"—she pushed him by the vanity and out the front door—"I can handle the hospital. You go. Find out what you need to know. This is important to you, and to us."

Outside, a handsome chestnut horse stood saddled and waiting. "Where did you get the horse?" Savannah asked with surprise.

"He belongs to the army. I delivered the granddaughter of the man who runs the livery stable. He repays me when I need to borrow a horse. Nice trade-off, don't you think?" Placing his foot in the stirrup, he threw his leg over the saddle. The leather creaked as he settled into it.

Savannah drew close to touch his boot. "Please be careful, Jacob. Hurry back to me."

He leaned down and lifted her face to his mouth, kissing her thoroughly as Miss Emma watched from the window. "I'm doing this for you, love, and for me. I'll be back tomorrow night. Leave the candle burning so I can see it from far off."

"Jacob," she called as he reined the horse toward the road. "I love you." He smiled, but did not answer. Standing on the steps, she watched as he spurred the chestnut into a canter and headed down the dirt road. Tears filled Savannah's eyes as Miss Emma joined her by the door.

There was definitely plenty to be done. Savannah unwrapped a day-old bandage to inspect a gunshot wound, her tenth this morning. All the patients needed attention of some sort. She had no idea how Jacob had managed alone. Smiling at the soldier in the bed, Savannah cleaned the wound carefully, dabbing it with whiskey to help prevent gangrene. There wasn't much left in Colonel Sanger's two bottles. She made a mental note to ask for some type of alcohol the next time she traded with Mathilde.

Her thoughts turned to the colorful time traveler and their next meeting tomorrow morning. Savannah still needed a Bible and a copper kettle to keep her end of the bargain. She supposed Miss Emma had an extra kettle in the kitchen, and she could probably find an old Bible buried somewhere in the attic. As she finished the bandage and moved on to her next patient, a thought came to her. One so simple it made her laugh.

Who said she had to steal? Why couldn't she go to the mercantile and buy a Bible and a copper kettle? Mathilde never specified they had to be used items, and Jacob had left her a few Confederate notes for the hospital. What better way to spend the money? Excited by her plan, Savannah grinned contagiously at the legless man lying on the bed. In spite of his misery, he returned her bright smile.

"You sure are happy today, Mrs. Cross. Makes a man long for his own woman. Would you like to see a picture?" he asked shyly. "Her name is Cynthia."

"Why, she's lovely!" she exclaimed, bending

over the daguerreotype he held out to her. "I know you can't wait to see her again."

She chatted with the man for a little while longer, then turned to the next patient. Looking up to see twenty more waiting to be tended, she sighed. It would be quite a while before she would have time to walk to the mercantile.

The afternoon passed quietly as Savannah examined the soldiers. Not only was healing their bodies part of her job, so was healing their minds. That meant care, attention, encouragement, and listening. It was what she loved best about medicine. The condition of the hospital had dramatically improved since her arrival, giving her more time to visit with the men. Cases of gangrene and severe infection had declined dramatically. She was certain half the men in the room were still alive because she insisted on stringent sanitary measures.

No fog darkened the morning sky as Savannah rose to meet Mathilde.

It was still chilly, and she longed to stay in the warmth of her bed, although with Jacob gone, the bed would never be warm enough. It surprised her how used she had got to lying beside him. Their last night together spoke for itself.

She moved to the mirror for her morning toilet, deciding on a French knot to contain her hair. Savannah reached on the dresser for a pearl-covered clip, another gift from Miss Emma. Still not awake, she fumbled in the morning light, accidentally knocking the clip to the floor.

"Damn!" She lifted the oil lamp to find it, lowering it close to the floor. There it was halfway underneath the dresser. When she bent to retrieve it, the light from the lamp caught the gold glint of Jacob's pocket watch laying well beyond reach underneath the dresser. He must have knocked it off and not realized it. Thankful she found his precious heirloom, Savannah happily got on all fours to reach the watch. Using the hairbrush, she managed to slide the timepiece to the side of the dresser where she could touch it. Once in her hands, Savannah stood and considered the watch carefully.

It was the same watch; of that there was no doubt. It was relatively new, though, the fine etching on the gold showing no signs of wear. She couldn't believe it had been almost three weeks since she walked into the antique shop to sell her father's collection. Three weeks ago in a time waiting to happen. Sighing, she closed her eyes, held the watch to her breast.

She dressed quickly, then dropped the watch in her apron pocket. She would have to hurry, or she might miss the weird woman from the future. Savannah quietly rushed down the stairs and out the front door. The morning air was calm as she made her way to the back of the barn.

She had managed to make a trip to the mercantile yesterday and had everything the old woman wanted. Savannah knew Mathilde would be pleased.

"Yoohoo," a voice called softly from behind the barn. "I'm here." The rotund figure quickly rounded the corner of the barn. "Sorry I'm running late." Mathilde was breathing heavily from overexertion. "I can't make these trips like I used to." She smiled at Savannah. "Did you get the lustre?"

"Yes," Savannah answered, smiling, surprised to find she was actually glad to see the woman. "And the copper kettle and a Bible." She led Mathilde into the barn where she had stored the three treasures, moving the hay that covered them.

At the sight of the lustre, Mathilde exclaimed in awe, "It's as beautiful as I remember! I do so love these little lamps." She took it to the open barn door and held it up to the light. The prisms sparkled through the attic dust that still covered them.

"Here's the Bible." Savannah held out a large leather-covered volume. "It was the only one the mercantile had."

Mathilde looked at her strangely. "You stole this from the mercantile?"

"Oh, no, I bought it," she replied defensively. "You said you wanted one in good condition. I assumed brand new would suit you fine."

"Certainly. Smart woman. Is the copper kettle new, too?"

"Yes, this is the only one the mercantile had. I figured it would be quite valuable in your time."

Mathilde raised her eyebrow. "My time? Don't you mean our time?"

Savannah looked at her carefully, then said, "I'm not sure anymore, Mathilde. I guess I've begun to think of this as my time."

The woman was quiet for a minute. "I see," she said slowly. "Have you determined your destiny yet?"

"I don't know. I believe it has something to do with Jacob rather than the hospital."

"What makes you say that?"

"There's only so much I can do at the hospital. Thanks to you, I can keep medicines arriving. But I can't provide medicines from the future. I'm restricted to what they already have. That being the case, am I really helping the hospital more than someone from this time?"

Mathilde shrugged, then moved to sit on a bale of hay.

"With Jacob it's different," Savannah reasoned. She lifted his watch from her apron pocket. "This watch is all he has left of his earlier life. He needs someone to restore his hope in the future. I can give him that, and I can give him love, something he desperately needs."

"I see," the old woman said, eyeing the gold piece speculatively. "You have definitely made progress."

"You mean I'm right?"

"As I've repeatedly told you"—she sighed in annoyance—"I don't know your destiny. It's up to you to figure it out."

"Mathilde." Savannah looked the old woman squarely in the he face. "Is it up to me to create my own destiny?"

The old woman shrugged again. "Of course. It's always been so."

"Does that mean if I make my own destiny, I

control whether I leave this century and return to the future?"

"Perhaps," she repeated, rising from her seat on the hay. "I wish I could tell you more, Savannah. I know you're frustrated, but you really must be sure of what you desire. Only then will you seal your fate."

The woman handed Savannah a heavy box containing surgical equipment and another containing bottles of laudanum. "What shall we swap next time? Are you willing to trade the watch yet?" Mathilde asked, changing the subject. The conservator had told Savannah as much as she intended, and there was no sense in pressing her any further.

"Of course not! I told you how Jacob feels about it. Besides, you said the watch has its own destiny. How can I send it with you to the future?"

"Smart girl." Mathilde offered the backhanded compliment with a sly grin. "You may just solve this mystery all by yourself."

With the skill of a seasoned antique dealer, she carefully placed the lustre, Bible, and kettle into a small box and turned toward the double doors. She hesitated at the opening. "I have been . . . er, fortunate, to come across a large supply of ether. I immediately thought of the hospital, of course. Ether, as you know, is a most effective—"

"Yes, I know, Mathilde. It's an early form of anesthetic. Where did you get it?"

"Never mind about that, but rest assured it's a large supply. I'll want something extra special for it."

"Not Jacob's watch again?"

She looked surprised. "Oh, no. That will come later. Right now, I want the vanity in Miss Emma's hallway."

Savannah gasped in horror. "You can't take that. It's my only link with the future. What if I need that to get back?"

"I thought you said you didn't want to go back."

"I . . . well . . . I'm not sure."

Mathilde sighed impatiently. "You must make up your mind, Savannah. Determine your destiny and decide your future."

Almost without question, Savannah knew she wanted to stay, even though a nagging doubt caused her to hesitate. In spite of the war, in spite of the shortages, in spite of the lack of modern conveniences, she loved it here. She felt so right, so complete, so fulfilled. Here her medical knowledge was put to good use, for people who desperately needed her. Especially the doctor. She wanted to be in his arms forever.

Reaching a decision, Savannah asked slowly, "When do you want to trade?"

"I've got another matter to attend to over the next couple of days. Another traveler. A most interesting man . . ." The corners of Mathilde's lips lifted with a knowing smile. "Ah, well, I know you're not interested in him. Let's meet in three days. You'll be here?"

"No, let's meet just before dawn on Miss Emma's front porch. That way I don't have to move it. How will you carry it, by the way?"

"Don't you worry about that. I'll manage." With

that, the old woman walked out the barn door.

By the time Savannah had collected Jacob's new instruments and the laudanum, Mathilde was gone.

As he walked down the steps of the prison and mounted his horse, Jacob shuddered at the thought of the men behind the thick walls. Callous individuals. Murderers, thieves, deserters. He had visited twice before and both times had left the compound with a vile taste in his mouth. He had also left empty-handed, his efforts to convince young Lawrence Hall to tell what he knew futile.

This trip, however, time was on his side. Over the past year, the boy had developed his own internal demons because of the raid, demons more frightening than any of Colonel Sanger's threats. The boy had anxiously wanted to make amends the minute Jacob and the warden had entered his dark cell.

The boy admitted that Colonel Sanger had ordered the men to bring back all of Riverlawn's horses. If there was any resistance, their orders were to burn the barn. While there was never an order for murder, he had said, it was understood that the act was to be carried out, too.

Tormented by what he had done, Hall had actually cried then. Surprisingly, Jacob had felt compassion for the young man. He had accepted the boy's remorseful story that his role was only to hold the horses. He had even believed that the fellow had no idea Nathaniel Cross would refuse to give his horses for the Great Cause. And, more importantly, he had claimed he didn't know a woman was hiding inside.

As he rode away from the prison, Jacob patted the sealed envelope in the breast pocket of his wool jacket. The warden had a statement written up immediately, and Lawrence Hall had wasted no time in signing it. The boy could finally rest, knowing he told the truth.

Jacob could rest now, too. Once Sanger was behind bars, he would be able to get on with his life, to start over, to build a new future with Savannah. Although it had been a marriage of convenience at first, he had fortunately found something worth keeping. He encouraged his horse into a trot, anxious to get back to his wife's arms. To share his news.

Savannah was a vixen, a fiery vixen, and he had branded her as his own. It had worried him a bit that she wasn't a virgin. He had known almost immediately. She had been too intent on his pleasure to be inexperienced. His anger had flared at first, then he had realized that it didn't matter. She was his now and forever.

From the very minute he first saw her, he knew there was something unusual about this woman. What was it she was hiding? Why didn't she think he'd believe her? The shroud of mystery surrounding his love was heavy but not unbearable. In time, she would tell him everything.

He looked up at the sun, noting that it was already past noon. If he hurried, he might make it back to the hospital by midnight. He felt a stirring in his groin as his thoughts turned to their wonderful night of passion. Savannah had promised to leave a candle burning to welcome him home. Giving the chestnut his head, Jacob urged him into a gallop.

Chapter Nine

It was early afternoon by the time Savannah gathered all of Jacob's old-fashioned surgical instruments into one box and carried them out behind the kitchen. She was pretty sure she had found them all with the exception of a small set Jacob had taken with him just in case he was needed somewhere between St. George and Memphis.

Using a small shovel she found in the barn, Savannah dug a hole underneath a huge bush behind Miss Emma's house. She planned to dispose of the gruesome knives and scalpels before Jacob returned and to replace them with the modern new ones that Mathilde had brought this morning. She grimaced at the equipment inside the box, shuddering to know she had used them over the past few weeks. Two wooden-handled bone saws were pushed up against a tarnished pair of surgical tweezers, while a rusty bullet probe and several dull scalpels rested atop a dozen other miscellaneous pieces. She, Miss Emma, and Deltry had done their best to disinfect them all after each use, but even those efforts were limited. The type of metal was unsanitary. They had spots of rust and the damp wooden handles were notorious for housing germs. The wounded soldiers desperately needed the new stainless steel probes and scalpels Mathilde had brought.

She lifted a knife for closer inspection, grimacing at several oxidized spots on the blade. What Jacob considered the latest in modern medicine was virtually barbaric by her own standards. Savannah dropped the knife in the hole, then dumped the rest of the instruments on top. Using her hands, she covered the metal with soil, then packed it down tightly. She pulled fresh leaves over the grave and stood back to consider her work. There was always a small chance that Jacob would object to the loss of his old instruments. She wanted to ensure that they couldn't be found.

The new scalpels, probes, and knives were wonderful by comparison. Made of surgical stainless steel, they were the best available in the industry. Although she deeply regretted stealing Miss Emma's lustre, replacing Jacob's old instruments with ones that could be thoroughly sterilized was one of the best long-term improvements she could make for him and the hospital.

Bending to smell the fragrant spring blooms on the bush, she thought of her husband. She hoped he had gotten the information he needed and was now on his way home.

Home. She looked around the expanse of Miss Emma's house and realized this was home. The only place she had ever felt so alive and needed. The thought of a permanent life with Jacob sent a flush of desire down her spine. It still seemed like the whole situation couldn't be real, but it was. So real that Savannah could almost feel his hands surrounding her in a warm embrace. A slow warmth spread softly across her face at the memory of his body possessing hers last night. Never before had she felt loved with such abandon, and never before had she given herself so freely. As she walked back toward the house, Savannah knew she wanted to stay. Jacob Cross and she belonged together no matter what century.

"Mrs. Cross!"

A commotion at the front door brought Savannah's attention from the supper she was feeding a bedridden Confederate private. Catching sight of her, Colonel Sanger pushed through the maze of medics and patients, ignoring everyone else in the room. Savannah stood to meet the colonel, irritation furrowing her brow. She didn't have to be a brain surgeon to know that deviously charming smile meant trouble.

As he neared, Sanger's eyes roamed up and down her figure, as if memorizing each curve. A sudden wave of distaste washed through her stomach. She nodded to a medic, who took her place by the soldier, then turned to greet the blond man. How could she have ever been enthralled with him?

Savannah smiled with forced politeness. "Good evening, Colonel. To what do we owe the pleasure of your visit?"

He took her hand and brought it delicately to his lips. "It's always a pleasure to see you, Savannah. I must say, you grow more beautiful each time we meet. I envy Dr. Cross." His eyes grazed over her once again as he held her hand in his.

In spite of her determination to remain reserved, a disbelieving giggle slipped from the back of her throat as she rolled her eyes at the saccharine sweetness of his manner. Sanger's eyes narrowed at the obvious insult of her laugh. He opened his mouth to respond when two uniformed soldiers barged through the front door. They carried between them an older man who looked as if he had been badly beaten.

"Our livery man was the loser in a bar fight," Colonel Sanger announced smoothly. "Would it be possible for Dr. Cross to see to his wounds?"

"Dr. Cross is not presently here, Colonel," Miss Emma interjected, coming through the hallway.

Savannah nodded coolly to the colonel, withdrawing her hand from Sanger's gloved ones. "Miss Emma is right, Colonel. I'm afraid Jacob has been called away for a few days. Perhaps I can help."

Sanger studied her carefully, his eyes clearly indicating he didn't consider her help worthy. Without saying a word, he slowly removed his buff-colored gauntlets, looking from her to Miss

Emma. He shrugged casually, not bothering a glance toward the injured man. "Whatever you say."

Savannah didn't know what she hated more: his obvious disinterest in his own man or his insulting chauvinistic attitude. She brushed by him, directing the soldiers to place the injured man in a chair near the surgery room. After carefully considering the man's bloodied and bruised face, she smiled at him, offering encouragement. "I'm sure it hurts badly, but the wounds are not that bad, I promise."

Dull brown eyes stared up at her as if they were trying to communicate an unspoken message. "He knows." The man whispered for her ears only, words so faint Savannah thought she imagined them.

Who knows what? she wondered. The man grimaced as Savannah bent closer to dab the dried blood around a nasty cut above his eyebrow.

"He knows I gave Jacob the horse," the man murmured.

Savannah stopped as the full impact of the man's injuries hit her like a blow to the stomach. She recalled Jacob's words about the liveryman loaning him a horse, and anger surged through her. The fine upstanding Colonel Sanger had punished Jacob's friend for giving him a horse.

"How did you say this happened, Colonel?" she called to him over her shoulder.

Colonel Sanger tapped his toe, looking slightly bored. "I told you. Bar fight," he said impatiently.

"I am surprised Jacob is not here to tend the wounded. Where did you say he was?"

Savannah returned his unblinking stare, barely concealing her rage. "I didn't, Colonel, and since he is not one of your officers, his absence is of no concern to you."

She reached for a white rolled bandage from a nearby table, then turned back to the liveryman to complete her ministrations. She squeezed the man's hand, offering a soft smile. "Take care to stay away from the scum who did this to you, sir," she said pleasantly, turning to look directly at Colonel Sanger. "You never can tell about such lowlife scoundrels."

Sanger's brown eyes narrowed as he undoubtedly caught the hidden meaning of her words.

"May I speak with you in private, Colonel?" Savannah motioned toward Jacob's office. His shoulders lifted in a bored shrug as he turned to follow her.

"I have only one question," she said, shutting the door behind him with a click. "Why are you here?

If the officer was surprised, he covered it well. "Although I must say it's not necessary that I explain myself to you, I believe I've already shared the reasons for my presence. My liveryman got in a fight and needed patching." The smile on his face was a silent warning. The simmering anger in his eyes confirmed that he owed no one reasons for any of his actions.

"His wounds are not serious, Colonel. You

could have doctored him yourself," Savannah pressed. "I ask again. Why are you here?"

Sanger ignored her question as he lifted a muddy boot to the lower rung of Jacob's polished oak chair. As he scraped the mud from the oiled leather, his eyes freely roamed over her body. Savannah felt her face flush as his eyes came to rest on her bosom. Refusing to be intimidated by his deliberate rudeness, she did not drop her gaze. The man before her was so much like her former fiance it sickened her. He could be charming when it suited him, but there was no doubt of his determination to promote his own interests.

"I'm pleased to see your medical skills match your unusual beauty, Savannah." He deliberately ignored her question. "It's a pity your hospital has no supplies. I might be willing to extend my offer once again." He drew his body within inches of hers, his mouth a breath's width from her own.

Savannah jerked away, flashing him a look of pure hatred. "I believe you and I both made the situation perfectly clear at our last meeting, Colonel. You will not help your own men, and I refuse to forsake my marriage vows."

Sanger lifted an amused eyebrow, ignoring her jibe. "You are quick to cut to the point, my pet, so I will be, too. I understand Jacob has received shipments of medicine. I want to know from where," he said, his voice hard.

She tried to show no emotion, to control her reaction. Of course he'd be curious as to where they'd gotten more supplies, especially since he controlled the deliveries. "I have no idea what you're talking about."

"Don't play games with me, Savannah," he said coldly, a flash of temper showing in his eyes. "I'm far better at it than you." The colonel walked around to Jacob's desk, rifling through the papers on the top as if they were his own. "Besides," he said brightly, looking up with a confident smile, "I still intend to have you in my bed." At her intake of breath, he continued, "I understand the upstanding doctor made a trip to Memphis yesterday. What better opportunity, I thought, to see you again, to see if you've changed your mind about my proposal. I was confident you'd have a change of heart, especially since you so earnestly claimed the hospital is in urgent need of medicines. I see now that you're just being stubborn."

Several of Jacob's new surgical steel scalpels lay in a box on his desk, waiting for Savannah to sterilize them. Colonel Sanger looked in the box with interest, then carefully lifted one of sharp instruments for closer inspection.

"Where did Jacob get these? They are most unusual."

"The scalpels are a present from me. A *wedding* present." She emphasized the word for effect.

His eyes widened in amusement. "You are most bewitching, Savannah. I wonder about you."

He replaced the scalpel and walked toward the heavy oak chest that housed Jacob's supply of medicine. Opening the door, he removed a bottle of aspirin, then read the label as she watched in stunned disbelief. The arrogance of the man was simply amazing. Quickly covering the distance between them, she grabbed the bottle from his hands and replaced it in the cabinet. With one swift motion, Savannah slammed the door to the cabinet, locked it, and dropped the key down her neckline. She stood before the chest like a guard, her eyes daring the man to object.

"What do you wonder, *Colonel* Sanger?" she snapped, lifting her chin to glare at him.

"Everything." The corners of his mouth lifted slightly. He seemed to be preparing for a verbal sparring. "Where you came from. Why you're here. Why you married Jacob." He touched a curl on her shoulder. "You and I are much the same, Savannah. We have our own purposes and reasons for our actions. You're not merely a nurse—you're far too cunning."

Savannah winced. This man was definitely in the same league with her ex-fiance.

"The bottle of aspirin is an Ohio product," he continued. "The only way this hospital could have obtained medications is through Yankee contacts." He hovered over Savannah like a lion with its prey. "That, of course, would indicate possible covert activity. Something that is certainly within my jurisdiction."

"Are you saying I'm a spy, Colonel?"

His eyebrows lifted again as he moved away. "A spy," he said with a calculating tilt of his head. "If I so much as suspected you of being a spy, I could detain you at Army headquarters. I'd be forced to keep you until I discovered your connections. That would probably take several weeks and many, many long nights of interrogation."

The reality of his words hung heavy in the air, and Savannah couldn't help the fear spreading through her body. This man was evil and would stop at nothing to get what he desired—and at this moment, he desired her. Their eyes met in silent challenge as seconds ticked away.

"Savannah is no Yankee spy, Colonel Sanger." Miss Emma threw open the door and barged in. Storming up to the immaculately dressed officer, she wagged an angry finger under his nose. "She has a moral code far superior to your own, I dare say." At his raised eyebrow, she continued, "I know for a fact that she comes from a fine, well-connected family in Atlanta. It would cause great offense to her father if he received word of your accusation."

Savannah smiled in relieved amusement. Miss Emma had obviously been listening to their every word from just outside the door. "Thank you, Miss Emma," she said with dignity. "My father would be most pleased to hear your kind words." She stared pointedly at Sanger.

The colonel considered both of them with a cold, calculating stare that quickly melted into a snake-charmer smile. "You misunderstand, Miss Long. I am not accusing Mrs. Cross of being a spy. I only question where your recently acquired medical supplies are coming from. As you may know, we have difficulty getting the same for our men in the field."

Savannah fought for self-control at the lie, knowing his office held an abundance of medicines, every bottle and jar doled out at his whim. The selfish man was hoarding what he had and would probably sell them to the highest bidder, even if the highest bidder was a Yankee.

"As I said"—Miss Emma's voice held a firm warning—"Savannah's family is well connected in Atlanta. Thanks to her, this hospital has received what it needs to treat our boys." She held the door open. "I suggest it's time you leave, Colonel."

Rage seared across his face at the dismissal, only to be quickly replaced with a smooth smile. His expression said he would finish this battle later. Slowly, the colonel picked up his hat and, nodding to them, walked through the door. The room was silent as they listened for the front door to slam, indicating the colonel and his entourage had departed.

Savannah shot a worried glance at Miss Emma's tense face. Miss Emma was a feisty lady, but it still took courage to stand up to Sanger. Touching her sleeve, Savannah offered silent gratitude. As the older woman regained her composure, Savannah saw the weathered eyes held questions. Questions she knew must be answered.

"Savannah, dear," Miss Emma queried, "what did Colonel Sanger mean about 'your arrangement?' "

Savannah sighed. Her friend had jumped in to protect her from Sanger; the least she could do was offer some type of explanation. "Shortly after I arrived, I went to see Colonel Sanger," she confessed. "The hospital was desperate for medicines, and I figured that as the commander of the post, he would be able to get us what we needed."

"You didn't think that Jacob had already asked?"

"At the time, no. I knew animosity existed between them, but I had no idea why. I figured if I were to ask, we might stand a better chance."

She nodded in understanding. "What happened?"

"He said yes," Savannah replied simply, "under one condition." She raised her eyes to Miss Emma's. "He offered to give the hospital all the supplies it needed if I became his mistress."

"No!" Miss Emma gasped, clutching her hand to her mouth. "Of course you refused."

"As a matter of fact, I slapped him good!" Savannah couldn't help smiling. "He was persistent, though. He gave me two bottles of whiskey to help me think over his proposition. I guess he wanted to sweeten the deal."

"Well, that accounts for the whiskey, but where did you get the other medicines? And the fruit the men so enjoy?" At Savannah's hesitation, Miss Emma sighed. She took Savannah by the hand and led her outside to the rockers on the porch.

"You know, Savannah, I feel I must apologize to you for my behavior the other day." Miss Emma hung her head shamefully. "I didn't know you were trying to save Ely's life. I thought you were hysterical. I'm sorry I doubted you."

Savannah sat her friend down in a white rocker. "Please, Miss Emma, I understand. Ely couldn't breathe because he was choking. Then we had to start his breathing again. It can be quite daunting if you've never seen that before. How is he, by the way? With everything that's happened, I haven't had a chance to check on him tonight."

"Resting comfortably." Miss Emma smiled, clearly relieved at the explanation. She patted Savannah's hand. "I have grown so very fond of you during the past few weeks. I've never seen Jacob happier, and the changes you've made here at the hospital are drastic. I'm so pleased. However"— she leaned back in the chair, her face serious—"I am worried." She held up her hand as Savannah began to explain.

"I don't need to know where you got the medicines if you truly believe it must be confidential, but there are other matters that don't seem to make sense to my feeble mind."

Savannah smiled. If there was one thing Miss Emma did not have, it was a feeble mind.

"It has bothered me, dear, that when you arrived, you were wearing . . . shall we say . . ." she hesitated as she searched for the appropriate words, "improper clothing. You had no trunks with you and claim everything you owned burned in Atlanta. While this is proving to be a vicious war, I know Atlanta has not fallen and, I hope, never will. I can't seem to make your story coincide."

She placed a weathered hand on Savannah's arm. "You know, my dear sister has six children. Four wonderful boys and two beautiful girls. Her eldest, John, is my favorite. Always into mischief he was, and always making me laugh. Her children are grown now, but, oh, how she talks about them in her letters!" Miss Emma dabbed away small tears. "It's just that they mean so much to me, that I also wonder about your family," she pressed, trying to be tactful. "Scarlett is a lovely name for a sister, but you rarely mention her. I also wonder how you knew what was needed to save Private Well's life. How did you know about germs and sterilizing? Jacob Cross is the finest doctor I know, yet he admittedly had no idea what you were doing. He's pleased now with the results, but he, too, was a skeptic at first."

Savannah hung her head, speechless. What was she to say? Miss Emma was slowly piecing together the puzzle, solving the mystery that surrounded her. It was foolish to think these people would not know something was amiss. But, as quick as she was, Miss Emma would never find the last clue. The thought that Savannah had materialized from the future would never occur to her.

Sensing her hesitation, Miss Emma pressed on. "I've overlooked everything because Jacob seems much happier with you in his life, but now I must admit I'm a bit worried. I love Jacob like a son, far too much to risk more of the terrible pain he's already suffered."

Savannah took a deep breath. "Miss Emma, as you may have guessed, Jacob and I have been able to settle the differences between us. He wanted to go to the prison immediately. He insisted that he had to resolve the murders before we could have a life together.

"I wanted to tell him the truth the night before he left, but he asked me to wait. He did that in order to show how much he trusted me. I've already made the decision to tell him everything as soon as he gets back. Please allow me to discuss this with him first. He is, after all, my husband. I think it would hurt him deeply to know I confided in you but not in him." She looked at the older woman, her eyes pleading for understanding.

Miss Emma nodded compassionately, patting her hand. "You are a dear, dear child, Savannah. I share Jacob's trust."

"You have my word that we'll talk after I speak with Jacob. And, Miss Emma, please rest assured I would do nothing to hurt him."

"I believe you, Savannah," the gray-haired lady said with a sparkle in her eye. "I trust you, too."

Just one more crest and Jacob would see the lights of St. George. It was late, and he was tired, but he longed to see the light shining in the window indicating that Savannah was waiting up for him. It was well past midnight as he rode along the darkened road. He hadn't passed a soul since the sun had gone down. Partly, he was sure, this was due to the threat of a brewing thunderstorm. Brilliant streaks of lightning had decorated the sky for the past hour, but as of yet Jacob had been spared a torrential downpour. He prayed he could make it home before the rain started.

The journey had allowed him ample time to think about his next course of action. He planned to contact Sanger's superior officer and personally deliver the sealed envelope now safely tucked inside his jacket. He would report Sanger's involvement in the murders as soon as he could, even if it meant going straight to Jeff Davis himself. This whole war was about Southern honor and traditions. Surely the Confederate president would not tolerate such dishonorable conduct within his own army. All he could do was trust that justice would prevail.

Trust. A picture of Savannah immediately came to mind. It had taken all his strength to admit his love, then turn away her willing confession. As much as he wanted to know her secrets, instinct told him patience was necessary if they were to build a future together. Once he had proven to her how deeply he trusted her, the night they had shared had been spectacular. He felt a tightening in his groin as he thought of her waiting arms. A loud clap of thunder sounded, and he urged the tired chestnut to give a little bit more and gallop faster.

This blasted war, there was no telling how much longer it would go on. Even though he obtained the information needed to convict Sanger, a heavy burden still weighed upon his shoulders. What kind of life could he offer Savannah when their country was so torn? He had no home or family to speak of, save for Miss Emma and the hospital, and he couldn't truthfully promise her any more until the bloody differences could be settled.

Thick sprinkles of rain began falling as he crossed the ridge overlooking St. George. Since

Miss Emma's house was on the west side of town, he could make out its shadow in the moonlight. It was completely dark save for one window. His heart swelled to see a bright light emanating from their room. He was sure Savannah had placed at least a dozen candles in the window.

In a very short time, his young wife had come to mean more to him than life itself, and the thought of a future without her was as dismal as the cloud-covered sky. He might not have much to offer her, but she had already given him everything he could ever hope for. Everything and more.

Reining up in front of the house, Jacob saw a familiar feminine figure curled up on the porch swing, wrapped in a patchwork quilt. At first he thought she had fallen asleep waiting for him. His heart pounded in a sporadic rush when she rose from the swing, delighted at his return.

"Jacob!" Savannah flew down the steps, impatiently waiting for him to dismount. Ignoring the beginning fall of raindrops, she rushed into his arms, and his lips found hers in a passionate meeting. "Oh, how I missed you! Did you get the information?"

He could only nod and crush her to him again. Wrapped in her arms like this, he thought he could almost forget about the war, forget about Sanger, and forget about the murders. Almost. Lifting his head, he nodded to the tired horse beside him, patting his neck. "I've ridden this fellow pretty hard to be back in your arms tonight. Let me take care of him while I tell you all about it."

He loosened the girth, then took her hand as they walked the exhausted animal to the barn. The soft sprinkle of rain fell in earnest, creating a soothing rhythm on the roof of the barn.

"The boy confessed," Jacob said as he unsaddled the horse. "It was really quite easy, too. He's a young fellow, only thirteen, and his conscience refused to rest. It was almost as if the time had come for him. He wanted to tell everything the minute the warden and I walked into his cell."

Bit by bit, Jacob recounted the details of his trip as Savannah listened quietly. She seemed to sense he needed to talk. To talk about the boy and to talk about the murders. To expel the demons that had tormented him for so long.

Savannah picked up a curry comb and began brushing the tired animal. Her eyes met his over the horse's back. "Your father was not a traitor, Jacob. Thanks to your determination to gain the truth, Sanger will pay for his murder. And for Anna's, too."

Jacob stopped what he was doing and walked around the horse to her. "Thank you, Savannah." She looked at him in surprise. "Thank you for understanding. For giving me the courage to resolve this." He dropped a quick kiss on her forehead. He turned slightly and headed for the hayloft ladder.

"Don't go away," Jacob called with a grin as he began to climb. "Did anything happen here while I was away?"

"No, nothing unusual," she answered as he threw down hay for the horse.

"Savannah, come look what I've found!" He watched her make her way to the ladder and saw a flash of worry cross her face. Briefly, he wondered what caused her frown. She held out her hand as Jacob helped her up the last few steps.

"What is it?" she asked in a small voice. "What have you found?"

"Only you, my love." He brushed a tendril from her face and gently pushed her down onto a soft bed of hay, kissing her as if he had never tasted such sweetness.

The rain outside continued to pound lightly on the roof, and the horse downstairs continued to munch contentedly on his dinner as they settled into the warmth of the hay. Words were not necessary when they began to communicate as only a man and woman can do.

Several hours passed before the rain let up and their passions were temporarily abated. Jacob carried Savannah into the house and deposited her gently on the feather mattress, then settled in beside her. Throughout the night, their bodies entwined in a comfortable, contented sleep. The sun hadn't begun to peek over the horizon when he arose and dressed. He was anxious to check on the condition of his patients since his absence, then draft the letter to send discreetly to Army headquarters. He needed an appropriate plan of action. Now that he had the information he required, Jacob knew he had to proceed cautiously. Sanger was a dangerous man when crossed. At this point, it would be foolish to allow Sanger to believe there was any evidence to link him to the crimes. He would be threatened, and there was no telling what he would do. Jacob had Savannah and Miss Emma to consider. He knew he had to be careful.

Jacob poured himself another cup of coffee, then sat down at the kitchen table. Sunrise was now breaking, and the first rooster was calling forth the day. He felt a warm hand on his shoulder and looked up to see Miss Emma wearing a clean white apron over her muslin dress. Deltry followed. Her path was straight to the stove to begin the morning meal.

"Jacob!" Miss Emma said, sitting down beside him. Her eyes shone in delight. "I'm so pleased you've returned. Savannah and I both missed your smiling face."

Jacob returned her greeting with a grin. "It's good to be back."

"Well?" Miss Emma tapped her fingers on the table. "Don't keep me in suspense. How did it go? Did the boy talk?" Despite her cheerfulness, her motherly eyes were filled with concern.

He nodded, smiling. "He did."

"What a relief! Now we'll see that horrible Colonel Sanger court-martialed for his crime. I never did take to that man," she added. "Never. Not since he came into town with the impression he owned it. I've had no patience for him."

Jacob chuckled at Miss Emma's rattling before he grew serious. "Yes, the boy admitted that Sanger issues the orders. Not only that, he said Sanger joined the group as the house was burning.

Told them to let it burn." His voice was tight with emotion as his hands tightened into fists. "If I didn't have Savannah in my life, Miss Emma, it's possible I might kill him."

The older woman captured his clenched fists in her hands. "I understand, Jacob. You've lost so much. But you are also right about Savannah. You have found love again, so fight for it.

"You would have been proud of her yesterday," Miss Emma continued. "Colonel Sanger brought in the old man who runs the livery, saying the man had been beaten in a bar fight. We suspected Sanger knew he loaned you the horse to ride to Memphis and gave him a going-over."

Jacob swallowed quickly as hot coffee scalded his tongue. "Sanger did what? He came here while I was gone? How is the liveryman?"

"He'll be sore for a day or two, but nothing serious," she assured him with a concerned smile, then frowned. "There was more to it than just the liveryman, though. Sanger knew you were gone. We supposed he came to find out where. When we wouldn't tell him, he began questioning Savannah about the new supplies of medicines. Savannah handled him with dignity, I might add, especially when he made . . . er, certain advances."

"He made advances?" Anger laced his words. "Savannah didn't mention it last night." Sanger's blatant desire for Savannah sent a wave of hatred through him. Sanger had relieved him of everything he'd ever loved once before. Jacob would be damned if he allowed it to happen again.

Worry settled on Miss Emma's face as she cast an anxious glance his way. "I hope I haven't spoken out of line. I assumed Savannah would have told you last night." At the shake of his head, she took a deep breath. "Considering how you feel about Sanger, I suppose Savannah thought it wise not to cause more trouble."

She rose from the table to help Deltry mix the flour for biscuits. Jacob stared silently for a few minutes. It was obvious Miss Emma knew more than she was telling. It was also obvious she had no intention of saying anything else.

The kitchen was quiet as Deltry added another few logs to the fire in the wood-burning stove. Jacob stared at flames through the open stove door, listening to the crackle of wood each time she added one of the small logs. His thoughts were in turmoil. Why had Savannah not told him about Sanger's visit? Surely she would have mentioned his appearance and, no doubt, his advances. Perhaps she had wanted to wait for a more appropriate time, he reasoned, remembering their passionate lovemaking in the hayloft. Still, it didn't make sense. There had to be more to Sanger's visit than Miss Emma had implied.

He turned to the motherly woman. "Finish it, Miss Emma. What else happened with Sanger?"

She glanced up in surprise. "I've told you what happened, Jacob. Savannah tended to the injured man. Then she and I sent Sanger on his way. What more do you want to know?"

"I want to know what was said," he stated firmly. "You said he wanted to know how we got medicines. He hasn't cared about this hospital in the past, why would he now?"

"You really should to talk to Savannah, not to me." Miss Emma nervously fidgeted with her hair.

"I intend to talk to Savannah . . . later. However, I want to know now and I want to know from you. What did Sanger say?"

"Jacob . . ."

"Now," he said firmly.

Miss Emma sighed, obviously knowing Jacob refused to accept her deference to Savannah. She sat back down at the table, while Deltry discreetly disappeared with her egg basket.

"Apparently, Savannah went to see Colonel Sanger. She asked him to provide the hospital with more medical supplies." The older woman took a deep breath.

"Yes, I knew that."

She nodded with relief. "I'm sure you know, too, that he agreed to do so under one condition. She had to become his mistress."

Jacob's jaw fell open as anger scalded him just as the hot coffee had earlier. That he didn't know. Who the hell did Sanger think he was? What in hell did Savannah think she was doing? She knew Sanger was a dangerous man, yet she still approached him for help. And now, a good supply of various liquids, powders, and tablets were inside his medicine cabinet just in the other room. Surely she hadn't agreed? Surely not.

"Your expression gives you away, Jacob," Miss Emma quickly scolded him. "How dare you assume such a terrible thing about your wife! Of course Savannah refused. In fact, she brought him down a notch or two from what I understand. I was quite proud of her when she made it absolutely clear that it was none of Sanger's business where we got the supplies."

Miss Emma rushed on. "Jacob Cross! I do declare you are pigheaded! Can't you see that Savannah only wanted to help you and the hospital? You have no right to be angry with her. She has done wonders since she's been here, and I will not have you doubting her intentions!

"She loves you, Jacob, of that I am certain." The elderly eyes flashed at his stone-faced silence. "I asked Savannah where she got the medicines. As much as she wanted to share her burden, she couldn't tell me. She said she had promised to tell you once you returned, and she will if you give her a chance." Miss Emma's wrinkled hand covered his.

"Don't go all obstinate on her. She's a good woman, Jacob. You know that. Give her a chance."

Instantly, he felt ashamed. Miss Emma was right. He still had questions and his wife had some mighty good explaining to do, but he told Savannah, not once but many times, that she held his trust. As confusing as the situation was, he had to live up to his word. He lifted the cup of still-steaming coffee to his lips. There could never be anything between them without trust.

* * *

Savannah smiled happily, watching Jacob tend the patients. She had missed him terribly while he was gone, and last night had welcomed him home so tenderly. His dark head lifted as she began to cross the room toward him. He shrugged with an apologetic grin as he turned to answer the call of a soldier on the far side of the room.

Undaunted, she joined him by the wounded man, squeezing her husband's hand in greeting. As their fingers touched, their eyes locked for an instant, causing a quiver of excitement to soar through her, the warmth of their joining last night still fresh in her mind. He bent to tend to the fellow in the bed, then glanced up again. This time his blue eyes were questioning, and from his expression it was obviously serious. Puzzled by his abrupt change, Savannah hesitated as another patient called her name. Dropping her gaze, she moved toward the man, hiding the disappointment she felt.

Savannah had been anxious to show Jacob his new stainless steel surgical instruments, but, since there were no surgeries planned for today, she knew the surprise could wait. Doctors could be stoic about their tools of medicine, and she didn't relish Jacob's reaction when he learned his old instruments were buried somewhere in Miss Emma's back yard. As much as he needed the scalpels, probes, and knives, he had a history of stubbornness. So, with not much more than a passing greeting, their day had begun.

* * *

The mantle clock had just chimed two when Jacob grabbed her hand and pulled her into his office. "I can't wait any longer," he said. "I need to talk to you."

With a sinking heart, Savannah recognized the seriousness of Jacob's tone. Her husband would wait no more to hear her secrets. There was no sense in delaying the inevitable; it was time to give him answers.

She withdrew her arm from his grasp and lowered herself into a chair. Jacob stepped around the desk and sat down. He leaned forward to place his arms on the heavy blotting pad. "I understand the good Colonel Sanger dropped by yesterday morning," he began, drawling Sanger's name sarcastically. "Miss Emma reluctantly explained to me how he made improper advances toward you. She also mentioned the conditions that must be met if we are to obtain medicines from him." Jacob looked directly into her eyes.

"Why, Savannah? Why haven't you told me before now?" He nodded toward the wooden cabinet in the corner. "Why do I have a cabinet full of medicines that Sanger once refused to give me?"

She stared at him blankly, reading the hurt in his eyes. Her intentions to explain escaped as no words came to mind. "Jacob—"

"I only wish you knew how happy you make me, Savannah," he interrupted. "You give me hope for the future. Before you came into my life, I had given up all hope. Now, I don't know what to think." He lifted his dark head to gaze at her.

Savannah gripped the arms of the chair so

tightly, her hands hurt. He was right. The time had come to tell her husband the truth. To tell him she was from the year 1996. It wasn't going to be easy. She felt confident in his love, that was true. But actually telling someone that she knew the future from history books was a bit daunting. She rose from her chair and motioned for him to stay in his.

"Jacob, I need to tell you a story," she began, pacing in front of his desk. "When I tell you this story, you must promise me that you will not interrupt until I finish. You must also promise that you won't make a rash decision based on something you don't really understand. And I do mean *really* don't understand." She stopped, placed her hands on his desk, and looked him squarely in the eye. "With all the love you feel for me, can you promise that?"

Jacob's expression was confused. "Savannah, you make this sound so terrible. Nothing can be as bad as you seem to think. Explain this to me. Help me understand," he demanded softly. "This is clearly something we have to put behind us."

Taking a deep breath, Savannah pulled the nurse's cap from her head and placed it on the desk. She reached into the pocket of her white apron and placed Jacob's timepiece beside the hat.

"You found my watch!"

"Yes, it was under the dresser upstairs."

He reached for the watch. "I must have dropped it."

"Probably." She nodded. "I found it while I was getting dressed."

"What does my watch have to do with your secret?" He tossed another worried glance as he polished the crystal with his sleeve.

"Your watch once belonged to my father."

He looked surprised. "No, you're mistaken. I purchased this watch from a reputable jeweler in Nashville. I gave it to my father for Christmas seven or eight years ago."

"Yes, that's true," she agreed, "but my father collected watches. This was his prized piece."

Jacob shrugged in confusion. "I suppose that could have happened, although the jeweler assured me it was one of the first made by Dennison, Howard, and Davis." He reached for a wooden letter opener on his desk, toying with it while he waited.

She took an even deeper breath to steady her nerves. "Jacob, my father had an impressive collection of *antique* watches." Surprise registered on his angular face. "In the year 1996."

"What?" he asked, shaking his head as if he hadn't heard her correctly. "I must have misunderstood. I thought you said 1996."

He could only stare at her affirmative nod.

"Savannah," he said, his patience quickly wearing thin. He held the watch in his palm. "I don't understand."

The room was heavy with silence as tears swelled at the corners of her eyes. Confusion filled Jacob's face. Of course he wouldn't believe her tale, and it was hopeless to expect any other reaction.

"I'm from the future, Jacob," she said softly.

Shocked disbelief crossed his face. "How can that be possible?" he asked, his voice barely audible.

"I only wish I knew," Savannah replied sadly. She picked up the cap and sat down on the settee in his office. This was going to be a long afternoon, she thought, closing her eyes under the strain. "You know that I arrived here suddenly." At his nod, she continued, "I was in the antique store waiting for a Civil War collector to come look at the watch. I planned to sell it and use the money to go to medical school to become a doctor."

Savannah realized she was babbling and fought her nervousness. If he was going to believe her story, it must be absolutely convincing. "While I was waiting, I found a collection of antique hats. I am a nurse, you see, and this hat caught my eye." She held up the cap. "I sat down at a vanity, the actual one that's by Miss Emma's front door. I was just playing around, you know, seeing how it looked on my head and all. Then a sense of peace came over me, and I couldn't keep my eyes open. I relaxed so deeply that I fell asleep."

She considered his reaction. He sat stoically; even the letter opener in his hands had been returned to its proper place on the desk. His forced composure indicated he doubted her story.

"A scream woke me. It was the scream of the man whose leg you amputated." She placed the hat on her head. "Now I'm here, and I have no idea how to get back." Tears filled her eyes at the memory of her desperation. "I sat at that vanity that very first night and cried. I hoped beyond hope that somehow I could get back to my own time. But I couldn't. I guess I gave up. From the moment I arrived, I saw you needed help and threw myself into nursing."

Jacob stared at her in stunned silence. She sensed there was not much he could say. She was sure he had expected her secret to be of thievery or even of spying. Nothing like this.

After several agonizing moments, he finally spoke. "Savannah, surely you don't expect me to believe such a story? It's ludicrous to think someone can travel through time."

She shrugged, suddenly calm. "I know it sounds impossible. If it hadn't happened to me, I'd never believe it, either. But, it is true. I *am* from the future.

"I'm afraid that's not all," she continued, figuring she might as well tell him everything. "The antique dealer followed me through time. The first time I saw her was the night we went to dinner at Rose's. In the sitting room." Encouraged by his lifted eyebrows, she pushed on. "I was ecstatic at first, thinking she could take me back and I'd wake up from this dream. I guess she had other plans, though. She knew the hospital needed supplies, and wanted me to . . . well, trade things for the medicines we needed. That's where you got the morphine, the aspirin, and the fruit. While you were gone, she brought laudanum and new surgical equipment. She's bringing us a large supply of ether next time." She looked cautiously at her husband.

Another lull of silence.

Jacob rose to stand by the window as Savannah sank back into her chair. For a long time, nothing was said.

"I thought that we had something special, Savannah. I thought we had a trusting relationship," he said, anger filling his voice. "Is the truth so horrendous that you must make up such an unbelievable story?"

"Jacob, it's not like that! I *am* from the future!" Savannah pleaded, rushing to the window to touch him. When he moved from her touch, she knew her worst fears had come true. It was almost impossible for him to believe her story, and there was nothing she could do to convince him. She wanted to stay in Jacob's time, but if he refused to believe her, refused to trust her, what would be the point?

Tears fell from her cheeks as she watched him by the window. His head was bent as if his heart had been broken. This man was her only hope of happiness; she couldn't just stand by and not fight for their love.

"Think about what I'm saying, Jacob! Please!" she cried. "Remember my clothing when I arrived? You said it was improper. I'm telling you it was fashionable in my time. The pressure points? A discovery of modern medicine.

"The CPR we used to resuscitate Ely? I learned the practice in college in 1988! The University of Tennessee, in fact." She opened the box of new surgical tools and pulled out a scalpel. "Look at the quality of this scalpel. It's surgical steel, and

271

it's from my time, from the twentieth century! Jacob, I am not lying!" She dropped the scalpel to the floor and ran to his medicine chest.

"Look at this bottle of aspirin! It expires in March of 1998. That means it can't be sold after that date. I promise you, I am telling the honest truth!"

He watched her without answering, his face expressionless. Savannah had no idea what he was thinking when a minute flicker of recognition rose to his eyes. Not much, she thought, but something.

"In my time smallpox has been virtually wiped out," she continued, this time more calmly. "I can show you my vaccination scar. My appendix burst when I was thirteen. You felt the scar where they removed it."

The spark in his eyes disappeared as quickly as it had come. He continued to stare at her, refusing to acknowledge the possibility of her words. "I don't believe you, Savannah. You're making this impossible. Ruining what could be good between us."

She sighed and sat down on the chair in resignation. "You promised you would," she softly accused. "You said you'd believe me no matter what. You said that, Jacob." Hopelessly, Savannah closed her eyes to fight her tears. "I guess it is too much to believe. I understand why you can't keep your promise. I suppose I would react the same way if I were in your position."

"Then why don't you tell me the truth?" he asked coldly. "There is no reason for you to lie."

"I am telling the truth, Jacob. I can tell you anything," she said sadly. "I can tell you most anything that's going to happen in the next hundred and thirty years."

"Tell me who's going to win the war?" Their eyes met in challenge.

"I don't think you want to know."

A sharp rap sounded at the door. At first, they ignored it. It came again, this time more persistently. Jacob shook his head, obviously thinking he knew who stood on the other side of the heavy wood. "Miss Emma," he said softly. He strode to the door, throwing it open wide. He stopped suddenly to see Colonel Sanger leaning against the wooden jamb.

"Who did you say was going to win the war, Mrs. Cross?" he asked, barging in uninvited.

Savannah gasped as she wondered how much Sanger had heard. Then her fear turned to anger at his obvious rudeness. "I am sorry, Colonel, my husband and I were having a private conversation. I don't know what you could possibly mean."

"What is it, Sanger?" Jacob snapped, interrupting their exchange. He glanced at Savannah, uncertainty on his face. She couldn't help but feel a small tremor of hope. There was a possibility, small perhaps, that he was considering what she had told him.

Sanger cleared his throat in irritation. "I have come to seek your assistance on behalf of the Confederacy."

Jacob cocked his eyebrow. "You know how I feel about serving in your army, Sanger. This better be important." This time Jacob did nothing to conceal his hatred for the uniformed man.

Surprisingly, Sanger ignored his jibe and pressed on. "I have received word from General Lee that both Confederate and Union forces have been building to the south of here." At Jacob's nod, he continued, "It's a small place called Shiloh, between Pittsburg Landing and Corinth, Mississippi. The battle began yesterday, and it's vicious. In less than twelve hours, we've had reports of at least four thousand Confederate casualties. I am here to request your assistance in tending to these men. You are needed at the field hospital and to assist in bringing back the casualties."

Jacob walked to his desk and sat down in the leather chair. "And if I refuse?"

Sanger shrugged. "You know as well as I that I have the authority to force your cooperation." His voice lowered as his eyes narrowed. "You also know that I will use any means necessary."

Savannah watched as the two men glared at each other, neither refusing to break eye contact.

"Jacob!" Sanger snapped in a voice filled with irritation. "I wouldn't be here if doctors weren't needed so badly. The destruction has been harsh. I must personally carry munitions to replace their depleted supply. We plan to move out at dusk and ride through the night to avoid detection. Should we encounter Yankee forces on the way, you know as well as I that they are more apt to allow a doctor and ambulances to pass through even though they may take officers as prisoners. We plan to hide the munitions—"

"Under a false floor in each wagon," Jacob finished for him with a nod of reluctant understanding. "Save your words, Sanger. I'll go, but not because of you. I'm going because my father would have thought it the honorable thing to do. He was, after all, a patriot." Sanger's eyes narrowed as the meaning of Jacob's words were clear.

"I'll go, too," Savannah piped in to break the tension. Both men looked at her as if she were crazy.

Sanger spoke first. "The battlefield is no place for such a charming and delicate lady, Mrs. Cross. I will not allow it."

Ignoring the officer, Savannah turned to her husband. "Jacob, surely—"

"For once I agree with the colonel," Jacob said tightly. "You will stay here and prepare the hospital for my return." Turning back to Sanger, he nodded. "I will be ready when you are." With that, Jacob turned and strode out the door.

Chapter Ten

"I don't understand why you won't let me come with you, Jacob. My skills will be needed."

Savannah watched her husband gather the medical supplies he needed from the large wooden chest in his office. Several hours had passed since Sanger's visit, and Jacob was preparing to join the colonel's entourage. She saw a good portion of the new morphine and a variety of other supplies set aside for the journey. His new collection of surgical instruments had been packed first, without comment, in his black leather bag.

"I'm not going to argue with you, Savannah," he said, not looking up. "The battlefield is no place for a woman. You will stay here and prepare the hospital for my return with the wounded. I have enough to concern me without your safety to worry about, especially in light of the circumstances."

"What circumstances? That I'm from the future?" Fury creased her brow. "It's not my traveling with you, is it? You're afraid of what I've told you. You think I'm lying or crazy or both, don't you?"

Her husband ran his hand wearily over his eyes, his lack of sleep obviously catching up with him. "The reason you will not accompany me to the fighting is first because you are a woman, and second because you are my wife. I will not allow you to be subjected to the dangers of battle.

"As for your story, I don't know what to believe," he went on. "You finally tell me your hidden secrets, something I told you I would believe no matter what. Now, I'm supposed to accept you've come from the future and that someone else has followed you offering medicines I can't get anywhere else." He sat down in his overstuffed leather chair and stared at her, his chiseled face strained. "Would *you* believe it without question?"

Savannah hurried to his side, instantly regretting her anger. "I wish there was something I could do to prove my story is true. I just don't know what would convince you." She picked up a bottle of aspirin, shaking her head sadly. "I'm afraid this aspirin will not be much help to those in severe agony. I wish I could have gotten something stronger."

He took the container from her hand. "If these

won't help serious wounds, why didn't your acquaintance bring something that could? If you have a smallpox vaccine in your world, surely it would be a small task to obtain something to numb pain."

"You're right, there are a variety of stronger, more effective painkillers. But the choices were limited. The conservator, as she called herself, said she could only bring back things that are available in your time." She held up her stethoscope from around her neck. "This stethoscope is from my time. You've seen for yourself that it's far superior to the one you use. The conservator was able to bring it back through time only because the technology has already been developed. This is just an improvement. It's the same with your new knives, probes, and scalpels. Aspirin is available in France, so she could bring it to me. She didn't want to, but I insisted. These soldiers had to have something for the pain."

"We have morphine."

"Yes, but you know that constant, repeated use of it is addictive. So is laudanum for that matter. It's going to be a big problem after the war. What she did bring were things you could have, medicines like the morphine and laudanum. The fruit was something special she brought the patients. Soon, you'll have ether, too. I may not have made the best of trades, but it was all I could do under the circumstances."

"What did this conservator want in exchange?" Disbelief riddled his face, but Savannah was heartened. At least he seemed to be considering her explanations.

She hung her head in embarrassment, knowing it was time to face the consequences of her thievery. "I had to . . . steal a few things to make the trade."

"You're a thief?"

"I did what was needed," Savannah replied indignantly. "She wouldn't simply give me the medicines. I had to trade for them. And, to make the trades, I had to take a few little things that didn't belong to me."

"Such as?"

"A Confederate hat from a soldier, a sword from your office, a few Confederate notes, Miss Emma's lustre from the attic, and one of her handsewn quilts. I bought a copper kettle and Bible from the mercantile with money you had given me." Her chin lifted as she met his eyes. "I hated myself for stealing, Jacob, but there was no other way."

He said nothing as he rose and continued to pack his medical bag.

"I must go with you, Jacob," she pleaded. "Don't you see? My knowledge of healing is exceptional simply because I trained in the future. I can help you with the wounded. You need me."

"Savannah," Jacob said, his voice conciliatory, "I agree you have impressive medical skills. I'd even say they're stronger than my own as a doctor. But you are still a woman and the battlefield is no place for you.

"I'm going with Sanger while you remain here

and get the hospital ready for the wounded." He snapped the bag with a click and turned toward the door. "When I get back, we'll discuss this further. Right now, I don't know what to think." His voice rang with finality.

Savannah fought back the tears that threatened to erupt. Jacob didn't believe she was from the future. Anger coursed through her. This man swore he loved her and promised to believe her secret. She had trusted him enough to share it. Now he was shutting her out.

It was an almost unbelievable story, except that the adventure had happened to her. In essence, it had happened to Jacob, too. Some force had brought them together over a span of more than a century. She'd be damned if she'd let him go without her. She had to prove she came from the twentieth century, a place where a man did not automatically assume a woman was incapable of more than staying at home while he bravely went to the battlefield.

Savannah rushed out of the office to formulate her plan.

Jacob looked toward the porch once again. Only Miss Emma and Deltry stood on the steps in the late-afternoon sun. Savannah had gone to her room after their conversation in his office and had not made an appearance since. It was obvious she was angry about not going with him, but surely she meant to come downstairs to see him off. After all, he was going to the battlefield.

He glanced toward their bedroom window, remembering how she left the candles burning for him just last night. A tightening in his groin reminded him of the love they had shared, the meeting of their hearts and bodies. Now, only a soft spring breeze fluttered the white lace curtains.

Jacob caught Miss Emma's eyes and smiled. Her look of encouragement was a bit apologetic for Savannah's absence. He knew instinctively that the old dear would share a word or two with his wife about her behavior. In spite of his bruised feelings, he hoped Miss Emma wouldn't be too hard on her. At least not as hard as he had been.

He had thought Savannah had finally gotten the courage to share the secrets she had been hiding. Jacob had actually looked forward to her trust, especially now that he could finally begin to put the murders to rest. Instead of honesty, she had invented a far-fetched tale of time travel. It was hard for any rational person to believe, even though many of the things she had said seemed to add up. As difficult as it was to admit, Jacob realized he wasn't certain he discounted Savannah's story. Yet he wasn't certain he believed it.

He untied the horse provided by Colonel Sanger and mounted. The animal was an unruly sorrel stallion with a flaxen mane and tail the color of Savannah's own tresses. A beautiful animal— and temperamental—just like his wife. The horse began to paw and prance before Jacob could settle into the saddle. Controlling a feisty animal caused him no worry. Controlling a feisty woman did.

At the far end of town, he heard Sanger's convoy of wagons begin to move out. A rebel yell sounded as the ambulances, soldiers, and horses began their journey.

He could wait no longer. It was time to go.

Jacob cast a last furtive look at the porch, but knew Savannah was not there. She was probably still up in their room crying because he refused to believe her. He didn't blame her for not coming to say good-bye. He could only hope she would forgive him when he returned.

The convoy made slow time as Jacob rode the sorrel near the front of eight ambulance wagons. Sanger and several of his men rode ahead of him. He glanced back at the trail of wagons and noted the group was limited to the drivers, Sanger, his men, and himself. All appearances had to show they were a medical detail on the way to the battlefield. A full patrol might raise a few eyebrows.

Although they had to travel a little more than forty miles, the convoy would move throughout the night, stopping only to water the animals. Jacob stood in the saddle to flex his legs. They had already been riding for more than six hours. If the battle was already raging as Sanger claimed, it certainly couldn't last much longer. A cold chill shuddered through Jacob as he thought of the destruction of men that lay ahead.

The sun had long since gone down and a bright full moon began to rise in its place. Heavy clouds drifted across the sky, occasionally blocking the limited moonlight. Once again Jacob's thoughts turned toward Savannah and the haunting memory of her lies. The educated man in him said it wasn't possible. There was simply no way she could have come from the year 1996. He pulled his father's finely crafted watch from his jacket and rubbed the gold etching, as he often did when something worried him. Looking at it carefully, he considered again what Savannah had said. Would the watch show up at some antique store in the future? He shrugged, supposing it was possible. If he were to believe that though, surely it meant he believed her story. He wasn't prepared to go that far. No, his rational side knew that whatever she was involved with had to be terribly serious if it merited such a convoluted explanation.

Jacob placed the watch back into his coat pocket. The night Savannah had given herself to him, the night she had reminded him how much he needed someone, he had promised he would believe her carefully hidden secrets. In spite of his promise, her story didn't deserve his unconditional trust. Surely she didn't expect him to believe it? It was too wild, too far-fetched.

He dropped his chin to consider the ground passing underneath the steady motion of the horse. Shame nagged at his conscience. He told her he would believe her, so why would she come up with something so amazing unless . . . unless she was telling the truth?

Her medical knowledge was certainly far superior to any he had known. He prided himself as one of the best physicians around, yet she practiced medicine with an advanced expertise and knew things he had never considered. Perhaps aspirin *was* from France, but how did she know about it? Where had she learned about pressure points? What about this cardiopulmonary resuscitation? CPR she had called it. Ely would have died had Savannah not intervened. Each day, he had learned something new. He shook his head, frustrated. No, her story could not possibly be true.

Jacob's eyes narrowed as Sanger pulled out from his men and roughly reined his horse around to ride beside him.

"How is your mount, Doctor?" Sanger smirked, obviously knowing the temperament of the unruly sorrel. "I understand you have an appreciation for fine horses. I chose him just for you." He popped his crop on the rump of his own mount, the sudden noise causing both horses to startle and prance.

Jacob quickly soothed the nervous stallion. "We've reached an understanding, Colonel. I'm pleased with him."

Irritation flickered in the colonel's eyes, then disappeared. "I imagine you are quite tired from your ride to Memphis," he said casually. "Did you have a pleasant journey?"

"Yes," Jacob replied. "It was most informative. Certainly worth the trouble of going." He met Sanger's steady stare with a bemused grin. He had the facts on the colonel, and, if all went well, it wouldn't be long before Sanger made his own trip to join the boy in prison.

"What did you say your business was in Memphis?" Sanger adjusted the leather reins in his gloved hands without looking at Jacob. The moon came through the clouds, casting an eerie glow on the colonel's blond hair.

"I didn't, Colonel. Why do you ask?" Jacob countered. He knew he was baiting Sanger but he didn't care. There was pleasure in watching the other man's discomfort.

Sanger didn't answer as he tried to appear cool. They continued to ride along in silence.

When Jacob heard about the liveryman's "bar fight," he figured Sanger surely suspected the purpose of his journey. Now, his suspicions were confirmed. The colonel could barely conceal his anxiousness.

"I'll be perfectly frank, Doctor," Sanger said in cold, clipped tones. "Your hospital has been receiving shipments of vital medications. Medications that are very difficult to obtain through the Confederacy. One in particular has all indications of being a Yankee product." He paused with a glance at Jacob's reaction.

"Since such supplies would normally come through my command, I question where you got them." Sanger turned in the saddle to stare at Jacob. He smiled smugly, as if he held all the cards in a high-stakes poker game.

"Should I so much as suspect," he stressed the unspoken meaning, "that you or someone in your hospital is receiving supplies in exchange for espionage activities, I can arrest you. Do I make myself perfectly clear, Doctor?"

"Perfectly, Colonel," Jacob returned with a controlled smile, his eyes narrowing almost to slits. "You have no idea why I went to Memphis and you're worried. In fact, you're threatening me."

"Oh, no, Doctor," Sanger said with practiced innocence. "I'm letting you know the outcome of rash behavior."

"You don't scare me, Sanger," Jacob replied, maintaining his calm demeanor. "Your kind never has." He turned his attention back to the road and began humming a tune. He could feel the tension in the air as Sanger fought to control his rage.

"We'll be stopping shortly to water the horses," he said through clenched teeth. "Then, we'll travel through the night. You'll need to be alert in case we encounter an enemy ambush. They come out of the woods so quickly, you'll never see them. It would be wise to watch your back."

"Another threat, Colonel?"

"Of course not," he replied tightly. "Merely a warning for your safety. I—"

"Colonel Sanger!" A soldier yelled from the rear of the procession. "We've found a pretty piece of baggage stowed away in the last wagon, sir."

The colonel glanced at Jacob, his mouth forming a knowing smile. "Do you suppose it belongs to you?"

At Jacob's shrug, Sanger signaled the men to halt, then dismounted from his black horse, looking down the row of wagons expectantly.

"Take your hands off me, you moron!"

Jacob inwardly groaned when he heard the familiar female voice. What else could possibly happen? He got off his horse, rubbed a weary hand over his forehead, then stared at the approaching figures.

"She was hiding underneath the canvas in the rear ambulance. Sound asleep." The private groaned as Savannah jerked her arm from his grasp and landed a sharp whack across his face. By now, the other drivers had dismounted and walked forward to see the excitement. Laughter filled the night as the young private stumbled from Savannah's swift kick to his shin.

She stormed up to Sanger, irritation flashing on her face. "I'll thank you to have your men keep their hands to themselves, Colonel. I am not a criminal. I came to assist the wounded."

Dismissing her without a word, Sanger turned to face Jacob. "I see you cannot control your wife, Doctor. She was instructed to stay behind; now she's a stowaway on a very important mission."

Jacob glared at his wife as she rushed to his side.

"As I mentioned earlier," Sanger continued, obviously pleased by the sudden turn of events, "I have the authority to detain suspected spies. Don't doubt that I will do so. However, since your presence is required for this journey and your medical skills are needed on the battlefield, I will overlook this incident."

He bent close until his face was only inches from Savannah's. "Were you mine, pretty lady, you would not disobey me." The threat in his words was clear. Sanger quickly straightened before Jacob could push him away.

"Were I yours, Colonel, I'd gladly slit my wrists." Savannah met his glare eye for eye as muffled laughter rose from the onlooking men.

A twitching nerve under Sanger's eye grew more pronounced. "This trip is no place for a woman, and your wife is here against my wishes," the colonel stated loudly for the group to hear. "Should anything happen to her, I will accept no responsibility. Keep her out of my sight."

Spinning on his heel, Sanger strode down the line toward the rear of the wagons.

"What the hell do you think you are doing?" Jacob hissed through clenched teeth as he dragged her away from the interested ears of the men.

"Jacob! Let go! You're hurting me!" She jerked her arm from his grasp, rubbing her bruised skin. "I came to help."

"I told you to stay behind," he said angrily as he walked away from her.

"Yes, you did, but you refused to listen. Next to Gettysburg, Shiloh is one of the bloodiest battles in the war. If I remember correctly, more than twenty thousand men are going to die in only a few short days. You need my help."

"I suppose you know this because you're from the future?" he queried sarcastically. At her nod, he rolled his eyes, clenching his fists so as not to throttle her. "Don't, Savannah. Don't say a word. Don't move—don't even breathe."

She opened her mouth to speak and he placed his hand over her lips. "I ought to turn you over my knee right here in front of God and everybody. I've a good mind to do it, too, so just be quiet."

He released her, then sat down on a fallen tree at the side of the road. Minutes ticked by as he glared at her. Savannah must have recognized how far she had pushed him as she stood quietly nearby. Several times she opened her mouth to speak, then quickly closed it at his warning look.

What the hell was he to do now? Sanger had made it clear he was only waiting for an opportunity to get rid of him. He knew he had to be on constant guard for his safety. The last thing he needed was one strong-willed female to look out for, too.

Taking a deep breath to calm his temper, he stared up at his wife. "The fact that you stowed away on a very sensitive mission does not look good, Savannah," he began. "Sanger has implied that the hospital is receiving supplies thanks to a spy. That spy being you, I might add. Now, here you are."

He flashed her a stern look to silence her protest.

"He's a dangerous man, not one to be taken lightly." For the first time, Jacob saw a glitter of fear in her beautiful eyes. He continued, "I don't understand why you're here. I don't understand where you've been getting the medical supplies, or why. I don't understand why you've made up such a ludicrous story to cover your activities. But I'm warning you that Sanger will find an opportunity and use it to his advantage. We must be very careful in both our actions and speech. This time, you *will* do as I say."

He rose from the log and walked away without so much as a glance.

Oh, was she miserable! For more than an hour, Savannah had ridden behind Jacob on the back of the spirited horse. Still angry by her appearance, he had pulled her up behind him on the huge animal without raising an eyebrow at her obvious fear of the beast. Being a city girl, she had never ridden a horse in her entire life, and the initiation was not pleasant. The horse she had brushed in the barn had seemed rather tame, but not this fellow. He was positively wild. Instead of subduing his nervous temperament, Jacob seemed to take pleasure in allowing him to prance about in the darkness. Unlike Savannah, he was a relaxed, confident rider. In less than a mile, her mood—and her behind—were terribly sore. Briefly, she questioned the wisdom of her decision to stow away in the wagon. Maybe this time she had acted too rashly.

"Jacob!" she whispered in fear, grabbing his shirt for balance. "Please don't let me fall."

He reined in the sorrel, bringing him to a halt at the edge of the road. The ambulances continued to rattle past.

"It would do you good to plop right down on your rear end." Jacob looked back at her, no sympathy showing in his blue eyes. "Perhaps it would teach you to listen."

"I—I've never ridden a horse before. What am I supposed to do?"

"Hang on," he said with a chuckle, urging his

horse into a gallop to keep up with the convoy. She threw her arms about his waist and gripped him tighter.

"Jacob, please, I'm frightened. I'm going to fall!"

Again he brought the snorting horse to a halt and turned in the saddle to look at her.

"You really have never ridden, have you?" he asked, clearly shocked by her trembling.

Mutely, she shook her head. Shame circled her heart as she realized her arrogance. Simply because she was from the future, she had considered herself superior to the things of this time. There was nothing in this century, she had childishly thought, that she could not do—and do better. Now, here she was, paralyzed in terror from what Jacob considered a normal, expected, even enjoyable activity. Horses were a vital part of his world. She was definitely out of her element. Savannah cast her eyes down, suddenly ashamed to meet Jacob's concerned gaze

"Mrs. Cross must rest a minute," he called to the passing soldiers. "We'll catch up before you're out of sight."

At their nod, he lifted her from the saddle, depositing her gently on the soft dew-covered grass beside the road. "I can't believe you've never learned to ride."

She sat silently for a moment, then looked up as he got back on the horse. He waited patiently, obviously expecting an explanation. "Where I'm from, we drive cars for transportation," she began awkwardly. "Those who ride do it for enjoyment rather than necessity." She rubbed her sore rear end. "Although I can't see how anyone enjoys it. It's too hard on the posterior."

He smiled then. "How do you drive this car?"

Hope replaced her fear. Perhaps he was beginning to think what she told him might be true. "I can't tell you all the ins and outs because I don't understand it completely myself. Basically, it's a horseless carriage made of metal with four rubber tires. People sit inside while an engine powers it, making it travel up to one hundred miles an hour. Sometimes more."

"What? More than one hundred miles in an hour? You jest."

Although it was dark, she could see the laughter in his eyes. She glared at him. "Yes, that fast. Far better than your old slowpoke horse. And it has cushioned seats."

Their eyes locked in challenge. Suddenly, he wheeled the horse within inches of her. Before she could protest, Jacob reached down and pulled her back up on the horse.

"Cars, indeed," he said tightly as he spurred the horse into a gallop to catch up with the moving wagons.

On into the night they moved silently, covering mile after mile. She and Jacob rode without speaking. Finally, out of exhaustion, she dozed. Her arms were still wrapped tightly about his waist as she leaned her cheek against his back. The horse had settled, and his constant movement was now relaxing, even a bit soothing.

In her semi-conscious state, she thought about the events of the past few hours. Jacob's eyes had been unfathomable as he had watched her approach with the rude private. She knew he would be angry that she had hidden in the ambulance, but she was not sorry. He had no idea what he was about to face, and he would need her help with the wounded. She had left Miss Emma a note explaining her absence and instructions to prepare the hospital for their return. More importantly, if Sanger was now threatening them as Jacob said, there was no telling what he might try. Yes, Jacob definitely needed her.

Their earlier conversation about cars flickered through her mind. Savannah longed to continue their talk, but knew she must wait until Jacob was ready. Oddly, she wasn't angry that he couldn't fulfill his promise to believe her secret. He had tried to find some explanation to account for what she said, something more logical, and Savannah had expected it. That's what had happened to her in the beginning, too.

She had dropped a bombshell on him. He needed time to adjust.

Jacob guided his horse alongside the military wagon train. The moon shown bright as the crickets and katydids called their songs. The road traveled through the midst of overgrown woods, and the gently blowing wind caused the rustling leaves to add a melody. In the distance, fireflies sporadically sparked their signal. Even the tired men traveling with him sensed the deceptive peace of the night.

Seeing Savannah had shocked him. Never before had he known such a woman, a woman who would have the courage to steal away on a dangerous journey just to be with her husband. Certainly Anna never would have done such a thing. Anna had been far too timid, far too proper for such a thing.

Proper.

He shook his head as he thought about the woman resting against his back. Her grip around his waist had loosened, yet her warm body was tightly drawn up against him. The proper thing would be to ride off into the woods and take her into his arms, to show her how their differences could be resolved. If only she would tell him where she had truly gotten the aspirin and morphine. Her body near his felt so right. But if she couldn't be trusted, what did they really have?

Nothing, he thought sadly. Nothing at all.

Suddenly, a thought left him cold. She believed she knew the outcome of this battle and was insistent he would need her skills. What if she were right? What if the battle ahead turned out to be one of the worst battles of the war? Would that prove she knew the future? Would that mean her incredible story was true? Of course not. Jacob shook his head, irritated the thought had even crossed his mind.

His muscles tightened as Savannah suddenly stirred. Jacob brought the horse to a halt so she could step down for a minute and stretch her legs.

He dismounted as well, nodding to the sleepy ambulance drivers as they continued by. Earlier, he had overheard two drivers talking about how the group would not see the ravages of war until they were almost to the battlefield.

He looked toward Savannah standing quietly under a large oak. She stared up at the tree deep in thought, seemingly oblivious to anyone around her. The moonlight filtering through the branches reached her face reminding Jacob of an angel. He sensed the prospect of morning terrified her, though she tried to hide it. The desire to protect her was overwhelming. He hadn't been there to protect Anna, but now he swore that no harm would come to Savannah. Sanger had almost destroyed him once. He'd be damned if it would happen again.

Jacob approached the vision from behind, standing close without touching her. For a minute he thought she was unaware of his presence. Then she slowly turned and lifted her lips to his. Ever so gently, he met her request, his lips brushing hers like the moonlight. He stood motionless as she withdrew and gazed into his eyes. This woman claimed he needed her. Yet she was silently telling him how much she needed him. It took every ounce of self-control he possessed not to crush her body to his and kiss away her fears. She wanted him to; it was on her face. But she had told him a horrendous lie, expected him to believe it, and then disobeyed him by coming along on this mission.

Suddenly annoyed, he turned toward the horse

and held out his hand to her. "We shouldn't let the convoy get too far ahead. You never know when Yanks could be hiding in the trees."

Disappointment shadowed her face as she stepped toward the horse. Jacob relented. Lifting her chin, he dropped a quick kiss on her soft lips. "You can sit in front of me for a while. It will be easier for you to sleep."

"Savannah," Jacob whispered in her ear. "Wake up. We're getting close to the encampment. You need to be alert in case of danger." Instantly, she woke from her fitful doze. She sat upright in the saddle, causing Jacob to shiver as his body lost her warmth.

"How much longer?" she asked, smoothing her tresses with a trembling hand.

"Close."

It was still dark, but pink streaks were beginning to lighten the sky. The quietness of the woods was eerie. The crickets and katydids had ceased their songs. Not even an occasional call of an owl indicated life anywhere around. Even the soft night breeze was gone.

Suddenly, a sharp chirping sound came from the bushes. Colonel Sanger returned the call with one of his own. After a long moment, a solitary man on a tired old horse emerged from the woods. One of the men nearby cocked his gun as the stranger approached the colonel.

Savannah and Jacob had been riding near the front of the group, but they were too far away to hear what Sanger and the man discussed in whispered tones. The man glanced back as Sanger pointed toward Jacob and Savannah.

The two pulled from the front and rode back toward them. Jacob recognized Sanger's irritation. Instinctively, his arms tightened around his wife. The men stopped next to Jacob's horse. "Doctor"—Sanger's words were quiet and tense—"you will ride with the sentry. He will take you directly to the field hospital. It's in a church not far from here."

The sentry gave a quick salute to Jacob.

"That's not necessary, soldier!" Sanger snapped with derision. "The good doctor is a civilian."

Jacob glared at Sanger but remained quiet. The sentry spoke quickly to cover his blunder. "I've been sent to advise the colonel of a change of plans. The battle has been more vicious that we supposed. There are many wounded and many more dead from the last encounter with the enemy. Your help is required at the hospital.

"There's talk of possible surrender at another church about eight miles away," the sentry added, turning back toward Sanger. "We've had serious rain the past three days, and there have been heavy losses on both sides. No one seems to know what will happen next, but my orders say we have to be prepared for another encounter this morning."

"You've said quite enough, soldier," Sanger retorted in a rushed whisper. He turned to Jacob. "We must take the munitions directly to the field. The ambulances will follow after we unload. You are to assist however you can, then ready the men and ambulances to return to St. George."

Expecting his orders to be followed without question, Sanger turned and motioned to his men. The sentry nodded his head, indicating that Jacob should follow. The convoy of ambulances began to move forward on the road as they pulled out of line and headed toward the woods. Savannah placed a shaky hand on his as he guided the horse through the trees.

"Be brave," he whispered.

Chapter Eleven

A soft persistent knock sounded at the door.

"Who could that be at this time of morning?" Miss Emma wondered aloud as she came down the stairs holding a lighted candlestick. It was just past five, not yet dawn. The hospital was still quiet except for the snores of the slumbering soldiers. It was time to start breakfast, not entertain visitors. She turned to Deltry, who followed her down the polished staircase.

"Go ahead and gather the eggs, Deltry. I'll get the door. It's probably someone needing to see Jacob." At Deltry's nod, she continued, "I certainly hope it's not serious since neither he nor Savannah are here. I still can't believe her note, especially after Jacob told her to stay behind." She smiled in spite of her irritation. "I'm glad we won't be around when Jacob finds her."

"That's the truth, Miz Em," Deltry agreed. "That's the truth." She disappeared toward the back door as the rap came again.

"Coming," Miss Emma called lightly. She glanced at the sleeping soldiers. The noise had not disturbed a single one. Moving to the thick door, she pulled it open. "I'm sorry to make you wait," she said before it had fully opened. "I do hope you haven't come to see the doctor. He has gone to help with the wounded and won't be back for a few days."

In the darkness of the morning, Miss Emma could barely see the figure standing before her. She squinted her eyes and adjusted her spectacles for a better look. "May I help you?" she asked cautiously.

An enormous, oddly dressed woman stepped into the light of the candle. "Yes, ma'am," she said politely. "I am here to see Savannah."

"Indeed?" Miss Emma responded with interest, lifting her eyebrow.

Savannah could hear the sounds of cannon fire in the distance. It was barely dawn, the pink sky peeking through the trees. She wondered if the battle had lessened during the night and was now growing again in intensity.

"Sanger told me that we won't be going that close to the actual battle," Jacob said in her ear. "There is a church nearby that's being used as a temporary field hospital. We're going there to help with the wounded until they unload the munitions and bring us the wagons. Then we'll take as many wounded as we can back to St. George."

Savannah nodded but remained silent. She was frightened, but not as terribly as Jacob seemed to believe. More apprehensive. It made her nervous to consider how many men had already died in this two-day battle.

"I wish I could prepare you for what you're going to see," Jacob continued, mistaking her silence for fear. "I'm afraid it will be the true brutality of war. The horror of men killing men. You'll see why I didn't want you to come."

In spite of his concern, annoyance irked her. "If you want me to be sorry I stowed away, I'm not!" she snapped at him, tossing her hair over her shoulder. "You are going to need help, and I'm a skilled nurse." The gallant man riding behind her was used to women of his time, she supposed, not someone who had seen all types of death and dying in an emergency room. She turned in the saddle, bringing her face inches from his. "As a matter of fact, I've seen some pretty gruesome stuff back in my century."

Jacob rolled his eyes. He tightened the reins, causing the sorrel to dance nervously. Savannah quickly straightened in her seat and grabbed Jacob's arms to steady herself.

"What about the men back at the hospital?" he asked in annoyance. "They need you far more than I will."

"There was no one in immediate danger. Miss Emma and the medics can tend to them. We'll be back soon anyway. Face it, Jacob, you need me.

Even though you're angry right now, you're glad I'm here."

"Will you place a wager on that, ma'am?" he drawled in a deeply accented voice.

Savannah leaned forward in the saddle, then slammed her body into Jacob's chest with enough force to knock the wind out of him. "That'll teach you to tangle with me, Doctor." Savannah giggled as Jacob took several deep breaths.

Instead of growing angrier as she figured, Jacob grinned. "With your medical training, I suppose I am glad you're here," he admitted. "That doesn't mean I'm not going to worry about you. You have a distinct knack for getting into trouble."

She smiled as the horse made its way through the brush. "Yes, I guess I do."

"I overheard Sanger say earlier that we've won this battle. It's just a matter of surrender. I don't know if I believe him. The sound of that cannon fire is still too strong."

Savannah nodded but remained quiet. She had tried to tell him about this battle. He had refused to listen. She wasn't about to bring it up again, not when it seemed they had finally called their own truce.

"If you're from the future, you should know the outcome of this battle," he pressed skeptically. "Have we won it?"

She glanced over her shoulder to gauge the seriousness of his expression. Was he baiting her, or did he really want to know? His eyes were dark, unreadable. Savannah bit her lip, suddenly unwilling to risk his ridicule.

"Just as I thought," he said tightly. "You have no idea."

The sentry leading the way broke through the forest into a clearing. Still uncertain of how to respond, Savannah rested her hands on Jacob's lean fingers.

Only a few short words and Jacob had made the decision for her. She might be able to prove herself to him using this unfortunate battle.

"It's hard for me to remember my history studies," she said softly. "But I do remember Shiloh. This battle and Gettysburg had the highest casualty numbers throughout the entire war. I don't know how many of them were Confederates."

"Did we win this particular battle?"

"Although it's not far from Memphis, it's been a long time since I visited Shiloh National Monument. As I remember, both sides claimed it a victory. The Yankees will get reinforcements from up the river just in the nick of time," she whispered.

"Shiloh National Monument?" Jacob questioned cautiously.

"Yes. About all of the major battlefields in both the North and South become national landmarks. It's part of our heritage."

He was silent as they rode along. She turned around and saw his furrowed brow.

"Does the North eventually succumb to the Confederacy?" Jacob asked after a moment.

She sat motionless as they broke through the tree line into the clearing. The church was just ahead, its white steeple crushed by artillery fire. How could she tell the man she loved that his country was being torn apart, and that his army was not going to win their cause? Was it even her right to tell him the future? She sat quietly, hoping he wouldn't ask again.

Her silence must have answered his question. "How long before it happens?"

Savannah closed her eyes as her internal struggle grew. She had no choice but to answer him. It was her only way to convince him she was from the future. "General Lee will surrender at Appomattox on April 9, 1864, two years from now," she replied quietly, almost hoping he wouldn't hear.

He rode along without acknowledging her words. She glanced back at him to see a worried frown marring his face. "Are you all right?"

Nodding his head, he sighed. "I suppose I've known all along."

"Does that mean you believe what happened to me? Do you accept that I came from the future?"

His mouth tightened to a thin line. "I don't know what to believe."

There was one thing Savannah would never forget, not even if she was sent back to her own time. That was the sound of men moaning in agony. The wind carried it like a siren. The sound of the dying became louder as they approached the church. Nothing in her emergency room training could have prepared her for the shock of what she saw as they broke through the trees. Row after row of wounded men, at least 300, probably more, lay on the ground. Some without arms, some without legs, some on the verge of death, some already with their Maker.

Jacob and she quickly dismounted and hurried to the church. Inside, an older man was removing a boot from a prone soldier. "At least he's unconscious," he said to another man working nearby. They were both dressed in the uniforms of Confederate medical officers, including blood-stained green sashes around their waists. Each man looked worn and tired, leaving Savannah to wonder how long it had been since either had slept. Glancing up at the open door, the first, a wiry-looking older man, caught sight of her.

"What's a woman doing here?" he demanded, his hand reaching for his forceps.

"You must be one of the regiment surgeons," Jacob responded, crossing the room with three strides. "I'm Dr. Cross. This is my wife. She's a . . ." His unblinking blue eyes locked with hers, a slight smile meant only for her lifted the corners of his mouth. "She's also a trained doctor. We understood you needed all the help you could get."

Savannah was stunned by Jacob's comment. All her life she had longed to hear the very words he so proudly announced. Love for him swelled in her heart.

The worn man looked baffled but didn't object. "I'm Major Reynolds. This is Major Smythe. Pardon us for not shaking your hand." He motioned toward the rows of bloodied bodies before him as he and Major Smythe laughed at the weak joke. "We heard you were coming in from St. George to pick up some of the wounded. It's a wonder any are still alive after all this butchery."

He turned back to the bootless man on the table. "Never met a female doctor," he added, glaring at Savannah. "You should be home making bandages, young lady, not out here in this horror."

"We've brought morphine," Jacob said quickly, sending Savannah a warning glance to keep her mouth shut. "Morphine, laudanum, and a mild pain reliever called aspirin."

"Thank God you're here is all I can say." Dr. Smythe cast a relieved smile to Savannah. "Can you and Dr. Cross see to the men in the corner? The group we're tending came in this morning. I haven't had time to check them since yesterday."

With a nod, Savannah and Jacob headed toward the other wounded.

"Go sparingly with your painkillers," he instructed. "No matter how much you brought, there are far too many men who need it."

It was early afternoon before Savannah was able to glance around the church, to see it for the first time. Like many of the men outside, the church, too, was a casualty of war. Its white-washed walls were splattered with blood. Empty windowpanes, one on each side of the building, held the shattered remnants of once-beautiful stained glass. A gaping hole in the ceiling opened the room to the sky, the crushed white steeple clearly visible through the opening. Dozens of polished wooden pews had been moved to one side, stacked to the ceiling in some places. The seats were too narrow to use as beds, but a few men were stretched on their uncomfortable length. Savannah's gaze roamed further. Only the altar remained the same, almost untouched by the brutality around it. A barefoot private in a badly torn uniform kneeled nearby, his head bent, his eyes closed. It was Sunday, she realized.

Jacob was right. She was not prepared for the realities of war. Neither was he. Nor was a single soul in this church. Nor those out there pulling the triggers. She felt a tug at her hem. Kneeling down, Savannah weakly smiled at the man lying on the floor. "Let's take a look at that wound, soldier."

"I'm going to check those outside," Jacob said, walking up as she began to clean shrapnel from a nasty gash in the man's side. "Call if you need me." He touched her shoulder as if knowing she was already exhausted. Nodding silently, she rubbed a tired arm across her eyes as Jacob made his way to the door.

"I told you this was no place for a woman," Major Reynolds called, smirking as she stood to stretch her back.

She glowered at him before turning her attention back to her charge. Try as she might, there seemed to be no way to be sterile. If she so much as headed for the water bucket, Major Reynolds would tilt an eyebrow with smug satisfaction.

"Just like a woman," he had snickered hours ago when she had made her first trip to wash her hands. "Always cleaning."

Ignoring the irritating man, she had continued

to wash between patients as best she could. It pleased her to see Jacob was doing the same. At least he took that seriously. Sighing, she focused her attention back on stitching the gash.

Without a doubt, Savannah Stuart Cross had more backbone and stamina than any woman he had ever met. Jacob glanced back at Savannah as he walked toward another group of men lying near the steps of the church. Admittedly, he had thought she would not be able to handle the gruesomeness of what lay before them. He had been wrong, he realized, shaking his head in amazement. At least on the outside Savannah had never flinched. She had worked as hard as the other doctors and never once stopped to rest or to complain.

Unfortunately, that only added to the possibility that her story might be true. She was certainly not the typical woman of his time. The soldiers in the hospital had often told stories of female bravery on the front. More often than not, the majority of women stayed home to run the farm. Praying for their husbands, sons, and brothers and making bandages was about the extent of their involvement in the effort. There was nothing wrong with that, though. It was his way of life, something he had never questioned. Now, this one small courageous woman gave him a new view of the fairer sex. Was that how all women were in the future?

Throughout the day, she had treated soldier after soldier without stopping to eat the meager dinner set aside for her. He had told her to rest for a minute but as usual, she had refused to obey him. There were too many suffering men, she had said, too much pain and agony for her to rest. Scrutinizing the scene around him, he understood only too well what she meant. Men littered the church grounds with everything from bloody musket and bayonet wounds to gruesome stumps of limbs blown off in action, or worse, limbs amputated with no anesthetic. There were even several tragic cases of dementia.

The rumble of approaching horses sounded down the road. Looking up, he saw Sanger and his men bringing the ambulances. Sanger's face was alert but relaxed, indicating the munitions had been safely delivered. Briefly, Jacob wondered why the colonel had not sent the ambulances on without him and stayed on the battlefield. Military reasons, he supposed, or cowardly ones. He turned his attention back to yet another soldier.

"We have wounded!" Sanger called casually as he rode his horse directly into a crowd of wounded cowering on the ground. His tired horse jerked, trying to avoid stepping on them, but it was no use. A howl went up from one of the men. Irritated, Sanger looked down, as if seeing the fellow for the first time. He backed his horse away without so much as an apology. The man shook his fist at Sanger's turned back.

Sanger dismounted as several stewards rushed to the wagons and began unloading the new arrivals. Jacob followed them, pushing his way through, barking instructions about each soldier after a quick examination.

"Doctor."

Jacob did not look up at the sound of Sanger's voice, but continued to go from body to body, checking the extent of injuries.

"Doctor!" Sanger repeated, his voice more forceful.

"What is it, Sanger? Is what you have to say more important than these men?" Jacob went on to the next person, still refusing to acknowledge the colonel.

"Doctor, I don't give a damn about your concerns," he stated cruelly. Jacob was astonished and noted that the men nearby were, too. "We will move out at dusk. Have the wagons full with those you're taking with us." Turning his back, he stepped away from the ambulance.

Instantly, Jacob grabbed the colonel's arm and jerked him around until he and Sanger stood face-to-face. Stunned, the colonel stepped back as Jacob brought his face inches from the blond man's. Without touching his still-immaculate uniform, Jacob used the force of his stare to push the colonel back against the wagon. Fear showed on the colonel's face, although his eyes narrowed to hide it.

"No, Colonel," Jacob said in a low, threatening voice. "I am not a member of your army. You will not order me to do anything. These men are dying. They need medical attention. There are too many here to be ready by dusk. Yesterday, I came at your call. Today, we are not bound by a rushed schedule. *I* will let *you* know when we are ready to leave." Jacob backed up a step, releasing Sanger from the wagon.

Taking a deep breath, the colonel regained his composure by arrogantly locking eyes with the onlooking men. One by one, he stared them down until, with a nervous cough, each lowered his gaze.

"A simple explanation would have sufficed, Doctor," he said tightly, adjusting the sleeves of his uniform. "There is the threat of Yankee ambushes on the return journey to St. George. Several have occurred on the road we traveled. I want to avoid the danger, especially since your lovely wife is traveling with us." He looked at Jacob, stressing each word deliberately, his lip curling in a dastardly grin.

"Take as much time as you need, Doctor, keeping in mind that we will be safer traveling at night."

Turning on his heels, Sanger walked toward the church. Several snickers came from a small group several yards away. He stopped, sending a menacing glare toward the offenders. The titters were silenced as quickly as they had arisen, and the colonel continued his pace.

The wagons moved out, carrying the pain of almost a hundred men. Each of the eight wooden wagons had bunks for eight men. They had patched up many during the day and sent them back to the battle, but still, there were so many seriously wounded. Jacob couldn't leave them. It was certain death. So, the men were packed in tightly, sometimes two to a bunk, as they started their journey back to St. George.

It was just past midnight when the wheels began to roll, Sanger impatiently in the lead. His men rode silently beside him, occasionally glancing back to check the progress of the wagons. Savannah had not objected when Jacob ordered her to ride beside one of the wagon drivers. His horse was still unruly, and he doubted she wanted to make the long ride home behind him on the saddle. Plus, the sky was about to let loose with a torrential rainstorm. Jacob reined to a halt at the side of the road as a streak of lightning flashed overhead. He watched silently as several teams of tired horses pulled the ambulances along. His eyes squinted in the dark to catch sight of his beautiful wife. Knowing how tired she was, he was not surprised to see her leaning on the arm of the driver, already dozing.

"She's all right, Doc," Caleb, the driver, called softly. "She's worked so hard. She needs a little rest."

Jacob smiled his thanks as the wagons rumbled by. Allowing all eight to pass, he settled in behind the convoy, surprised that the sorrel he was riding had calmed down to a steady walk. He was glad Savannah could get a little rest. It was going to be tough going for some of the wounded. He would need her. He rubbed his hand wearily over the stubble on his chin. There was no way he could rest. The lives of too many men were at stake. Each jolt of the wagon caused a series of pain-ridden groans that hurt him as it did the men.

He also saw the look in Sanger's eye. As a doctor, Jacob had seen the eyes of many men. The happiness of seeing a newborn child for the first time; the fear when that child has been hurt or is in danger; even the resignation when a man accepts his own death.

Sanger's eyes were different. They held revenge.

Jacob had embarrassed him in front of the wounded. Most were privates and corporals, men Sanger considered to be his inferiors. For that reason alone, the colonel would get even. Plus, if Sanger had any idea about the sealed envelope carefully hidden in Jacob's desk, Jacob was certain his eyes would read murder.

Jacob's grip unconsciously tightened on the reins, causing the sorrel to toss his head angrily and to sidestep down the road. "Easy boy," Jacob murmured, stroking its neck with his gloved hand. The horse settled down to a walk.

He and Savannah had been through so much over the past twenty-four hours. Seeing the damaged church for the first time with all the wounded men lying outside on the ground had a chilling effect on both of them. Jacob had offered to stay behind and help the two doctors, but his offer was refused. "No, son," Major Smythe had said. "There are eight doctors up at the battle lines and two of us back here. That's enough. We would rather see you take as many of these boys as you can back to your hospital."

As he turned to walk away, Major Smythe had grabbed his sleeve. "Send us morphine when you can spare it. That would help the most." Jacob had opened his bag and gave him most of what he had brought. "I'll get more to you, sir. You have my word."

Rain began to pour as they traveled into the night, each step bringing them closer to St. George. In spite of the storm, the drivers were alert to the woods around them. Sanger had said this road was notorious for Yankee ambushes, and the men had taken him seriously.

Jacob glanced up against the wind as one of Sanger's men came into view. He was one of the more pleasant men in Sanger's command, a young fellow who had introduced himself as Louis. He waited on the road for the wagons to pass, then joined Jacob and the other two sentries at the rear.

"Doctor." Louis spoke in a friendly voice, rain dripping off the brim of his hat. "The colonel sent me to advise you that we will be stopping shortly to water the horses. He assumed you would like to check the wounded."

"Thank you, Private," Jacob answered.

They rode in silence for a few minutes. Several times, the private opened his mouth to speak, then closed it without saying a word.

"Was there something else, Private?"

"Well . . ." The young man hesitated, clearly unsure of whether to proceed. "The men have been talking . . ."

"Yes?"

Glancing back to ensure the three sentries behind them were out of earshot, the private continued, "It's just that . . . well, we just wanted to let you know that we admire you for standing up to the colonel the way you did."

Although he was surprised, Jacob merely shrugged.

"I know he's my commanding officer and all," the private went on, slowly shaking his head, "but he's got one hell of a mean streak. We were glad somebody brought him down a notch or two," he finished awkwardly. "It needed to be done."

"You're right," Jacob agreed, "he does have a mean streak."

The long line of wagons came to a slow halt.

"The colonel and I will be scouting for Yankees while we're stopped." He spoke loud enough for the other sentries to hear. Then, guiding his mount next to the sorrel, he spoke again, this time lowering his voice for only Jacob to hear. "One more thing, sir. Watch out for him. You showed him up back at the church. That means he'll get even. He always does. You can bet on it."

The young man spurred his horse and galloped through the mud toward the woods to their rear.

Quickly and efficiently, the drivers began to water their horses. A creek ran near the road, offering sweet water to quench the thirst of the long journey. The rain lessened, but the black sky overhead offered no moonlight.

Jacob needed to check the more seriously wounded men, but all he could think of was Savannah. If the young private was right, and Sanger had something planned, she might be in jeopardy, especially considering the colonel's blatant desire for her. Grabbing a lantern from the rear wagon, Jacob rushed to the front of the convoy. His heart raced. How foolish it was to let her out of his sight. She had been riding in the third wagon near the front, closer to Sanger than to him. Jumping from the horse, he rushed around to the driver's seat. Empty. *Where was she?*

"Dr. Cross." Colonel Sanger approached from the darkness, a calculating smile lifting his lips. "I assumed you would be checking the men."

"Where is Savannah?"

"Your wife has disobeyed you again?" he asked, sarcasm dripping from his words. "You really must take a firm hand with a headstrong woman like Savannah."

"If anything has happened to her, Sanger . . ." Jacob let his words drop off, but his threat was clear.

"I can assure you that Mrs. Cross will always be safe in my care, Doctor," Sanger replied smoothly.

"If you two are quite through, I would appreciate some help," Savannah snapped, coming up from the first two wagons in time to overhear their conversation. "Not only are we soaked to the bone, we have wounded men here. This is not the time for you two to stand around letting testosterone and that lousy Y chromosome rule your heads."

They stared at her in confusion.

"Colonel, I believe your men are waiting for you

to scout the area. And you"—she turned to Jacob—"I thought we stopped so you could check the wounded."

With a tip of his hat and a snicker, Sanger headed toward his waiting men.

"Where were you?" Jacob snapped as soon as Sanger was out of earshot. "And what, may I ask, is a Y chromosome?"

"It's that part of a man that makes him act like a jerk. The part that makes you think you have to protect me from danger," she answered his second question first, poking her finger into his chest with each word. "I was in the wagon tending to the men. I know enough to avoid him, Jacob. Give me some credit."

Jacob lifted the lantern to stare down at her face only inches from his. The rain and the light combined to cause a pale aura about her golden hair. God, she was beautiful. Beautiful and gutsy. Of its own volition, his head bent, allowing his lips to touch the soft, damp smoothness. As the heat of her flesh met his, a familiar burning began in his groin. It had only been two days since he had held her in his arms, but it felt like a lifetime. He couldn't wait any longer. He had to kiss his wife and kiss her thoroughly. He had to feel the warmth of her breath caressing his skin if only for a moment.

Savannah started to protest as he pulled her away from the lantern into the shadows of the trees. Jacob silenced her, putting his finger to her lips. He encircled her with his arms and brought the full force of his body up to hers, searing in her

317

mind what he craved. They were both soaked from the driving rain, yet the heat of their bodies chased away the chill.

Winding his fingers through her long hair, Jacob again lowered his face to kiss the raindrops from her cheeks. Her irritation melted as her mouth widened to meet his. For a brief moment they stood entwined, hidden by the low-hanging branches.

"Jacob," she protested softly, "there are wounded."

For a second, her words didn't register. It had been so easy to lose himself in her arms. To forget the horror of what they had just been through. To forget her story of being from the future. To forget Sanger and this blasted war.

But she was right. They had almost a hundred men in their care. There was no time to get carried away. He lifted his head and smiled regretfully. "You're right, of course."

Standing on her toes, Savannah answered him with a light kiss and a smile that promised all he longed for. She stroked her fingers along the side of his neck. "We have forever, Jacob. Some of these men might not—"

Suddenly, a nearby shot rang out from the silence of the night.

Savannah jumped, clinging to Jacob's shirt. He could see the terror in her eyes before a mask of calm came over her. She turned for the wagons, clearly expecting him to follow.

"No," he whispered firmly. "You stay here until I see what's going on. It could be an ambush. Stay

318

hidden until it's safe." He looked deeply into her eyes. "If anything happened to you, I'd never forgive myself. Neither would Miss Emma. Will you promise to stay put? Please?" He gripped her arms tightly, bruising the soft flesh underneath her blouse.

Something must have been in his eyes, he thought, because she nodded quietly as a commotion began around the wagons.

"We need Dr. Cross!" a voice called from the distance.

With one last glance at Savannah, Jacob quickly headed toward the excitement.

"Dr. Cross," Colonel Sanger called, leading his horse behind him. "A man's been shot. I didn't see anyone, but it has to be an enemy attack. Probably scouts or a small band of soldiers." He gave the reins of his horse to a waiting sentry. "Follow me and stay down. You never know what awaits."

Briefly, Jacob questioned the safety of walking into a darkened woods with Sanger. He did not have a pistol, and there would be no way to protect himself. He would be completely at the mercy of the colonel. Still, a man lay dying out there. He had to go; he was sworn to save lives.

"This way," Sanger whispered as he crouched along.

They were less than one hundred yards from the wagons, but the night was dark and the undergrowth so dense, Jacob could not see anything but the man beside him. Sanger moved along with stealth, with a confidence that indicated he was good at this.

Instantly, Jacob sensed Sanger was not afraid. He was not creeping along as cautiously as someone who was wary of being shot. Sanger was about to make his move.

Clutching his small medical bag tightly, Jacob foolishly realized he had been set up with careful cunning. There probably wasn't even a wounded man out there. He had followed Sanger willingly into a trap. Sanger could get rid of him with virtually no questions asked. He had nothing with which to protect himself except Savannah's stainless steel scalpels.

They heard a muffled groan. Instantly, Sanger was alert.

A break in the clouds sent moonlight streaming through the trees. Jacob saw the body of a man lying face up in a small muddy clearing. He brushed by the colonel. It was Louis, the same private who had warned him earlier, barely breathing but still alive. Even in the patchy illumination, Jacob could see a huge red patch of blood covering his side. The young man's dark eyes filled with pain. He looked up to Jacob, trying to speak. No words would form.

"Don't talk, son. We'll get you out of here." He kneeled to loosen the man's uniform and inspect the wound.

"I'm afraid that won't be possible, Doctor," Sanger said, moving to stand behind him.

"Explain, Sanger."

"I shot him." Sanger shrugged calmly. "With this." He held up a Union pistol. At Jacob's incredulous stare, he recited a carefully planned statement. "We were ambushed by a band of Yankee soldiers. It must have been a small group, because when they saw our numbers, they retreated before we could apprehend them. Not before they got two of our men, though, one of my sentries and the brave doctor who went to save him."

Jacob heard the cock of the gun and felt something hard pressed against his back. "If you'll kindly step this way, Doctor."

Jacob had done it to her again, Savannah realized. Whenever the going got tough, he ordered her to stay behind. This time though, she had been scared. When the shot had rung out of the darkness, she had had no idea if the bullet had been destined for them. Jacob had evoked her promise to stay before she had been able to think clearly.

She stood alone in the forest, the same place where Jacob had so thoroughly kissed her. Savannah ran her tongue along her bottom lip, still feeling the pressure of Jacob's touch. The darkness, coupled with the overhanging limbs from the trees, made her virtually invisible to the men at the wagons. They had already taken precautionary measures. Every able-bodied man sat with a loaded weapon pointing in different directions toward the darkness. Were she to step toward them now, she might be mistakenly shot as the enemy. She stamped her toe quietly in frustration. There was no choice but to sit and wait for Jacob's return.

That, or go find him.

She had followed the sound of his voice as he left a few minutes earlier. Apparently, Sanger had told him one of his scouts had been ambushed and asked Jacob to see to him. He and Jacob had headed off toward the man, back into the woods to her left.

At first, there had been excited activity around the ambulances as the men had taken their places to protect the wagons. Now, they sat silently, apprehensively. The damp night air became tense with fear; even the normal calls of night animals were quiet. There was no telling how many men were out there, ready to ambush the group.

As she stood there considering the situation, a question dawned. If an unknown number of men sat waiting for the right time to seize their horses and what little supplies they had, why hadn't Sanger ordered his other sentries into the woods to find them? Although some would need to stay and protect the ambulances, surely he would have sent more.

Unless Sanger already knew how many Yankees were out there. Unless there really wasn't a wounded man out there at all. A sudden terror clawed at her. What if Sanger had fired the shot as a means of getting Jacob into the woods alone? Away from the eyes of his men, he could murder Jacob, report that they had been ambushed. If so, he would conveniently get away with murder, just as he had with the killing of Jacob's father.

If Sanger had somehow learned that Jacob had the evidence needed to convict him, he would take drastic measures. He had murdered to get horses; he would definitely murder to save his neck. Savannah clenched her fists in determination. Maybe she had promised Jacob she would stay hidden, but that was before she suspected his life was in danger.

Quickly, she gathered the folds of her skirt and quietly moved away from the wagons. A bush rustled drops of water as she brushed by, the noise riveting through the forest.

"Who goes there?" a voice called from the wagons.

Savannah turned and hurried away. She would have to be careful. She planned to stop Sanger, and surprise would be of the essence.

"I will repeat again, Doctor. If you would kindly step this way, we have some business to settle." Sanger pushed the gun deeper into Jacob's back.

It would be certain death just to cooperate, Jacob realized. He would have no fighting chance, no way of defending himself. If he were to stall Sanger, drag this thing out a bit longer, he might see an opportunity to disarm him.

"Your man is hurt, Sanger. Let me tend to him. Then you and I will take care of matters."

"He's a dead man, anyway!" Sanger snapped impatiently. "He knows too much as it is." He prodded Jacob with the pistol. "Move, Doctor, and I do mean now."

Jacob grabbed his bag, moving slowly to considher everything around him. Sanger followed closely.

"Right here, if you don't mind." Sanger prodded

him with his gun. "I want you to fall here. That way it'll look like they got you from behind." His voice held a giddy sound of excitement to it as if he were savoring every word.

Now, Jacob thought.

In a split second, he turned and swung his black leather bag at Sanger's blond head. Surprised, the colonel reacted quickly, jerking his head back so that the bag caught only his nose. Sanger cursed in pain as the sickening thud of impact crushed the bone. For an instant, he lowered the pistol, giving Jacob the opportunity he needed. He lunged for the gun, but Sanger held the advantage. Before Jacob could wrestle the weapon from his hands, Sanger lifted it toward Jacob, this time only inches from his face, their eyes locked in another battle. Sanger held his free hand over his battered nose as blood seeped through his fingers and began dropping on his uniform.

Sanger dropped his gaze first, glancing down at his blood-soaked blouse. His lips twisted into an treacherous grin.

"Thank you, Doctor," Sanger snarled, still breathing heavily. "This will only add to my story of attack. I tried to fight them off, but was knocked unconscious with a blow to my head. When I came to, the good doctor, who tried so valiantly to save my life, was dead."

He laughed sarcastically. "I had hoped to get this over with quickly and easily for Savannah's sake. I would hate for her to dwell on the fact that her late husband was brutally murdered. It might take her a long time to get over her grief. I'm a patient man, but not that patient."

Jacob glared, but said nothing.

"She will get over it, though, and then she'll be mine."

The thought of Savannah in Sanger's arms created more anger than the gun. He would rip Sanger to shreds before he'd allow one of Sanger's fingers to touch Savannah's soft skin.

Keep calm, Jacob thought. Keep him occupied. He's too confident. He'll make a mistake.

"She'll never have you, Sanger."

"Of course she will. She and I are much alike. We do what it takes to get what we want."

"What's that supposed to mean?"

"Don't you wonder where your supplies have been coming from?" he asked, an evil gleam in his eye.

At Jacob's shrug, he continued, "She and I discussed an arrangement."

"An arrangement?" Jacob asked to keep him talking.

"Of course. Every new bottle of morphine you got, Savannah paid for. Paid for in my bed. Surely she told you?"

Jacob took one step back as Sanger came closer with the pistol.

"No, she didn't tell me." *Keep him talking.*

"Ah, that doesn't surprise me. She's far too cunning to let details like that slip."

"Where did you get the morphine? You told me there was none to be had."

"None to be had for a cowardly doctor like yourself." Sanger laughed. "You and your father, both refusing to fight for the Confederacy. Both cowards."

Rage coursed through Jacob, but he fought to keep it under control. Sanger was growing boisterous, unwittingly allowing Jacob an edge. He couldn't lose it now. A movement over Sanger's shoulder caught his eye. He glanced at Sanger, then to the wounded sentry on the ground. The man lifted his head, then dropped back with a groan.

"I wouldn't worry about a dead man, Doc. I'd worry about myself were I you."

"I'm not frightened of you, Sanger," Jacob baited him, "because I'm not the coward. Neither was my father. You ordered your men to murder him. It's just like you pulled the trigger in cold blood."

"Yes, it is, isn't it?" Sanger agreed with a callous shrug. "He refused to give us his horses. We had every right to take them."

"You had no right to burn the house, or murder him and Anna."

"Oh, yes, your dear, dead first wife." He shrugged. "I do apologize for her. I didn't know she was in the house."

"You still ordered the raid."

"Oh, yes, I did do that. And, for the record, I pulled the trigger on your father just like I'm going to do to you. I truly didn't want to, your being the only doctor in St. George. But you have forced me."

"How's that?"

"Please, you insult my intelligence." Sanger

rolled his eyes in disgust. "You forget that I'm a powerful man in this army, Doctor. I know you went to see the boy, and I know what he said to you."

"I don't understand." Jacob acted surprised.

Sanger sneered. "I would not be in my position if I were a foolish man. Prison guards can be bought for as little as a bottle of whiskey." He laughed. "For two, you can learn all you need to know. Surely you know I will not allow you to ruin me. I've worked too hard, come too far.

"Besides," he continued, "you didn't need to make such a journey. Had you asked, I would have told you myself that I ordered the men to take your father's possessions. He was a stubborn old man, and he refused to give for the cause."

"That's not true, Sanger. You took what he had before the war had been declared. Just like you did to every other family in St. George. As far as my father was concerned, you were nothing but a thief. I agree."

Sanger's face turned red in anger. "We took what was needed! Your father refused to support our army. That makes him a coward."

"No, Sanger," Jacob replied as if he possessed a greater knowledge than Sanger. "You shot him in the back. You're the coward."

Rage contorted Sanger's face. "I don't believe you fully comprehend the situation, Doctor. I have the gun, a Union gun. We are standing in the midst of woods known to be partially surrounded by the enemy. When everything is over, you and the private back there will have been the unfortunate casualties of an ambush." He raised his pistol.

"You planned all this, didn't you?" Jacob taunted.

Sanger chuckled with a cruel lilt. "I didn't plan the battle, of course, but when the order came to bring more munitions, I couldn't think of a better cover than getting the wounded. I saw a golden opportunity to get rid of you and used it to my advantage.

"And now, Doctor, I'm sure you'll understand that I must hurry back to my command and to tell Savannah the horrible news about her husband." He lifted the pistol and aimed.

"No!" A female voiced screamed through the trees as Savannah raced into the clearing.

Quickly, Sanger fired, the distraction obviously startling him. Jacob felt a searing pain through his left shoulder as the bullet rammed into his body.

"Jacob!" she cried, rushing to his side. "No!"

"I had so wanted you to be mine, Savannah," the colonel said regretfully. "I can see now that would never be possible. My men will be here momentarily, and now you are a witness. I'm afraid that just won't do."

As if moving in slow motion, Jacob watched as Sanger purposefully lifted his weapon to fire again. Taking careful aim, he pointed the pistol directly at Savannah. With all his might, Jacob flung Savannah to the ground just as the second shot rang out.

"Savannah!" he cried as she fell on top of him.

He was certain Sanger shot with a practiced aim. Quickly, he searched for the telltale sign of death. Feeling her breath, he knew she was alive. He made a move to drag them both to safety when he realized Sanger was no longer standing over them. Looking up, he saw the colonel lying in a crumpled heap on the ground.

Slowly, from the other side of the bushes, Louis dropped his weapon, too drained to do more. "I told you, sir. He had a mean streak."

Then Louis fell back in the mud.

Chapter Twelve

Jacob drew a quick breath as Savannah doused his wound with whiskey. She knew the fiery liquid had burned his injured arm.

"Almost, Jacob." She breathed quietly, probably in as much agony as her patient. "I'm almost done. Sanger got you good, that's for sure. I can't believe you wouldn't take any morphine," she softly chided.

"This is just a flesh wound." He shook his head and gritted his teeth. "What little we have is needed for the other men."

The bullet had passed through the fleshy part of his upper arm, leaving a horrendous gash close to the bone. Savannah had to snip off the dried edges of skin, then sew as much as she could back together. Thankfully, the bullet had not shattered the bone, and Jacob would recover quickly.

He lay his head down on their bed and closed his eyes. "All the casualties have been unloaded and settled into the hospital," Savannah said, hoping to take his mind off his pain. "I've got Miss Emma and the stewards cleaning wounds and re-bandaging. Will you please rest for a little while?"

"How many died on the trip back?" he asked quietly without lifting his head.

"Ten." Savannah picked up the scalpel and needle she had used to close the gaping hole. "They just weren't strong enough, Jacob. Don't blame yourself."

He nodded, his eyes still shut. "It's hard watching them die, knowing there's nothing you can do."

She understood all too well. He drifted off to a restless sleep as she walked to the bedroom and opened it. They had all been through so much the past two days. It was time for all of them to rest. Closing the door behind her, she leaned her head against the cool wood.

The sun had been high as the ambulances had rolled to a stop in front of the hospital earlier that day. Savannah had ridden with the first group of men, sitting up beside the driver. Despite his injured arm, Jacob had insisted on riding the sorrel beside the detail. Sanger's feisty black stallion had been led by an officer, the lifeless body of the colonel bundled across its back.

Space had been made for Louis on the floor of the first wagon. He had saved their lives, and was a true hero as far as Savannah was concerned. His safe return to the hospital had been her personal mission. She had flinched every time a jolt of the wagon had caused him to grimace. As the wagons finally had ground to a halt in front of the hospital, she had noted the pallor of his face. If the trip had been any longer, he might not have survived.

It was actually miraculous he was still alive. While they were searching for deserters, Sanger had fired his pistol at the private at almost point-blank range. Thankfully, Sanger had miscalculated his aim. The bullet had missed the heart, passed through Louis's body, then out the other side.

"Get these men inside!" Jacob had ordered as he lifted Savannah from the wagon. His lips had been drawn in a tight line from the motion. His would was not life-threatening, but the constant bouncing of the horse had been hard on him.

"Jacob, please, watch your arm. I can get down on my own." Savannah had tried to brush away his help, but he would not hear of it. Dropping a quick kiss on her forehead, he had hurried off to the rear of the wagons.

She had turned to supervise as Louis was carried into the hospital on a stretcher. Resting her hand on his shoulder, she had smiled. "You saved my husband's life today. I owe you one."

His face had been contorted in pain, but he had managed to return her grin. "My pleasure, ma'am."

Before they had headed home, the private had told them all how he and Colonel Sanger had been scouting the area. The colonel had nodded for him to go ahead of him through the brush. Without warning, Sanger had spurred his black horse directly into the private's, causing both horses to ram together.

"I figured the colonel was giving chase to deserters, and I was in his way," he had explained. "Then I saw an evil look in his eye, something I'll never forget no matter how long this war goes on. When he pointed his pistol at me, I couldn't believe I was his target, even after I took the bullet and I fell off my horse." He had shaken his head sadly. "I guess it knocked me out when I fell, 'cause when I came around, he was gone."

The wounded man had closed his eyes against the pain. For a long moment, Savannah had assumed he had passed out, the bumps and jolts from the wagon being too much to bear. She had lifted her eyes in surprise when the soldier's soft voice had continued, "When I heard you coming, Doc, I figured it out. He was gonna get even for what happened at the hospital, just like I told you." He had looked directly at Jacob, regret filling his eyes. "Me and the other fellas . . . we had no idea he ordered the raid that killed your pa. I'm sorry, Doc. Real sorry." Those listening nearby had nodded in silent agreement.

"It's okay, son," Jacob had said as he bandaged the boy's wound. "You just hang on until we get to the hospital."

His eyes had found Savannah's, a comforting smile on his lips. She had known it was finally over. While Sanger would never stand trial for his part in the murders, justice had been served. Sanger's own men knew the truth about their leader. It was unlikely he would be remembered with honor.

"Doctor," Jacob had called when he finally had gone to their bedroom, his voice weary with fatigue. Savannah had hurried to his side. "I think I'll take your advice and rest a minute. Can you see to those men downstairs?"

With a nod, Savannah had smiled. Jacob had no way of knowing how much his comment had meant. She should have been a doctor in her own time, but the possibilities of becoming one were slim. Through fate, she had finally become the doctor she was destined to be. A surge of happiness had shot through her soul as she had overseen the medical detail. Jacob's words, his trust, and his confidence in her were everything she could have hoped for.

"Savannah!" Miss Emma now called from the bottom of the stairs. "How is he? I've been so worried . . . I do declare! I can't let either of you out of my sight without there being trouble! His poor mother, God rest her soul, would turn over in her grave if she could see him now. What happened?"

"It's a long story, Miss Emma," Savannah replied as she began her descent.

By the time all the men were settled inside the hospital, the late-afternoon sky had faded from pink to gray bringing the dusk. Savannah stretched her tired muscles, not remembering a time when she had worked harder. Every able body, including Miss Emma, Deltry, and the medics, had seen to the injured, then found them all a place to lay their weary heads. Even Jacob, with his wounded arm, had tried to help some. Cots had been reserved for the most serious, the others finding an empty spot on one of Miss Emma's wool rugs. Once settled, Deltry and Miss Emma had offered supper to the hungry men. While the stew wasn't much, it was the first decent meal some had eaten in a month.

Surveying the scene before her, Savannah couldn't help thinking about the widows of the ten men who died. Their husbands would never come home. She sighed inwardly, feeling very old. When would mankind ever learn? Obviously not in Jacob's century, and not in hers, either.

Her century. She hadn't thought about that in several days. Jacob had not yet proffered his belief in her. In spite of all that had happened, if he couldn't, there was nothing for her to do but go back. To tell Mathilde she wanted to return to her own century. Like the ten widows, she would lose her love, too. Not because of war, though. It was a lack of trust that would drive them apart.

Walking past the darkened foyer, the realization dawned that something was missing. The duties of the day had kept her busy, but each time she had passed the room, an eerie feeling swallowed her. Something was not right.

Reaching for an oil lamp, Savannah walked cautiously into the small area. As the shadows settled into images, the heavy front door stood like a silent monster. She turned slowly to head back up the stairs, figuring her tired imagination was

335

working overtime. Everything seemed okay. Then she saw it, or rather didn't see it. The pounding of her heart echoed around the room as she stared at the empty wall. Miss Emma's treasured vanity, with its polished marble top, was gone!

How could that be? In the impetuous excitement of stowing away with the medical detail, she had completely forgotten about Mathilde's next visit. It appeared that the conniving old woman had taken it anyway. *Damn her!*

Leaning back against the now-empty wall, she gave up. How was she going to explain this? The story of trading a quilt for morphine was odd, but at least the morphine offered proof. There was nothing now to convince Jacob she wasn't a common thief. He would never believe her, and she couldn't blame him.

Sadly, she dimmed the oil lamp and set it on the floor, then opened the front door. She might as well find Mathilde and leave before he found out. It would be easier this way.

The evening darkness wrapped around her like a cloak. Savannah didn't even know how to find the old woman. She had a mysterious way of showing up only when it benefited her.

"Savannah, dear," Miss Emma called softly from the darkness.

Startled, Savannah swung around, barely able to make out her friend in the shadows. She moved closer, sitting down on the swing.

"While you were gone, a friend of yours came calling."

Savannah lifted her hand to fidget with her

hair. She had hoped to get away before anyone knew, but it was not to be. "She did?"

"Yes. A most interesting woman, I might add," Miss Emma went on in her usual cheerful voice. "An antique dealer."

"Interesting isn't quite the word I'd use," Savannah said sarcastically, her eyes downcast. "What did she want?"

"She brought us a large supply of ether," a male voice answered. "There's none to be had in these parts, either."

Astonished, Savannah stared as Jacob came close, holding a large amber bottle in his good hand. Looking back and forth between the two, she stuttered, "She—she did?"

Hope dawned, then died in the same instant. It was all too unbelievable. Her voice edged with caution. "She just left it?"

"Actually, no," Miss Emma interjected. "She told me you had arranged a trade. We had a most interesting conversation."

That's it, Savannah thought sadly, Miss Emma knows. Everything. Fitfully, she wondered if Jacob knew, too.

"What did she want?"

"Can you believe she wanted that ugly old vanity I had in the foyer? I certainly can't imagine why anyone would want that thing. Jacob and I intended to burn it for firewood the next cold winter."

Savannah stared at the elderly woman blankly, knowing the vanity was a precious heirloom.

Miss Emma rose as Jacob remained still. She

walked to Savannah, placing her hand into hers. "Your friend wanted something else, too, my dear. I thought it most unusual, but she said you'd understand. She wanted your nurse's hat."

Surprised, Savannah glanced up to see the concern in Miss Emma's eyes. "I told her you had it with you. Something about it didn't seem quite right."

Savannah nodded silently. What did it matter now? She looked up at Jacob's unreadable face. There was no reason for explanations; he would never believe she was anything more than a common thief.

"Miss Emma says the woman will be back for the hat, Savannah," Jacob added at last. His voice was reserved, cautious. "She wants to trade one more thing. She told Miss Emma you would know. Apparently, it started your destiny, and it will complete it, too."

Savannah withdrew her hands from Miss Emma's and leaned back in the swing. She did know what Mathilde wanted, and it was impossible.

The cunning old woman who started her on the journey wanted Jacob's watch. How could she ask him for something that meant so much to him? How could she now ask him to give up his father's last remaining possession? A tear trickled down her cheek.

In her motherly fashion, Miss Emma leaned forward to hug her. "Trust him, Savannah," she whispered in her ear. Turning, Miss Emma walked back inside the house, leaving her and Jacob alone on the porch.

For a long while, nothing was said as Jacob continued to stare at her, his face masked by the darkness. It was obvious he had no idea what to say.

"How is your arm?" she finally asked.

He shrugged, then rose to join her on the swing. His good arm went about her shoulder.

"Could this be it, Savannah? Is this what the woman wants?" The gold pocket watch lay in his palm.

Savannah stared at the watch. A huge lump in her throat refused to let her speak. She looked away with tears in her eyes.

"That's what I thought," he said sadly. Still holding the timepiece in his hand, he brought her chin around until her face was only inches from his. "This is the only thing I have left of my father, Savannah. It's my only connection to the past."

"Yes." She shook her head in despair. "It's also my only connection with the future." Another tear slipped from her eye. Jacob bent forward and kissed it away.

"I know."

"You do?" She looked at him in sad amazement. "You believe I've been telling the truth? You believe I'm from the future?"

Silently, he nodded as a finger stroked her cheek. "I can't explain it. I suppose you can't, either, but I accept it."

"What made you change your mind?"

"I wish I could tell you that it was all you." He looked a bit ashamed. "That wouldn't be honest. When I saw you working by my side at the

339

church, I knew you were no ordinary woman, but to believe that you came from the future . . ." He dropped his gaze back to the watch. "That was still too much to comprehend."

"How then? I tried everything I knew to convince you, and you still didn't believe me."

"Miss Emma." A sheepish smile spread across his face. "Her conversation with . . . Mathilde. Isn't that her name? What they discussed was enlightening to say the least. You might say Miss Emma enlightened me as well."

In spite of her fear, Savannah laughed as she imagined a conversation between the two women.

"I guess I'm really not surprised. Everything about you is different. That's why I love you. But this watch . . ." He shook his head sadly.

"Yes, I know," she said, taking it from his hands. "I understand, Jacob. I understand if you can't let it go."

He met her eyes in confusion. "Savannah, the watch is not important. I'm trying to tell you that I love you enough to let you go home."

"You want me to go?"

"Of course not," he said with a trace of irritation at being misunderstood. "Nothing is more important to me than you. This watch can't help me survive this war or build a new life once it's over. But it can make you happy. It can send you home." His lips met hers tenderly, then he pulled away. "I can't kiss you. Each time my lips touch yours it would be to convince you to stay." He drew away.

"Oh, Jacob! If you only knew, my love! I don't want to go back! Ever!" Her happiness brought a lilt to her voice. She reached for his hands and brought them to her heart. "At first, I wanted to, probably more than you could imagine. Then I fell in love with you. You're my life now, and there's nothing I want more."

In spite of his injured arm, Jacob encircled Savannah, bringing her body close. His lips brushed a gentle kiss across her forehead before descending to press against hers, gently covering her mouth. Lowering his head, he nuzzled her neck. "I'm afraid if I kiss you, you'll disappear from my life as quickly as you came into it."

"Then we have to do it, Jacob. Surely it all needs to come full circle. We have to give Mathilde the hat and the watch. I think it's the only way I can stay."

He nodded. "Miss Emma say this Mathilde woman will be at your usual meeting spot. She said you're to call whenever you're ready."

"Then let's go. It's time to break the connection."

Together, they walked to the back of the barn, the stars above twinkling in the dark sky. It didn't seem possible what was about to happen.

They stopped just beyond the bush, as Savannah always did. She released Jacob's hand and started to walk away.

"Oh, no." He grabbed her hand before she could protest. "I don't know how all of this happened, but if we do it, we do it together." Stepping forward, he dropped a quick kiss on her mouth.

"Mathilde?" Savannah called softly. "I'm ready now. Mathilde?" As usual, there was no answer.

"She's done this to me before," Savannah explained. "She shows up whenever she wants to. She's never answered when I call."

"I take exception to that," Mathilde said sternly, coming around the side of the barn. "Besides, you broke the rules when you went to the battlefield. That was never in your destiny."

"How was I supposed to know my destiny?" Savannah snapped in irritation. "You certainly didn't tell me. You said it was up to me to figure it out, so I did."

Ignoring her outburst, Mathilde looked Jacob over carefully, then smiled devilishly. "I can see why you followed him, though." She walked toward Jacob. "Oh, if you had only been my destiny . . ." Her words trailed off as Savannah jumped between the two.

"Well, he's mine, so tell me what we need to do."

With a sigh, Mathilde stepped away. "You're right. It is time to bring this to a close. I'm tired of hopping back and forth to help you out."

"To help me out?" Savannah could not believe her ears.

"Ladies, please," Jacob interceded, clasping his hand over Savannah's mouth. "Let's get on with this."

Mathilde held out her hands for the two last items. Jacob passed the watch over Savannah's shoulder to Mathilde's outstretched hand. Savannah held out the hat. "The hat makes no difference." She brushed it aside. "It was only to get you here. It's this." She held the watch gently before them. "This watch belongs to both of you, although in different times. It was part of the past." She gave Jacob a long considering look, then turned to Savannah. "And part of the future. Sometimes, those merge together and you can't always tell which is which. It was destined to bring you together.

"Although the watch was the means that brought you here, Savannah, you created your own destiny. It's up to you to decide whether to stay."

She looked at Jacob to be sure he was real, to be sure he wanted her to remain. The love on his face spoke volumes. "I stay," she said firmly.

"Perfect!" Mathilde said, opening a small velvet cloth to drop the watch inside. "I know the most suitable collector!" She handed the watch back to Savannah.

Savannah looked confused. "What am I supposed to do with it, kiss it good-bye or something?"

"No. The watch doesn't return with me. It's already in the future, locked up in my vault, as a matter of fact."

"I don't understand, Mathilde. You told me this whole journey revolved around the watch and the hat. They were my destiny."

"Don't take what I say so literally! It's hard to believe that two brilliant doctors can't figure this out." Mathilde took a deep breath, obviously growing weary of Savannah's questions. "Surely Miss Emma told you about her nephew, John?"

Savannah nodded.

"This will be his watch," she explained patiently. "He will pass it down through the Stuart family to your father."

"You mean Miss Emma is my . . . aunt?" Savannah looked back at Jacob with excitement.

"Nothing gets by you, does it?" Mathilde grinned. She turned her attention to Jacob. "You and Savannah must give this watch to Miss Emma. She will eventually leave it to her favorite nephew, John Stuart, who will in turn leave it to his son. That's how it becomes an heirloom."

"A full circle then," Savannah said, reaching for Jacob's hand. "Everything is now in order." They turned to go. "Are you sure you don't want this?" She offered the nurse's cap once again.

"No, dear, that's your hat. It doesn't belong in the collection any longer." Savannah looked at the hat, hesitating. "Well, if you insist," Mathilde said, grabbing it quickly. "I can always get a good price from the Civil War museum. Are you quite certain staying in this time is what you want? You're giving up a lot."

"I know," she said, smiling at Jacob, "but look at all I'm getting in return."

Now And Then

TIMESWEPT

BOBBY HUTCHINSON

Indian legend says that the spirit can overcome all obstacles, even time itself. Yet Dr. Paige Randolph doubts that anything can help her recover from the loss of her child and the breakup of her marriage. But when a mysterious crop circle casts her back one hundred years, her only hope of surviving on the savage Canadian frontier is to open her heart to the love of the one man meant for her and the powerful truth of the spirit world.

_51990-9 $4.99 US/$5.99 CAN

MIRIAM RAFTERY

Taylor James's wrinkled Shar-Pei, Apollo, is always getting into trouble. But the young beauty never expects her mischievous puppy to lead her on the romantic adventure of a lifetime—from a dusty old Victorian attic to the strong arms of Nathaniel Stuart and his turn-of-the-century charm. One minute Taylor and Apollo are in modern-day San Francisco, and the next thing Taylor knows, a shift in the earth's crust, a wrinkle in time, and the lovely historian finds herself facing the terror of California's most infamous earthquake—and a love so monumental it threatens to shake the foundations of her world.

_52084-2 $4.99 US/$6.99 CAN

TIMESWEPT TRAVELER ELAINE FOX

With a thriving business and a stalled personal life, Shelby Manning never figures her life is any worse—or better—than the norm. Then a late-night stroll through a Civil War battlefield park leads her to a most intriguing stranger. Bloody, confused, and dressed in Union blue, he insists he has just come from the Battle of Fredericksburg—more than one hundred years in the past.

Maybe Shelby should dismiss Carter Lindsey as crazy—just another history reenactor taking his game a little too seriously. But there is something compelling in the pull of his eyes, something special in his tender touch. And before she knows it, Shelby finds herself swept into a passion like none she's ever known—and willing to defy time itself to keep Carter at her side.

_52074-5 $4.99 US/$6.99 CAN

ELIZABETH CRANE

Bestselling Author Of *Time Remembered*

When practical-minded Renata O'Neal submits to hypnosis to cure her insomnia, she never expects to wake up in 1880s Louisiana—or in love with fiery Nathan Blue. But vicious secrets and Victorian sensibilities threaten to keep Renata and Nathan apart...until Renata vows that nothing will separate her from the most deliciously alluring man of any century.

_52089-3 $4.99 US/$6.99 CAN

TIMESWEPT

A Time to Love Again by Flora Speer. When India Baldwin goes to work one Saturday to update her computer skills, she has no idea she will end up backdating herself! But one slip on the keyboard and the lovely young widow is transported back to the time of Charlemagne. Before she knows it, India finds herself merrily munching on boar and quaffing ale, holding her own during a dangerous journey, and yearning for the nights when a warrior's masterful touch leaves her wondering if she ever wants to return to her own time.

_51900-3 $4.99 US/$5.99 CAN

Time Remembered by Elizabeth Crane. Among the ruins of an antebellum mansion, young architect Jody Farnell discovers the diary of a man from another century and a voodoo doll whose ancient spell whisks her back one hundred years to his time. Micah Deveroux yearns for someone he can love above all others, and he thinks he has found that woman until Jody mysteriously appears in his own bedroom. Enchanted by Jody, betrothed to another, Micah fears he has lost his one chance at happiness—unless the same black magic that has brought Jody into his life can work its charms again.

_51904-6 $4.99 US/$5.99 CAN

Dorchester Publishing Co., Inc.
65 Commerce Road
Stamford, CT 06902

Please add $1.75 for shipping and handling for the first book and $.50 for each book thereafter. NY, NYC, PA and CT residents, please add appropriate sales tax. No cash, stamps, or C.O.D.s. All orders shipped within 6 weeks via postal service book rate. Canadian orders require $2.00 extra postage and must be paid in U.S. dollars through a U.S. banking facility.

Name _____

Address _____

City _____ State _____ Zip _____

I have enclosed $_____ in payment for the checked book(s).

Payment <u>must</u> accompany all orders.☐ Please send a free catalog.

BITTERROOT

VICTORIA CHANCELLOR

Bestselling Author Of *Forever & A Day*

In the Wyoming Territory—a land both breathtaking and brutal—bitterroots grow every summer for a brief time. Therapist Rebecca Hartford has never seen such a plant—until she is swept back to the days of Indian medicine men, feuding ranchers, and her pioneer forebears. Nor has she ever known a man as dark, menacing, and devastatingly handsome as Sloan Travers. Sloan hides a tormented past, and Rebecca vows to use her professional skills to help the former Union soldier, even though she longs to succumb to personal desire. But when a mysterious shaman warns Rebecca that her sojourn in the Old West will last only as long as the bitterroot blooms, she can only pray that her love for Sloan is strong enough to span the ages....

_52087-7 $5.50 US/$7.50 CAN